Terra Firma

STEPHEN PLATT
Terra Firma

www.leveretpublishing.com

First published in 1992 by
Leveret Publishing
56 Covent Garden, Cambridge CB1 2HR, UK

www.leveretpublishing.com

This edition 2018

Hardback ISBN 978-1-912460-37-3

Paperback ISBN 978-1-912460-38-0

Typeset in Janson Text

Cover photographs of El Avila, Caracas, Venezuela

1

The wind had the hot, rasping taste of furnace ash and David screwed his eyes against the brightness. People crowded on to the small platform, pushing him forwards, down the steps, and he had to grab the handrail to stop himself falling.

He stepped out of the line of passengers and looked around. The airport buildings shimmered and melted into the concrete runway. The back of his shirt was sopping wet and he could feel a cold trickle down his spine. In front of a building site a large sign read Terminal Internacional and, rising into the bare dirt hills, he saw thousands of small shacks of mud red block.

His first view of the continent from the plane had been of endless forest, deep green near the coast then purple as trees rose into mountains and soft slate grey in the far distance. He had never imagined anything so immense. Back home every-thing was so ordered, everywhere so shaped and moulded. Even his Scottish hills seemed circumscribed and tame. From three miles high there had been no sign of settlement or road, only the broad muddy fan of some great river and a succession of tiny white sand beaches.

The clamour of a near riot greeted him in the customs hall as people fought over their mountainous luggage—an incomprehensible babble overlain with shrieks that grated on his nerves. David waited patiently, watching for his case over their heads. Gradually the hubbub died away and he was left alone; the conveyor continued revolving, empty. The men in green fatigues fingered their machine guns.

A soldier shouted at him.

'I'm sorry. I don't speak Spanish. I'm waiting for my case.'

'Closed, senor!'

He turned to the customs bench in the hope they would speak English.

'Can you help me, I don't speak Spanish.'

'Senor?'

'I can't find my case.'

'All gone, Senor. Go ask aereolinea.'

The airline's desk was closed so he tried to go through to the unloading area but a soldier barred the way. 'Terminado, senor!' he said, pointing to the exit. Finally David admitted defeat and left the empty baggage hall.

Outside there was no sign of Jordi. The taxi-drivers pestered for a while and then ignored him. Sitting on a low wall by the side of the road he noticed his new shoes were covered in a layer of fine dust. He folded his jacket carefully over his knees to keep it out of the dirt.

As well as the clothes he was wearing he had two hundred pounds in travellers cheques, which was all he had been able to raise for the trip. He wondered if he was crazy: it wasn't like him, he was usually very cautious. Now he was totally dependent on Jordi, with nothing in writing about the job. What if it had all fallen through and Jordi didn't turn up? He didn't even know where Jordi lived.

He felt in his jacket. In the inside pocket he had his passport and a wallet which, apart from the money, contained two photographs: one of his mum and dad in the garden and another of himself and Nikki, taken by a street photographer, holding hands outside the National Gallery on a weekend trip to London. In the side pockets he found a Spanish phrase book and a toothbrush and razor he'd intended to use on the plane. Not a lot to start a new life. He could go straight back home, of course, but he didn't intend to, not unless he could help it.

He waited, losing track of time. Now and then he felt anxious, wondering if Jordi had forgotten, or if he had sent him the wrong flight number. No, he was sure he had sent the right details; Jordi was late, that was all.

§

It was nearly year since Jordi had invited David to his flat and had first mooted the idea of his going to Venezuela.

'Olá. Entra.' The woman said, pushing the hair from her face. Her eyes were black. David put out his hand, which she took, smiling beneath the hair.

'You English, so formal.' Jordi lounged in front of the

3

television.

David had gone in his one good jacket and wore a tie. They were both in jeans, laundered and pressed. Mariella wore a cricket sweater, several sizes too large, with the sleeves rolled up. Jordi's check shirt was pulled tight over his heavy muscled chest and thick hairy arms.

'Do you watch this?'

'What? I haven't got a television.'

'Star Trek—it's brilliant. Their starship is exploring space. Do you mind, while it finishes?'

They watched. It looked pretty childish to David, but then he found most science fiction boring. Captain Kirk was a bit like Jordi, he thought. When Jordi was doing his project he loved all the gadgets and being in charge. David found the fake technology got in the way. Maybe he disliked it because it was so unreal. He hated television; it made you feel you had been somewhere or understood something when you hadn't.

When he was young they would watch television on Sunday evenings at the dinner table. High tea of ham, lettuce and salad cream, served on green crockery. Then to evensong at the church round the corner, with a guilty, Monday morning feeling creeping up because he hadn't done his homework, and after, the bus ride down-town to the espresso bar and the bored tightness in his head as they sat, boys and girls, unable to think of anything to say.

'Do you like Chinese food?' Jordi asked when the programme had finished.

'Sure,' said David, snapping out of his reverie.

Jordi picked up the phone from the floor, next to his chair, and ordered a take-away.

'Drink? Beer, whisky, rum, coke?'

'Beer, please.'

Mariella fetched a pack of German bottled beer from the fridge, and poured for them both.

'How's work?' asked Jordi.

'The University's offered me a new contract, but I'm not interested.'

'Why not?'

'Ray's leaving—it won't be the same when he's gone. And we're getting thrown out of our building.'

'They're clueless—they deserve to get taken over. Ray's a genius, he could have earned them a fortune in consultancy. And that guy in graphics, what a gold-mine he could be. What will you do?'

'I'm not sure. I've been applying for jobs. In fact I've just been to an interview today.'

'And?'

'There were two of us, being interviewed together, which was odd. I was doing all right, better than the other person I think. Halfway through another candidate turned up—a woman in a big hat and gloves and within five minutes we both knew she'd got the job. We were there to make up the numbers.'

'Tough,' said Jordi, opening another bottle and filling David's glass. 'Have you ever thought of working abroad?'

David said, yes, as a matter of fact, he had. He'd applied for a lectureship in Vancouver and was still waiting for a reply.

'What about South America?' asked Jordi.

'I don't know. Why?' He was interested. He had read a lot about South America, but hadn't thought of going there. Jordi suggested he could get a job in Venezuela. David nodded, he wasn't really taking the conversation seriously, and mentioned having seen an article in the *Observer* about trouble there.

'It's nothing,' said Jordi. 'There was a chance in the late sixties, but protest won't change the system; revolution is the only answer.'

'What sort of revolution?'

'Marxist, like Cuba.'

David glanced round the room. It was a large flat. There was a curved four-seater sofa in yellow Harris Tweed, two black leather armchairs on chrome swivel bases and a number of glass-topped tables. Jordi's new MG was parked outside.

'I could leave all this tomorrow,' said Jordi, waving his arm expansively. He ripped open the top of a packet of cigarettes and offered one to David. David shook his head. The gold lighter made a loud snap when Jordi shut it. He glanced at Mariella and she got up and fetched an ash-tray for him.

'I prefer evolutionary change, it's less hard on the common man,' said David.

'Something you should understand,' said Jordi, leaning back in the armchair and blowing smoke at the ceiling. 'My country is yoked by Yankee imperialism. We are the richest country in Latin America, but we buy everything from the States—not just manufactures, but much of our food supply. It's fertile; we could grow many things: sugar, rice, mango, banana, anything, and our coffee is the best in the world. We nationalised the oil, limited foreign imports, but the factories are just assembly plants. It's a joke; the cars come in crates, they just fit the engines into the bodies. The system is one of social injustice, poverty, corruption. Only a small minority benefit. So you see a Marxist revolution is the only answer.'

'You swap one set of rogues for another.' He remembered the Communist party meetings he'd been to when he was an undergraduate. 'Communism's too bureaucratic: equality can't be programmed.'

Jordi ignored him. 'My uncles helped overthrow Perez Jimenez. They chased him to the airport and tried to stop his plane taking off by blocking the runway with their cars. But he got away. And grandfather was in the Rotunda while Goméz was president, in the thirties. His ankles are swollen from the *grillos*, how you say?'

'Manacles?'

'Yeh. He was chained to the wall.'

'There are communist tyrants too.'

'People are like sheep, they need a strong leader.'

David didn't agree: he believed in change from the bottom up, but he kept his mouth shut.

'We are forming a research group in the Central University in Caracas, to work under contract from the Ministry of Public Works. Listen, I have an idea.' Jordi stroked his thick moustache and looked at David. 'How would you like to work with us, in the university? I could write to my uncle, Manuel, he's Director of Planning.'

My God, this evening wasn't just a casual invitation, thought David, realising that Jordi was offering him a job. 'What sort of research?' he asked, his heart thumping.

'Urban planning. There is pressure on the capital—it's surrounded by mountains, everyone wants to live there and there's no room,' he shrugged. 'The question is where to direct development, near the capital or in the regions and Manuel wants us to help him decide. What I want you to do is join the research team.'

'I don't know much about town planning.'

'No problem; you're an architect and you can programme.'

'What do you want programming?'

'A computer model—a simulation that will allow us to test various alternatives. We need to anticipate development before it happens, to decide whether to develop the regions or build a new city near the capital, while there is time to direct the process.'

David absorbed what Jordi was suggesting. He had worked with Jordi before, helping him with his dissertation. Instead of the usual academic study, Jordi had devised a simulation involving dozens of people: the staff and students from the department and a party of girls from the local high school. David had been involved over three hectic days—inventing new twists to the plot, organising media coverage, as well as keeping score. Jordi persuaded the departmental secretaries to type up the transcripts in their lunch breaks and, almost unheard of, he got the lab technicians to edit the video tapes in a matter of days rather than months. And the beauty of it was, Jordi had just to write up all the material to get his dissertation done. Jordi was special—he had energy and enthusiasm, he'd go far.

'I've read a lot about *ranchos*. I'd love the chance to work on low-cost housing,' said David, starting to get interested.

'Splendid! There will be lots of opportunities for stuff like that,' said Jordi airily.

The meal arrived in carrier bags, delivered to the door by someone in a motor-bike helmet with the visor down. Jordi unpacked the bags and spread the cardboard containers on the long coffee table while Mariella fetched plates and cutlery. It smelt wonderful and David realised he was hungry. They helped themselves. Jordi hummed something that might have been a tune as he ate a pancake roll with both hands.

'Tell me more about your country, what's it like?' asked David.

'It is undeveloped and the population is quite small. There are high mountains, in the Andes; a Caribbean coastline with tropical beaches and palm trees; the llanos, the flood plain of the Orinoco and, in the south, the Amazonas with sandstone table mountains and jungle.'

While he talked, David dreamed. Unspoilt, virgin territory: every-thing he did would be new.

Jordi talked about politics, about urban planning and about himself. There had been trouble in the university there. David gathered that Jordi and his friends had been mixed up in student unrest. Jordi spoke of Simon Bolivar, the Liberator, and about his exile abroad and how he had lived in England too.

Little men dreaming of changing the world, thought David. 'Is there any climbing?' he asked, changing the subject. He spent most of his spare time rock climbing in Wales, Scotland or the Lakes.

'Maybe. Yes, in the Andes.'

'Have you been exploring?'

'I was in the Rescue Team in the university. See!' Jordi pulled out the identity tag on the chain round his neck. 'Sky-diving, rescue work. We discovered an unknown tribe.' Jordi told how he had been on an expedition that discovered a totally isolated tribe of Yanomamo in the Amazonas Region.

'And you discovered this tribe?' he asked.

'Yes, they'd had no contact whatsoever with white men,' said Jordi dramatically. 'We parachuted into the middle of their village!'

'Why?' asked David, incredulous.

'They were totally isolated—their *shabono* was miles from the nearest navigable river.' David was tempted to ask if they got back by parachute, but he kept quiet. Jordi was a braggart, but although he might exaggerate, David did not believe he lied. More importantly, Jordi had succeeded in capturing his imagination; places David had only read about became real and attainable. He wanted to go there and explore for himself.

'Have you any family?' asked Mariella.

'Both my parents are dead.'

His dad died of lung cancer the previous year. As long as David could remember he had smoked three packs a day of Players Please or Capstan Navy Cut. Knowing it might kill him, he said it was worth it and wouldn't smoke filters, maintaining it was like making love in spats. In the last month, before he died, David could lift him like a baby. Strange, he had seemed so huge when David was a boy.

His mum had died of a couple of years before.

'And a girlfriend?'

'She went to Ethiopia, on VSO—voluntary service?'

'Will you marry her?' asked Mariella.

Am I attached, you mean, he thought. Perhaps Jordi needed to know, or maybe she was just nosey. 'Neither of us wanted to settle down,' he said. 'We met when we were students. She writes long letters and I find it increasingly difficult to write back.'

In the last few weeks before Nikki left it had felt as if

they were moving inexorably apart, like trucks on diverging railway lines. Yet now, suddenly, he felt that he could have said or done something that would have made the difference.

Nikki was his first girlfriend. He'd met her in the climbing club and they had finally moved in together. But it hadn't worked. She was very independent and, he felt, maybe she just didn't need him. Often she would wake in the middle of the night and dance round the house. She never cooked and lived off nuts and fruit and herb tea. He had felt lost when she left but now, when she came into his mind, the main emotion he felt was curiosity. He could imagine her out in the bush, living in a thatched hut, tanned, fit, working hard teaching children in a corrugated tin shed or managing some civil engineering project. About now she might be sitting in a canvas chair writing her journal by the light of a Tilley lamp.

'Would you like to get married?' asked Mariella.

Maybe all South Americans are this direct, he thought.

'One day,' he said, smiling.

'When will that be?'

'When I find someone I love.'

'Oh, you're so serious, and those blue eyes,' she teased, 'I bet all the women fall for you.'

'What d'you think?' Jordi asked, after David had gone.

'He's neat,' mused Mariella, in the mirror, brushing her hair.

'So!'

'A neat and tidy Englishman—never been kissed! What Aurora wouldn't do to get her hands on him.'

'I wish your sister would control her fucking instincts!'

Mariella pulled a face. 'The English understatedness …'

she said, 'the old clothes—he's together—on him they work.'

'And on me?'

'Oh Jordi! You look crumpled two minutes out of the laundry.'

'Will he fit into the set-up? There's a lot at stake …'

'You may get more than you bargained for.'

'How?'

'Have you noticed the way he walks?' Jordi nodded, but she knew he would not have. 'He plants his feet firmly, not heavily, just well balanced.' She walked across the bedroom, imitating him.

'He's no push-over you mean?' laughed Jordi.

'He may look cool, but he's passionate,' she said, raising her eyebrows.

Although doe-like in public, playing the part of the attentive Latin wife, Mariella had a keen intuition which Jordi relied on heavily in private.

'Could he survive out there, that's the question?'

'Can you trust him? That's the real question.'

'He's tougher than he looks, sure, but he's an innocent!' said Jordi.

At home, that night, David was unable to sleep under the heavy pile of blankets. The flat was cold and damp and he drifted in and out of wakeful sleep, his mind ablaze with images of mountains and jungle. Finally he got up . There was ice on the window and he pulled on his old dressing gown and went to the kitchen to make some tea. It would be hard at first, if he went, but at least it would be hot. He cupped his hands round the mug and looked out. He rubbed his palm on the window to clear the condensation. The grey dawn revealed an ugly garden with cracked paving and a bald patch of grass that he cut in summer for Miss Ollerenshaw, the old lady who lived downstairs.

Everything seemed such a dead end. He wasn't getting anywhere at work. Even Ian, his friend, with whom he'd been climbing since he was at school, had married and moved to Glasgow.

Why not seize this opportunity then? Jordi was a bighead, but he was vital, he made things happen and he couldn't help liking him.

When he saw Jordi later that morning he said he was interested. But then nothing happened for three or four months and so he couldn't believe it was real. Then, just before he was due to go back to Venezuela, Jordi rang late one night and read a letter from his uncle over the phone offering a job.

'What about a contract?' he asked.

'Manuel says he'll fix things when you get there.'

'Will he send money for the fare?'

'Sure. I'll ring him.'

Jordi left at the beginning of June. David waited, but there was no news for weeks. Although he could not quite believe it was happening, he handed in his notice rather than start the new academic year. He felt he ought to be applying for jobs, but could not summon up the necessary enthusiasm. He felt in a state of limbo, of suspended animation, not yet committed to going but losing interest in staying. And there were doubts and fears. What would he have to do at the University in Caracas. How was he going to cope when he couldn't even speak Spanish. For a week he was hardly able to function. Even the most routine actions, seemed impossible and, although he still managed to get to work on time, he stopped shaving. Deciding what to eat when he got home from work and having to go out shopping became an intolerable chore and he lived off peanut butter and banana sandwiches. Despite the good weather, even climbing seemed to have lost its attraction.

Then, one Saturday morning, he took himself in hand. He cleaned the flat and polished the furniture. The lavender smell of the furniture polish and the fresh air pouring in through the open windows acted like a tonic. He bundled up the piles of dirty clothes that were strewn about the bedroom and headed out to the launderette. On the way back he bought fresh salad and some nice cheese for lunch. Imperceptibly he stopped worrying. If Manuel sent the money, he decided, that would make it real and he would have to go. He applied for a Venezuelan visa, but when he rang the consulate the man on the phone was rude and off-hand.

Just when he was convinced it was all off, a money order arrived in the post from Venezuela. Manuel had sent the money for the fare. He booked a flight and decided to go to the consulate in person to try and get the visa.

The clerk was a balding man dressed in a dark suit with shiny elbows. David recognised his voice as that of the man who had been so difficult on the phone. David explained that he had a job waiting for him and that they had sent money for the flight. The man said he couldn't help. A door opened and a fat man in tweeds came through carrying a golf bag.

'Good-morning,' said David. The man stopped.

'Que pasa aqui?'

'Me disculpa, su excellencia,' said the clerk. The man edged past them.

'Manuel Romero is going to be very disappointed if I don't get my visa.'

'Manuel Romero?' said the consul.

'Yes the minister of planning. Look, he's sent the money for the fare,' said David, showing him the money order. 'I have to pay for my ticket today.'

'Manuel Romero,' said the consul again. 'An old friend. Why didn't you say! Idiota!' he barked at the clerk. 'Hazlo. Rápido!'

'Give him my regards. Tell him how well we treated you,' he said, looking at his watch. 'I must be going.'

He confirmed the flight and sold his car to a colleague at work. A firm of packers arrived and took away the few things he'd decided to keep—his wood-working tools, books and climbing gear—which would go by sea. He bought a new suitcase and some clothes.

Ordinarily he didn't like shopping, preferring to manage with the clothes he had rather than battle his way round the shops on a Saturday morning. Ideally, when his things finally wore out, he would have liked to have replaced them with exactly the same. But for once this time, getting ready to go, he overcame his antipathy and took a real interest in assembling a complete new wardrobe.

In a men's boutique, a shop he had never dreamt of going in before, he bought three shirts: one with a yellow and pink flower pattern that came complete with matching tie, the other two in a plainer pattern for work. In Marks and Spencer he bought blue socks and underpants and in

Burton's he found two pairs of light weight grey slacks and a grey jacket in a herringbone pattern with high lapels which the assistant said was the height of fashion, a phrase that would normally have put David off. Only in his choice of shoes, sensible English brogues, did he indulge his usual conservative tastes.

Ray invited him to a farewell dinner the night before he caught the train to London. And then he was on the plane, fastening the seat belt, telling himself it was really happening.

A battered grey Volkswagen braked violently in front of him; Jordi jumped out, grabbed him by the shoulders and kissed him vigorously on both cheeks.

'Cómo estas? Great to see you. I'd hoped to bring the Mercedes. Sorry I'm late, there's been another landslide. How are you? Where's your luggage?'

'I don't know. It's lost.'

'We'll find out about that tomorrow. First, let's eat.'

They drove from the airport, past the port and out along the narrow coast road. David could not take in the details, he was tired and the glare of the setting sun hurt his eyes. Jordi drove fast, cutting the bends. Trucks, coming in the other direction, would force Jordi back on to their side of the road. David shut his eyes to blot out the sickening sensation as crumbling cliff walls slewed by.

Jordi swung off the road and parked next to a log cabin at the waters edge. David got out, shaking and stiff. There was a strong peppery smell of frying fish.

'This is one of the best fish restaurants in the country.'

'I'm not sure I can eat anything.'

'You'll feel better with food inside you. And anyway we have to wait while the traffic dies down after the landslide.'

David learnt that this happened all the time on the few roads through the coastal range.

Two hours later he could no longer concentrate on what Jordi was saying. Unless he got to bed soon he would curl up under the table in the sand.

'There'll still be traffic on the autopista, but we can go anyway.'

They ran into the queue as they approached the first tunnel. David felt sick with the oily fish and lack of sleep. They slowed to walking pace, then ground to a halt. Exhaust fumes made him dizzy and he began to retch.

'Jordi, stop here. I'm going to get out and walk. I'll wait for you up the road.' Anything was better than being stuck in the car.

There was no sidewalk and the cars were using the breakdown lane. It was pitch dark and his head swam with the lights, the blare of car horns and the revving engines. Gradually he climbed higher, picking his way round the stationary cars. In the tunnels he had to flatten himself against the wall as cars accelerated on each surge forward. The air began to feel cooler and he could see broad belts of fairy lights on the hills ahead. The traffic started to speed up and he rested on the crash barrier at the side of the road and waited for Jordi.

'We've found a hotel for you. Its reasonably priced and very convenient.' David had hoped Jordi would put him up until he found somewhere. As if reading his mind, Jordi said, 'Our flat only has two rooms—you know how it is,' and switching subject, added, 'That's the University and the Botanic Garden.' It looked like being the only green space in a jungle of concrete sky-scrapers.

They arrived at the Hotel Piccolo and, in a daze, David signed the register. His room was stifling and when he opened the window there was a strong smell of hot fat and garlic. He pulled off his clothes, put a towel round his waist and returned to the startled concierge at the desk. Holding up his soiled shirt, socks and pants he said, 'Mañana', one of the few words he knew in Spanish. Back in the room he collapsed on the bed and pulled a sheet over his naked body.

2

David had always wanted to try and find his mother. After Nikki left the idea that he might be able to see her kept coming back with increasing strength. He couldn't remember when he first realised that he was adopted, or stopped believing the story that his parents had been killed in a train crash. But three years ago, in her last illness, his mother told him about the young woman who had held him and cried when she handed him over.

Not that David was obsessed with being adopted. He loved his mum and dad. Occasionally his mum worried but his dad would say, David's all right, he's a bit solitary that's all.

But David held the idea of his other mother inside himself, hidden like the birth certificate he had found when he was about eight while rummaging in the large tan handbag in his mum's wardrobe. When he looked again it had disappeared.

A year after his father died he wrote to Somerset House for a copy of the missing document. When it arrived it was the same green form with the spidery writing he remembered and he felt the same mixture of excitement and bitterness.

There were two clues: his birthplace in Southport and his mother's address in the Midlands. He wrote and a reply came from the address in Southport saying that it had been a WAAF nursing home during the war but that they had no further information. So he decided to go and visit the town where she'd lived.

At eight o'clock on Saturday morning it was already hot and David was glad to be getting out of the city. He folded his jacket and tie and put them on the back seat. He filled up at the local garage and drove south through sweaty suburbs of rhododendron and sycamore, joining the motorway at Knutford. It was strange to be doing something after all the years waiting.

There was heavy traffic on the M6 but this disappeared once he left the motorway. Although the map showed a confident red line, the road was narrow and winding with dense overhanging trees, more like a country lane than an important 'A' route. Bowling along, preoccupied, perhaps he missed something or failed to take in some vital clue that would have alerted him to the danger. He came round one of the succession of bends and saw a stationary lorry less than fifty yards ahead.

A number of things happened automatically: his feet moved to brake and clutch and he changed into third; he saw that there was a cream, single-decker bus coming towards him in the other lane and that the trees—sycamore again, he realised, with a sense of absent-minded hysteria—formed an effective wall on the left. Some part of his brain simultaneously computed the length of empty road between his bonnet and the fast approaching lorry; the speed he had been travelling, about 45mph, and came to the simple answer, communicated as an imprecise but certain understanding, that there wasn't room to stop in time.

The engine screamed in protest as he forced the gear into second. His right foot did clever things with the brake pedal, easing off as the wheels skidded, braking harder as they bit. All this had taken perhaps a second and there was plenty of time to examine the lorry's tailgate in detail. The number plate was held on by a single screw and would shake loose soon; the red plastic cover of the right rear light was cracked and had been repaired with sticky tape; there was a neat pile of empty coal sacks on the flat-bed trailer—originally pillar box red, now streaky black—that was about to hit him in the throat and messily decapitate him.

The car stopped with at least a foot to spare. The lorry driver leaned his head out of the cab and shook an angry fist. David thought he should have blown him kisses or at least waved. The lights changed and the queue moved, leaving him sitting alone. He was all right, the car was all right, nothing had happened. He concentrated on unlocking his hands from the steering wheel and massaged them to get the pain out. The lights were green and he put the car in gear and drove through the road works and parked in a small lay-by alongside a road roller and a yellow compressor. He got out and walked back. The road was empty and peaceful; there was no warning sign. He looked about, then climbed into the hedge and began pulling out dead wood and branches with leaves to make a pyramid in the road. Returning, he saw long black streaks on the road and discovered that the two new remoulds he had bought for the trip were quite bald.

In the town centre he found a parking space in the main square. Right in front of him was a bookshop called Sparldings, his mother's name. He went in and bought a street plan of the town. Within an hour he was back having failed to get anywhere. The people who now lived in the detached house that had once been her home had never heard of her.

David sat in the car, undecided what to do next, but reluctant to give up and drive home. He felt lousy, he had exhausted the clues on the birth certificate and had failed to find anything. There was nothing left to try, he would never find her now. He was crazy to have imagined he would find her so easily.

On an impulse, he went back into the bookshop and asked them if they knew someone called Gwen Spalding. The manageress came over and said that she thought he must be looking for the daughter of the founder. Her married name was Dutton and she lived in a village nearby. It didn't take long to find her address in the telephone box in the square.

He drove slowly along the country lanes, through fields of blazing corn, feeling as though he was doing something dangerous and not just pottering along in his Morris Minor. In a few minutes he would see her. A sign read 'Battle of Bosworth Field 1485' and he stopped for a moment on the verge by the side of the road. There wasn't much to see: a low ridge of ripe corn bending in the breeze, a gentle slope down to trees marking the line of a watercourse.

The address was a thatched cottage in a tiny village of half a dozen houses. David drove past and parked up the road. He sat still for a while looking at the fields, then he got his tie from the back seat and knotted it carefully in the rear mirror. Taking a couple of deep breaths he got out of the car, slipped on his jacket and walked back up the road to the gate.

The garden was full of flowers – hollyhocks and lavender, roses and catmint. The scent was overpowering and he felt faint as he rang the bell. He waited, listening to the hum of insects on the flowers and the geese in the pond over the way. The cottage was bigger than he first thought and constructed from rough limestone. The woodwork was painted white and the curtains had a flower pattern. He rang again but there was no answer. He looked back once or twice as he walked back to the car, wondering what else he could do. A neighbour was working in her garden and David said hello. The woman got up off her knees and came to the wall. She said that the Duttons were away on holiday; they went away every summer and would not be back till September.

The rest of August dragged on interminably. There was hardly anyone around in the department and the library was virtually empty. David still needed six months to complete his probationary year as assistant lecturer and had to work. He tried to get on with taking notes for the next term's lectures but it was difficult to concentrate and he spent hours just looking out of the window or fiddling about.

September arrived at last. He thought of telephoning but despite the journey it seemed easier to go and visit her again. He took a day off work and drove down the M6 and the A5, then through Sheepy Magna and Sheepy Parva direct to her village. The harvest was in now and the fields were bare. Again there was no answer. The neighbour told him that the water main had burst and that they had gone to a hotel till it was fixed. David drove back feeling frustrated and stupid for not having rung first.

On the way back he came round a blind bend on the wrong side of the road and realised he was driving too fast. He was angry and pent up inside, taking his frustration out on the driving. If he was to get home in one piece, he decided he had better stop and calm down. He pulled into a lay-by and got out of the car. So stupid for not having rung first, he thought, as he kicked loose stones across the road.

Term started, the students arrived and there was a lot of work, so it wasn't until late Autumn that he had time to contact her again. He was going through his desk to find a cheque book stub when he came across the map he had bought and her address and telephone number. At home that evening he sat in the kitchen unable to decide what to do. He went out into the street holding the piece of paper and walked up the road to the telephone box. Without any clear idea of what he would say he picked up the receiver, put his money in and dialled.

A woman answered and, without preamble, he said, 'My name is David. I was born in Southport in 1946. Are you my mother?'

There was a pause and then simply: 'Yes, I've been expecting you to telephone. I always knew you would come one day.'

David closed his eyes, steadying himself against the wall of the telephone box. 'Can I see you?' he asked. They arranged for him to go the following day at twelve.

This time the drive felt different. The radio blared pop music and David beat time with his bare arm on the car door.

She met him at the door, a small robust woman with thick grey hair. They held hands, then David put his arms round her and she burst into tears. She took him into the living room and introduced her husband, Harvey.

While she served coffee Harvey asked him why he had come. It felt like he was being interrogated. He sat on a green velvet armchair trying to balance his cup and saucer and a plate of cake. 'Why dig up the past?' asked Harvey. 'Anyone would be curious,' said David, turning to his mother. He explained how his adoptive parents had both died, how he had always wanted to try and find her, but hadn't been able to until now. He told them how he had come twice before. 'Third time lucky,' he said, but Harvey didn't smile. He learnt that they had lived in the cottage most of their married life and had brought up four children there. So he had half-siblings, he wondered what they looked like. David wanted to ask who his father was and why she had given him away.

'You were happy?' she asked, and he said yes cheerfully, thinking it was more complicated than that.

Harvey asked what he was doing now and he told them about his job in the university.

'The education system's all wrong,' said Harvey, unbuttoning his jacket. 'School leavers we get for interview can hardly read or write never mind do arithmetic.' David was finding it difficult to concentrate on what Harvey was saying. This wasn't why he'd come, this hadn't anything to do with the tumult inside him.

David looked across at his mother and she got up and began clearing away the coffee cups. 'Isn't it time you were getting back to the office?' she suggested gently. She explained that Harvey was semi-retired, since the doctor had told him to slow down last year, but that he still popped into the office most days. They shook hands and Harvey said, 'I hope you know what you're doing, this is causing my wife a great deal of pain.'

David followed her into the kitchen and hung his coat on the back of a chair. 'Are you hungry,' she asked, and he said he was famished. So she got a steak from the freezer and fried it with mushrooms and tomatoes. He watched her cook, enjoying the intimacy of being together. They sat across the table from one another chatting as though they had known each other all their lives.

'My father?' asked David. She said that they had been in the air force together. It was different then; so many of her friends were killed, you never knew if you would see each other again. Yet she remembered it as a happy time, so full of life. 'We were in love, we lived each day at a time.'

She got up and took out a photo album out of one of the window seats and showed him a photograph of herself seated at a table in a bar, head turned to the camera, laughing. Then another of young men standing in front of a fighter plane. 'Your father, David Menzies,' she said pointing to one of them. 'Dad liked David. He hoped we'd get married and take over the business.'

'Why didn't you … ?' he asked, then saw she looked upset. 'I'm sorry, I …'

'No. Well we didn't. Things were different then, at the end of the war. Everything changed. David went off to Canada, before you were born. He couldn't settle, he'd have gone out of his mind, living here in the Midlands.' David wondered why she hadn't gone with him. Hadn't he wanted her? So many questions bubbled up. Why couldn't she have kept him? What traumas did she go through? Did she already know Harvey? How did it all happen? Where was he conceived, what was the weather like then?

'I needed security,' she said simply, getting up. 'Do you paint? Your grandfather painted … landscapes'. She pointed to a water colour and he recognised Ullswater. When she was a child they spent most summer holidays in the Lake District, staying in the Duddon Valley because her father's family came from there. It was one of David's favourite places and he had stayed in the climbing hut there many times.

Too soon she said it was time he was going; Harvey would be back from work. David said he'd telephone. Perhaps she could come and see him in Manchester or they might even meet in the Lake District. Then he was driving home. The moon came up, although it was still light, like a ripe tomato in the evening sunlight and he felt warm inside and happy.

Momentarily he worried about all the things he could have asked her but hadn't. He could hardly remember what she looked like. He had been concentrating so hard on just being with her, absorbing what it felt like, watching the expression of her face and the way her hands moved, that he had failed to take in the ordinary details of her appearance. But it didn't matter. He would be seeing her again soon, there would be plenty more opportunities.

He rang the following evening, having found out about trains on Saturday and intending to take her for lunch to a nice Italian place on Deansgate. As the phone rang and he waited for her to answer he had to take deep breaths to calm his heart.

This time her husband answered. 'Oh it's you is it?'

'Can I speak to Gwen,' David asked politely, sensing the

worst.

'What's your motive? that's what I want to know.'

David said nothing. He'd already explained once. His mother would know he wasn't after money. 'I'd like to speak to my mother,' he insisted.

Gwen came on the line and said, 'I can't see you. I'm sorry ... but I promised Harvey, all those years ago, so I just can't ...'

David felt as if he had been violently hit. From the moment they'd met, from the first words they'd shared, he had felt completely at home with her, as if the years of separation had no effect whatsoever on the empathy he felt for her. It was as if they had known what each other was thinking, how they felt and what they were about to say before they said it. And now she was denying that shared consciousness, pushing him away again. He was her child, she couldn't turn him away again.

'But, why not ... I don't want anything ... just to see you, that's all.'

Harvey took over. 'We discussed this last night and decided that it's best for all concerned if you don't see each other again.'

He could hear them arguing and Harvey saying that he would deal with it.

'Let me speak to Gwen.'

'I agreed to the meeting yesterday against my better judgement. Your visit has upset Gwen dreadfully.'

'We enjoyed seeing each other, she was fine,' David burst out.

'This is intolerable. I've told you I'm not standing for you persecuting my wife in this way ...'

'Can I speak to my mother.' David forced himself to keep calm. 'I'm sorry but I'd like to speak to my mother.' Gwen must have been listening because he heard her say, 'Harvey, let me ...'

'David ...' she said.

'I wanted to invite you. I thought we might have lunch together, next Saturday,' he said diffidently, because it mattered so much to him and because he felt her slipping away.

'It's impossible. Harvey ... he's not been well. Last night, after you left, it was awful ...'

David could feel himself giving up. 'Can't I see you?'

'No, it's best not to.'

He asked if he could write and she was saying yes when Harvey took the phone. 'Now listen to me, I'm not standing for this. I have to think of others.' You can't stop someone seeing their mother, thought David. Keep cool, don't get angry, he told himself. He wasn't going to be browbeaten. 'I want to see my mother,' he said forcefully, 'there are things I need to know, things I have a right to know. She wants to see me. I know she wants to see me.'

Harvey's tone changed. 'I've been very ill. My heart won't stand this. I've just had one attack, if I have another there will be no one to blame but you.'

That's blackmail, thought David, feeling sick. Harvey started to shout and lose his breath. Then Gwen took the receiver and said goodbye and then there was nothing. He felt himself slipping as if the hands that had held him were letting go, then he was falling. He closed his eyes and dropped into blackness. All that effort to find her only to lose her again. How could she be like this. She just wanted a quiet life. Surely she had more guts. He went home to bed and fell asleep curled into a tight ball.

The following day he wrote to her pouring out his feelings and begging her to see him, but he never posted the letter and it got lost in his drawer along with his old bank statements and cheque stubs.

He started a letter to Nikki. He wanted to tell her how thrilled he'd been and then how disappointed. He wanted to ask her to help him. But he couldn't put it all into words and anyway how could she help, she was in Africa.

Momentarily, he saw it from Harvey's point of view, but anger swept away any understanding, casting him into a maelstrom of recrimination and self-pity, leaving a metallic taste like battery acid. He abandoned the letter.

For days he felt numb, in shock. To escape, he buried himself in his work, hiding his grief from friends and colleagues who began to find his behaviour increasingly odd. Yet on the surface he thought he was coping. After all he had managed without her for the first twenty-six years. He was being melodramatic, he told himself.

Wanting to meet his mother had, he realised, been the most important thing in his life. Having to wait until he felt the time was right had made him more passive than he might otherwise have been. Unconsciously, everything was judged against the supreme importance of meeting his mother. Usually the active, practical side of his nature predominated. But now that she refused to see him again he was thrown into a kind of paralysis of spirit that left him hardly able to function.

It was in this mood that Jordi invited him to dinner and offered him the job in Venezuela.

3

David woke surprisingly early. His clothes, smelling freshly laundered and pressed, were waiting outside his room. He showered and then lathered his face. The sharp new blade left his face tingly tight, as if he'd sloughed off a layer of old skin. The shirt felt wonderful: the collar was slightly starched and there was a sharp crease down the arms.

The same porter was still on duty and he mouthed 'café' and mimed raising a cup to his lips.

'Si, señor. Sales de aquí, a mano derecha.'

He didn't understand but his arm waving suggested a cafe round the corner. Outside the leaves of the acacias shone with last night's rain and, turning on to the main street, he smelt fresh baked bread and coffee. It was a new day and he was doing fine.

David sat on a stool at the bar and started to plan the day.

He ordered a coffee by learning the words from the phrase book and the waiter taught him to pronounce it correctly—'Café con leche, señor'.

Jordi had given him a plan of the city. He had to find the airline office and report his case stolen. He had to find a flat, fix up Spanish lessons, start work. Don't worry, one thing at a time. He wasn't meeting Jordi till seven.

The cafe had filled, and there were couples at the tables on the broad pavement. People were hurrying to work, or sauntering in the sunlight: older men in suits, younger men in jeans and open necked shirts. The women were less forward than the men, their self-conscious poise more restrained.

Standing on the corner outside the cafe, David watched the traffic. He knew about the por puestos, taxis that ran on a fixed route and filled up with passengers. Every few seconds a car pulled into the curb: Chevrolet and Dodge, Packards and Fords—fifties cars with massive chrome bumpers and cracked windscreens. The signs on their roofs indicated their destinations; 'Silencio', 'Carmelitas', 'Sabana Grande'. One read 'Avenida Urdaneta', the address he had for the airline office, but he dithered and someone took the only place. Affecting confidence, David held his hand out for the next car and grabbed a seat.

He saw the BOAC sign as they climbed a hill into the city centre and asked the driver to stop. The woman on the front desk took him round the back and upstairs to a shabby office. The manager was tall and black with an aquiline nose. David explained that his luggage had been lost. The man didn't answer at first, then he said, 'So you've lost your case. Fill in this form.' His manner was imperious. He offered no apology and appeared to accept the loss as normal, even inevitable.

David could sense angry words forming on his lips: I haven't lost my case, you have!

Reason came to his rescue. How many years had the man worked in this seedy office? Taking the form, David asked, 'From your experience what is likely to have happened to my case?'

'Ah, well, your plane was delayed in Antigua and arrived half-an-hour behind schedule. I believe your case may have gone on to Jamaica and then Florida.'

'When will you be able to get it back here?'

'Not until next week.'

'I have nothing to wear', David said, his exasperation returning.

He could see the manager hesitate, he was going to say something offensive, disdain showed in his eyes. But he said, 'In the circumstances I believe we can recompense you for the inconvenience.' He opened a drawer in the desk with a key, took out some bills which he handed over. 'Two hundred bolivars.'

From the airline office David caught a por puesto back to the Plaza Venezuela where a broad avenue led past the Botanic Garden to the University. From the plaza near his hotel David had seen the palms and the cool trees. He wanted to sit in the shade and wait for the heat to go.

He was jostled by crowds of students running towards him. A line of blue and yellow trucks blocked the avenue and dozens of uniformed police, some with large plastic riot shields were standing around. David stopped by the low concrete wall bordering the road to let the crowd pass. A sudden whiff of turbid waters below made him look over the edge and he saw that the river was an open sewer flowing in a concrete canyon. Looking back the way he had come, three office towers formed a backdrop to the fountain in the middle of the plaza; behind them the chain of mountains David had come through the previous night were pale violet, their tops indefinite in the heat haze. A sign on one of the buildings said Cerveza Polar and flashing lights gave the time and temperature—14.45:32°.

A high wire fence separated David from the garden. The grass looked lush and inviting and the tall stands of bamboo made a musical sound as they rustled in the breeze. But the fence seemed endless and there was no sign of an entrance. He stopped a young woman and asked: 'Dónde está el Jardin Botanico?' She stared, uncomprehending, seemingly worried and preoccupied. He repeated his question and she laughed hysterically. Maybe it was his accent. Then he noticed they were standing by a gate into the garden, chained and pad-locked and, half hidden in the forest, he saw light armoured vehicles and soldiers in camouflage battle dress and suddenly he realised why she'd laughed.

About fifty yards ahead he could see the university gates, like a toll entrance, and lying face down, four or five young men, their arms straight ahead, pointing along the road. He could hear muffled cracks and realised they were firing. He looked round and saw the police had taken cover behind the vans. The gate to the botanic garden was being opened and the soldiers were moving into position. David knew that he had to move or he would be caught in the cross-fire. Turning immediately, he walked briskly back the way he had come. 'Don't run, just don't run!' he said, cursing himself for a fool.

As he got nearer to the police vans he could see armed men, their faces excited behind the visors. One of them came out from behind a vehicle, raised a gun to his shoulder and fired at David. A canister arched over his head and he turned and saw it explode on the road.

He was stopped and searched by a sergeant. A small crowd of police gathered round him and asked him questions he was unable to answer. He showed his passport. There was a sense of released tension as the men pulled off their helmets and made jokes. They let him go and he walked back to the hotel.

Meanwhile, in the university, Jordi pushed back his chair and strode back and forth, agitated by the disturbance outside. The other two members of the unit sat still: Alejandro, tilted his chair back and looked out of the window; Luis Carlos sat with his elbows on the table, his fingers making a steeple in front of his lips.

'The police found pistols taped behind the toilet cisterns,' said Luis Carlos, biting off the words. 'They're searching for more weapons.'

'We've got to get the contract settled before we go,' said Jordi impatiently. 'We agreed to form this unit to test alternatives for the capital.'

'No, we agreed to direct investment to the regions,' said Luis Carlos sharply.

'Manuel wants us to model development of the Tuy,' said Jordi, glaring back.

'So?' said Luis Carlos.

'We need this contract to pay David's salary,' said Jordi belligerently.

Alejandro smiled. 'Did he arrive safely?' he asked, deflecting the imminent conflict.

'Yes, I collected him from the airport last night,' said Jordi.

'Does he know you're planning to go to England?' asked Alejandro.

'Not yet. I wondered about putting him off coming when things turned risky, but I thought it would be useful having him here with you and Chelo. We'll only have to stay away till after the election. Things will settle down then,' said Jordi.

'What about Chelo?' asked Luis Carlos.

'She stays. You know she can't come,' snapped Jordi.

'He'll need to be a survivor, the money's very tight,' said Alejandro.

'But the money's not coming out of the same pot,' said Jordi.

'Has he got a contract?' asked Luis Carlos.

'I got a letter of appointment from the dean and a promise of one year's funding from Manuel.'

Luis Carlos tapped his baldhead with his fingertips.

'He either takes a chance and starts work, or he goes home,' he said.

'Let's get him started and worry about paying him later,' said Jordi.

'What's he going to live on, thin air!' said Alejandro.

'My father will help out and David is a resourceful character,' said Jordi, confidently.

§

The bar was dark after the brightness of the street. There was a maze of tables and chairs—heavy, fake colonial furniture. A row of brightly coloured beer steins with silver lids hung above the polished counter. He recognised Jordi's distinctive outline on a tall stool. Seated, he appeared a big man. Sensing someone behind him, he swung round off the stool and embraced David in a bear hug.

'Olá, cómo estas? How was your day?'

'Amusing', said David. 'It's good to see you.'

'And you. Want a beer? Germans know about beer.'

Jordi ordered two beers and a plate of spicy meatballs.

'They do good tapas here.'

'Tapas?'

'Hors d'oeuvres. These meatballs are fantastic. What a day … I'm destroyed … the traffic—it was almost impossible to get out of the university: the police had two of the gates blocked. Half the students didn't get into classes.'

'I nearly got shot!' David related his tale.

Jordi looked concerned and then laughed uproariously, 'I told you not to come into work today.'

'What's happening?'

'It's always like this before the elections. The opposition organises the students to make trouble for the government: they barricade the entrances, throw stones at the police. The police fire a few tear gas bombs.'

'But the students were shooting, and the army was in the Botanic Garden.'

'Yes, well it's a little difficult at the moment. There was a group hiding out in the Garden, being supported by elements in the university.'

'What sort of group?'

'Revolutionary—a guerrilla group. Things got rough a week ago—those bastards—some of them used to be guerrilleros—they're the worst: they take people up in helicopters and drop them out.'

David was horrified, yet sceptical still. 'I didn't realise …'

'The police weren't supposed to enter the university—it's all fixed. But the muchachos were firing on police cars on the autopista and they raided the School two nights ago and found arms and ammunition. Some people will have to lay low for a while.'

'What about you? Are you involved?'

'I'm all right. I'm going back to England next week. There's a conference in Cambridge and I'll stay on till the heat's off.'

'Cambridge! Next week!'

'Don't worry, there's plenty of time to get you settled in. Mariella's going to help you find a flat and I know my parents will give you a hand.'

David felt the same hollow apprehension he had sometimes on a long difficult climb. We were going to work together, he thought.

'Don't worry. We'll work together when I get back,' said Jordi, as if reading his thoughts.

But David did worry. It wasn't how he had imagined. He took a deep breath and asked, 'What's the conference on?'

'Computer modelling. They've got the urban models in Cambridge. Luis Carlos is coming too.'

David found it hard to concentrate, his mind was on his own problems. 'Who's Luis Carlos?' he asked.

'We're co-directors of the unit,' said Jordi, smiling.

David sensed Jordi wasn't happy with the arrangement. 'When can I start flat hunting with Mariella?'

'Come to the apartment tomorrow afternoon, about three. Buy the *Daily Journal* and she'll drive you round.'

§

'Did you tell him?' asked Mariella, when Jordi got home.

'Sure.'

'How did he take it?'

'He went quiet, you know the way he does.'

'Just so long as it's understood he doesn't stay here. I've promised the flat to Aurora while we're away.'

'I don't think we should be encouraging your sister.'

'Jordi … '

'Okay!'

'I said you'd help him flat hunt tomorrow.'

'What time?'

'I told him to come at three.'

'All right, but only tomorrow. I shall be busy all next week packing. What about our arrangements?'

'Everything is taken care of.'

'And the grant?'

'Luis Carlos nearly screwed it up today, but the Minister signed the applications and the money will be through before the election.'

Early the following morning David sat at a table under an awning outside the cafe he was beginning to think of as home.

'Hey Jude! What's this blackbird singing in the dead of night?' Franco, one of the waiters, came over to practice his English. He was self-taught from pop records.

'You know, Franco, it's like poetry.'

'Poesía, si, tu eres un poeta. Ha, Ha.'

David had been working methodically through the three papers he'd bought at the kiosk, marking advertisements for flats within a mile or two of the university.

'Franco, where should I look for a flat?'

'Maybe you like the old barrios like San Bernadino? San Roman is expensive, Caurimare and Chuao are new; many new building.'

Gradually David began to build up a pattern of the city: the government, the university, the industry, the commerce; where the rich lived and where they used to live; where the traffic was likely to be worst and where there might be trees and quiet at a price he could afford.

At two o'clock he decided it was time to go. He waited fifteen minutes but there were no cabs to Caurimare. In frustration, David boarded the next car going in the right direction. He checked the map—the mountains were on the left, they were heading east on the autopista down the centre of the broad valley that cradled the city. So far, so good. In the distance he could see Petare and the ranchos—hundreds of thousands of shacks rising in terrace upon terrace until they reached the municipal dump, smoking like a dormant volcano.

They were driving fast, in the breakdown lane, to avoid the queues of cars in the other three lanes, having to swerve every hundred yards to avoid the deep rainwater grids in the side of the road.

Looking across the river, David saw a long hoarding announcing 'Caurimare—Luxury Apartments'. He suddenly realised his mistake: this was an express car which went direct to Petare on the autopista without stopping in Caurimare.

He glanced at the map, saw a bridge over the river at

the next intersection and shouted, 'Stop here!' The driver objected and there were protests from the other passengers, but he stopped and let David out.

David crossed the river and found a dirt track where the map showed a road to Jordi's apartment. A construction site blocked his way but the gates were open and a path led through to the made road on the other side. He shouted hello, but no one answered.

They're all at lunch or sleeping, he thought.

Halfway across the site two large Alsatian dogs bounded from the timber huts to his left. He was terrified of dogs. For a second, as he watched the two dogs bearing down on him, he debated whether to run or stand. He could run fast, but the gates were too far away. The dogs were almost on him, he watched, fascinated, as great gobs of spittle flew from their jaws. They neither barked nor halted their charge. At the last second he leapt sideways, sprinted to the river and, without stopping, plunged down the steep bank.

The drop was much greater than he had realised. From the bridge, the river had looked no more than thirty feet wide. Now at the river's edge the scale expanded dramatically and he saw it four or five times as broad and the bank towering more than a hundred feet above him. The dogs had stopped on the brink, barking wildly. Carefully, he picked his way between the mud banks and rotting garbage. Well past the building site he began to climb. The shale and baked mud broke away under his feet and there was no solid purchase for his hands, but the angle was reasonable and he felt exhilarated to be climbing again.

He came over the edge on to the road and walked along until he found Jordi's building. He rang the intercom and a woman answered.

'It's me, David,' he said.

'Olá, come up.'

Mariella opened the door. 'What happened to you?' she asked, her nose wrinkling in disgust.

David's jacket and trousers were streaked with clay and his shoes were caked in foul smelling slime.

'I got attacked by dogs.'

'Stay there,' she ordered and disappeared, returning with an armful of newspapers. 'Walk on these. Don't touch anything!' She led him through the flat to a balcony by the maid's room. 'Here, use this to brush yourself down,' she said, handing him a stiff brush.

When she had shut the door, David took off his shoes and washed them in the stone sink. He brushed his trousers and jacket and finally used the block of coarse blue soap to wash his grimy hands.

'That's better. Coffee?' Mariella was sitting on a white leather sofa. She wore a plain black dress with thin gold straps. In England she'd always worn jeans and bulky sweaters. She crossed her long bare legs with ostentatious slowness and looked at David with an amused, almost calculating smile.

'Yes thank you. I'd love some.'

A sliding window ran almost its full length of the L-shaped room and, through the window, there was a wide balcony. The far end was lined with bookshelves and contained a desk heaped with journals and reports. The floor tiles, the colour of rose hips, were freshly polished and a Chinese silk carpet in soft pinks and yellows hung on one of the plain white walls.

Mariella yelled for the maid to bring coffee. 'They are all unreliable and want paying the earth,' she said while they waited.

The maid brought the coffee on a round silver tray. There were two small cups and saucers, a sugar bowl and a tall porcelain jug—all intricately painted with a gilded rim.

'It's Turkish,' said Mariella, noticing his interest. 'It was a wedding present. It's old and very valuable. But the coffee is fresh and very good,' she said with a laugh. 'We'll go out on the balcony,' She told the maid to carry the tray through.

The balcony was roofed by the flat above and shaded by a criss-crossed timber frieze. Slim steel railings supported a polished mahogany handrail and the end of the balcony was filled with plants. There was a panoramic view of the coastal mountains with the distinctive col, *La Silla de Caracas*, directly in front of them.

'Where to find a flat for you?' Mariella mused as she poured the coffee. 'Have you got the papers with you?' From his jacket he pulled out the pages he had torn from the newspapers.

David moved his chair so he could look at the view while she studied the lists of flats. He began to distinguish features on the mountains. The bright sun washed out all detail, but he could see the darker green of forest trees marking the ravines.

Across the avenue he could see down into the river. There was no sign of the dogs movement on the opposite bank caught his attention. At first he couldn't identify the small grey animal, maybe it was a rat or a lizard. Then he realised with shock that it was a horse.

'How do you like the coffee?' she asked.

'Very much,' he replied. 'It's strong, but not at all bitter.'

'It's a tragedy really; nobody can be bothered to grow it. There are just so many easier ways of getting rich.'

He wondered if she was bemoaning or celebrating the country's easy prosperity. She was completely different from the image he had formed in England. There she'd been slavishly attentive to Jordi. The biggest change was in her voice, soft and melodious when speaking English, she became shrill and carping when talking to the maid.

Mariella manoeuvred her car out of the underground car park and into the traffic.

'I think we should start by looking in Caurimare and Chuao,' she said. 'There are lots of new apartments and we can call in at the supermarket on the way.'

'I'd prefer somewhere nearer the University.'

'Yes, we'll see,' she said.

'Why do you have such a large car?' he asked, feeling irritated.

'I feel safer in a big car and, anyway, the air-conditioning never works on European cars.'

The first flat was all blue—speckled terrazzo tiles on the floors, baby-blue paint on the walls and aquamarine in the bathroom. The rubbish chute stank and a strong smell of cabbage and salt fish wafted up from the apartment below. David couldn't hear what Mariella was saying   over the noise of the engines and blaring horns.

'Let's go,' he said.

'What's wrong?'

'Everything,'

'Well, if you're going to be this picky it's going to take for ever,' she said, marching out of the flat and back to the car.

They looked at three other flats, all equally unattractive. By six o'clock David felt prickly and despondent.

'Come on cheer up, I'll buy you a drink,' she said, driving into a large shopping centre.

She led him to a restaurant and found a free table.

'Where are we?' asked David.

'Chacaito. Our first centro commercial. There are a lot of nice shops and a good cine. What would you like?'

'A beer, please.'

The trees under the high roof created the illusion of being outdoors. Inside it was cool and spacious, while outside, in the street, it was noisy, bustling and smelly. There was a sign over the entrance to the cafe which read: Papagallo. Like Papageno in the *Magic Flute*, thought David. Then he saw the sign depicted a parrot and realised that he'd learnt another word.

'What are you going to do next?'

'Sorry?' said David.

'About a flat. I'm afraid I'm going to be busy packing.'

'Jordi said he'd find someone to help me in the University.'

For some reason Mariella looked annoyed. 'Yes, well. ¡Mira! Por aqui. Una lisa y una Pepsi.'

He left Mariella shopping. Outside, right next to the shopping centre, the main road crossed a deep gorge and, far below in amongst the heaps of rubbish and scrap, David saw dozens of toy shacks. Tiny people were sitting outside their houses or climbing the steep flight of steps to the road. In the dry river bed children played in pools of fetid green water and mangy dogs fought vultures for scraps.

When David got back to the hotel, his case was waiting for him in the hallway.

4

At six o'clock on Saturday morning he was up and waiting
outside the hotel. A station wagon pulled up and a man
climbed out and shook his hand. 'David! I am Alberto, Jordi's
father. And this is Christina, my daughter.' David opened
the back door to get in but Alberto said, 'No sit in the
front, there's room for three. Jordi and Mariella are coming
tomorrow.'

At the Plaza Venezuela they joined the autopista,
following the course of the river past the Botanic Garden and
the old city centre. There was little traffic that early in the
morning, the sky was clear and, through the open windows,
there was a satisfying hum of tyres on the road. David sat
back in the seat and relaxed.

Alberto was powerfully built, like Jordi, and dressed in a
bush shirt, work trousers and heavy boots. Behind his dark-

rimmed glasses his eyes had a gentle twinkle, and in contrast to Jordi's ebullience, he seemed reserved. Christina also wore boots into which she had tucked her tight jeans. An emerald tennis shirt and a wide leather belt completed the outfit. Her skin was olive, like Jordi's, and her thick dark hair was swept back and held by a band, accentuating the patrician line of her nose.

It was clear they enjoyed each other's company and that Christina often accompanied him to the farm.

'This is the main road to the west. It was built by Perez Jimenez—one of the few good things he did,' said Christina.

'The city's getting awfully crowded,' said David, looking back at the maze of skyscrapers.

'It has changed so quickly,' said Alberto 'We built our house less than twenty years ago. It was a paradise then— ciudad de primavera—city of springtime.'

'It's impossible to control the pace of change,' said Christina.

'That's why I like the farm—it's peaceful. I love the horses, but I never go to the races,' said Alberto. 'That's the Hipó-dromo, the race-track, over there to the right.'

Alberto said he had bought the farm eight years ago to breed race horses, but had only begun to build up the stock in the last four or five years since he had more spare time. He now had over forty brood mares and three stallions. The farm was six thousand hectares on the south side of Lake Valencia. Half was good pasture and the rest chaparral, up to the ridge, to safeguard the water supply. He came most weekends, but his wife, Mildred, only came now and then. She was a biochemist doing cancer research and by the weekend all she wanted to do was rest.

They reached the edge of the city and began the steep sweeping climb into the mountains. At first the vegetation was lush, but as they crossed the watershed the land became much drier. The trees were confined to the valleys and the grassland on the intervening ridges looked brown and tinder dry. Ugly scars, where fire had left black stumps of trees, sometimes disfigured a whole hillside. David suddenly felt homesick for green fields and gentle rain.

'Is it always this dry?'

'It's the dry season. This will all be green when the rains come,' said Alberto. The valley they were descending began to widen into a fertile plain. The small vegetable plots of the upper valley changed to broad sweeps of sugar cane. David could see the ruined chimney of a sugar mill and the long straight avenues of palms dividing the valley into rectangular plots.

They left the autopista and pulled up at a service station. People crowded three deep yelling their orders to the hurrying waiters. Alberto levered a way to the bar and was recognised immediately by one of the men serving. He ordered arepas—flat round cakes made from white maize flour. David had tried them with spicy fish or meat, but here they were filled with chunks of roast pork sliced from joints sizzling on rows of spits.

David downed his coffee and, eating his sandwich, strolled round, absorbing the sights and sounds.

There was a constant coming and going of vehicles: long-distance buses, heavy lorries, beat-up trucks and hundreds of cars. The noise was intense: shouted orders, street vendors, the klaxons of the buses and lorries as drivers tried to steer through the press of people. The whole place seemed to be in boiling, bubbling turmoil.

Produce and money changed hands at bewildering speed: commerce conducted with such zest and enthusiasm that it left him breathless. Street vendors of all description touted their wares: women with baskets of steaming yellow pancakes, boys selling hot pork crackling, fruit sellers, some with bags of oranges, others with mangos, pineapples and many fruits he failed to recognise; sellers of beads and amulets, potions and herbal remedies, plastic crucifix and Madonnas, photographs of bleeding hearts, of presidents, of saints in robes and saints in trilby hats; a hotchpotch of the sacred and profane, promising health and fortune, luck, love and a safe journey.

There were dark-skinned women in headscarves and coloured caftans, men from the Andes with black felt hats and Hitler moustaches; sharp men from the city, peasants from the country; some in rags, others in the height of fashion. People leant out of buses to buy cans of drink and hot food, drivers stopped in the middle of the road to exchange news or shout abuse and everywhere there was the smell of diesel exhausts mingled with tropical fruits and cooking food.

A heated exchange between two drivers over a dented wing erupted into a fierce argument. A man leaned out the window of a station wagon to threaten a truck driver, who, in turn, climbed down from his cab and pulled a heavy tyre lever from under his seat. The man in the station wagon produced a squat revolver. The truck driver stopped, looked at the gun and climbed back into his cab and drove off. The man put away the gun and swaggered to the bar.

The crowd now appeared more alien and dangerous. Men at the bar with paunches bulging over trouser waists displayed guns, stuck in their belts like combs in back pockets. Lean youths with hard eyes cruised through the crowd and on the outskirts unshaven men moved in twos and threes like jackals.

'Why were there were so many soldiers on the road?' asked David.

'There are many … cuartel?'

'Barracks,' said Christina.

'Yes, many barracks here. This is where the road west meets the route south into the *llanos*, the flood plain of the Orinoco River. Throughout our history, leaders have been afraid of insurrection from the Andes or the plains and this area has always been a military stronghold.'

Although out of practice, Alberto gave the impression that he had once spoken English fluently and David asked him where he had learnt it.

'I did part of my medical training in Canada. It is curious going to live abroad—people thought we all went naked with bows and arrows. I remember a consultant asking if we had cars. I said yes we had one but the Indians came from the jungle and captured it!'

David smiled; although they were very different, Alberto reminded him of his own father. His aunts had told him that his dad had always been good at telling a tale and this talent had been honed to a fine art selling jewellery out of suitcases in the north of England.

He had beautiful hands, David remembered. His fingers were nicotine-stained from heavy smoking, the nails strong and wellformed, and the backs of his hands were covered in sun freckles and a patchwork of fine lines David used to try and trace when he sat on his knee.

His father was a thinker rather than a doer—he had David doing the garden while he leaned on the fence chatting to the next-door neighbour. The son of a coach painter in St Helen's, he left school when he was eleven to sweep up and make tea in a solicitor's office. He educated himself from books bought on the street market and continued to buy second-hand books all his life that David's mum used to throw out or hide away in a cardboard box under the stairs because she couldn't stand untidiness. David could still remember the slightly mildewed smell of the paper and the pleasure of unearthing some literary treasure.

When his dad died there were so few possessions: a couple of suits, two or three ties. They looked worn out, but David remembered him looking smart, elegant even. The only thing he had of any value of his father's was his retirement watch—22 carat gold, 24 jewel movement in return for 25 years loyal service. They had taken it out of stock, his company made them, but his dad was proud of it anyway, and David had got it after he died and worn it. It had an expanding gold bracelet, which was the company's main line, and had a nice clean face with bold Arabic numerals.

There was a diary, written in pencil while his father was a prisoner of war in Leipzig; and a tiny photograph of him on leave in Durban, in shorts, standing, with his arm around a tall woman with blonde hair and a beautiful strong face.

They turned off the road. A small man in a sweat-stained shirt, his trousers rolled up to the knees opened the gate. Alberto leaned out of the car and they talked quietly.

'That's Vincente, he's father's foreman. Alberto's asking him if there have been any problems. One of the mares has been ill.'

David admired the order and efficiency of the new fencing and the well-made track. The white gate was freshly painted and the meadows were luxuriant. David noted the clean irrigation ditches and the sprinkler systems operating in the distance. In the fields nearer to the track, sleek fine horses were grazing or nuzzling each other under the shade of saman, wide spreading rain-trees.

Vincente said goodbye, nodding to Christina and David. He told the night-men to bring in the herd and bed them down for the night and set off on foot to his home in the village.

They drove up to the house and Alberto unlocked the door. They entered a large room, empty but for a long wooden table and eight or nine rustic chairs.

'I'm afraid the house isn't much. All the money goes into the farm. I'll make some coffee,' Alberto said, and went off to the kitchen.

Christina unrolled one of the bundles hanging on rings along the wall. Looping the rope expertly through a ring on the opposite wall, she opened out a woven hammock of bottle green and blue. David thought it was beautiful.

'You sleep diagonally in them like this,' she said swinging into the hammock in one graceful movement. 'You try.'

David lowered himself gingerly and, after some wriggling, found a comfortable position.

Night had fallen and he could hear Alberto and Christina talking in the kitchen. There was a cool breath of air from the lake and David fell asleep to the chorus of night sounds that had seemed so strange a week ago. In the night he sensed someone fold the long fringes of the hammock over him.

It was barely light. David found Alberto in the kitchen, spooning fresh ground coffee into the tall cafetera.

'Would you like to come down with me to the stables?'

'Yes, I'd like that. Who's coming this weekend?'

'Besides Jordi and Mariella … Aurora, Mariella's sister, and her husband Angel. Also Julio, another one of the group at the University.'

'Is your wife coming?'

'Mildred. No, not this week-end. She's very busy, her research is going well. The farm is my thing. She is not so keen to … rough it.'

They left the house quietly and walked down to the stables: two rows of stalls, and between them a concrete trough filled with hundreds of young plants in black plastic containers.

'This used to be a cattle ranch … that's the old manger we're using as a nursery. We propagate from cuttings and in three months they are ready,' said Alberto. 'You will see later what a garden we have made.'

A lad was leading a string of horses out towards the paddocks. Alberto gave each an appraising pat on neck or rump.

'Why aren't the others going out?' asked David.

'They are mares in foal—the vet is coming to see them this morning.'

Alberto showed him round and introduced him to each of the remaining horses. They were big beautiful creatures and David let them nuzzle his face as he reached over to stroke their necks. It was clear that Alberto loved them and wasn't running the farm purely to make money. He had a game, letting the horses bite the back of his hand over the knuckles and laughing uproariously even though the strong teeth left deep impressions.

There was the sound of a vehicle skidding on the steep slope up to the house. A bright red sports car swung into the yard and a tall young man climbed out. He was wearing grey overalls and Wellington boots and carried a smart plastic case. Vincente brought out the first of the mares. Padded loops were slipped over her hind fetlocks by two stable-lads and Vincente whispered in her ear. The vet pulled on surgical gloves and, leaning into the mare's rump with his shoulder, he gently inserted his hand into the anus. He felt around and withdrew a handful of dung which he dropped into a bucket. Having cleared the intestine, he inserted his arm to the shoulder and felt for the foetus. He seemed satisfied and, having scrubbed his arms with brush and soap in a bucket of hot water, gave the animal a vitamin injection.

David was shocked by the matter-of-factness of it all. In spite of his mountaineering, he was a city boy and knew nothing about animal husbandry. 'Is it all right if I look round the farm?' he asked Alberto.

'Yes, sure, but look out for snakes. Vincente, get him a machete!'

David was wearing an old pair of Alberto's boots and didn't feel too worried. He set off on the track that climbed into the hills behind the farm. After a two or three mile walk along a narrow path he reached the small reservoir that provided water for the farm. The water looked cool and he made for the dam where he could dive. There was a sudden movement in the long grasses five or six yards ahead and he saw two dark brown snakes as long as a man move away at speed. His first thought was to go back, but the snakes obviously wanted to keep out of his way.

He climbed onto the dam and, stripping off his clothes, plunged into the water. He crossed the pool with strong, easy strokes. Afterwards, he lay on the dam and while his body dried in the sun, he tried to take stock.

He liked Alberto and felt comfortable with him—he was calm and dependable. And Christina—so relaxed and assured. What a family! He was glad they had invited him, but for a moment he wished he could just stay there by the dam and not have to meet more new people: he would have preferred to spend the weekend with Alberto and Christina.

Before leaving the dam, he cut a straight staff with the machete and used it to beat the path where the vegetation was thickest. Nearing the house he could hear laughter and splashing from the swimming pool—Jordi had arrived.

'David! Where have you been? Come and meet the others.' Jordi put his arm round his shoulders and introduced him round. Aurora removed her sunglasses and, remaining stretched on the sun-lounger, offered him her hand. A man at the other end of the pool did a graceful swallow dive off the springboard, as if he had been waiting for David's attention. He swam powerfully and, streaming with water, lifted himself out of the pool.

'Jose Angel Mendoza. A sus ordenes,' he said, giving a little flourish with his hand, which seemed to David ridiculous from someone in swimming trunks.

'Hello, pleased to meet you.'

'He's a banker; very boring. What do you do David?' asked Aurora.

'He'll tell you at lunch, Aurora. Come and meet Julio,' said Jordi.

Julio was still in the pool. He shook hands vigorously and told David to get changed and come and play water polo.

The game appeared to be an excuse for extreme physical contact. A number of times he felt himself drowning under Jordi's over enthusiastic bulk and had to use all his strength to throw him off. There seemed no logic to the game, and he neither knew nor cared how they were scoring or who was winning. Mariella shouted that lunch was ready and, with the camaraderie of a rugby team after a hard match, the four men climbed out of the pool, dried themselves and went in.

The long table had been laid.

'This is the national dish, papellon,' said Mariella.

'Like roast beef and Yorkshire pudding,' said her sister.

Papellon, he discovered, consisted of rice, spicy shredded meat, fried banana and sweet black beans. He liked it.

'And what brings you here?' asked Aurora.

'The short answer is Jordi. I was interested in working with him at the university on housing problems.'

'You are an architect?' asked Angel.

'Yes, although I am particularly interested in social patterns,' said David.

'Ah! A sociologo,' said Angel, disdainfully.

'More of an amateur anthropologist. I was also fascinated by what I'd read about South America and I'd like to explore a bit.'

'The spirit of adventure. You English … ,' said Aurora.

Jordi, who had been conversing quietly with his father at the other end of the table, saw David's discomfort.

'Yes, David is a great climber. By the time we get back from England he'll know more about the interior than any of us,' he said, laughing uproariously.

'I'm really envious,' said Aurora. 'When we were in London we had a marvellous time, didn't we Angel? We were there three weeks, before we went to France and Italy, and managed to see everything: Londres, Cambridge, Oxford, Stratford-upon-Avon ...'

'Yes that's about everything,' said Christina.

After lunch Alberto asked David to bring his coffee onto the porch.

'Jordi says things may be difficult at the University, that there may be delay in your contract. I want to tell you that if you need any help, a loan or a place to stay, Mildred and I would be honoured to assist you.'

David said he was very grateful for the offer and they sat in silence for a time, looking at the lake away in the distance and at the coastal mountains beyond. The sun at this time of day blurred line and washed out colour. The lake looked as heavy as jelly, but as he stared, it seemed to evaporate. It was a mirage, a lake of fable, shrouding the spirits of the tribes that had inhabited this fertile plain. He could imagine the phantoms of armed conquistadors rising up out of the water, helmet and cuirass gleaming in the sun.

'Goméz had a launch to take his concubines out on the lake,' said Christina, joining them.

'Goméz?'

'General Goméz, the dictator. He looked just like Stalin— the same uniform and moustache, and the same knowing eyes. His nickname was El Bagre—Catfish. He lived in El Limon on the mountain road to the coast. He was very security minded, he ruled a long time.'

'And the launch?' asked David.

'Yes, like a paddle steamer. He never married, but fathered

hundreds of children by his many mistresses. The story goes that he always slept alone, he would never wake in the morning with a woman in his bed.'

'How did he die?'

'Of old age, with his grandchildren round him, I suppose.'

'We've had a long line of military dictators,' said Alberto.

'We are a democracy, but the people still love a strong leader. The whole political structure is based on patronage.'

'But isn't that open to corruption?' asked David.

Christina laughed out loud. 'You would see it as corrupt of course. But that's the way people expect things to be done. Patrons are called caciques. It's an Arawak word meaning chief. Jovito is a cacique, he leads a tiny party which often holds the balance of power in national elections, but his interest is in local politics. His party deals in favours in return for support. People living in ranchos are not stupid, they're just poor. The only power they have is the block vote, and they use it.'

'You mean patronage is really democratic!' said David.

'Patronage in England exists as strongly as here, it's just more covert. Class regulates and is accepted unthinkingly.'

'Is there no class distinction here?' he asked.

'Yes, of course,' she said. 'Family matters, your name matters. If you can trace your ancestors back to the time of the Spanish Colony, if your family is one of the important land-owning families, then you are someone in society. But what really matters, what our class system is based on, is wealth. With wealth you can buy a good name, marry into a good family.'

'What about the people in the slums, can they break into the economic system?' asked David.

'Not easily. But you have to realise that people are getting rich there, like anywhere else, off the backs of their neighbours. They are acquiring land and property, starting businesses. The tigers eat the lambs.'

He wanted to refute her bleak view of human nature but his thoughts slid around: the heat, the heavy lunch, the strain of so many new people. He looked at Alberto who laughed and said, 'Don't worry, she puts everyone to sleep.'

There was a wild shout from the direction of the stables and Jordi and Angel appeared racing, bareback. They were neck and neck. Angel began to pull ahead. At the long bend before the steep rise to the house Jordi rode wide, forcing Angel off the track. Angel had to rein his horse to avoid going over the edge.

'The winner,' shrieked Aurora.

Jordi fought to control the excited gelding, which pranced and turned, its flanks foamy from the effort of the race, great gouts of spume spraying from its nostrils. Jordi sat, head thrown back, chest slicked, face flushed and triumphant. David could imagine him leading a column of irregular cavalry out of the *llanos* to seize power.

5

Jordi said that later they planned to drive over to the coast where they had a house in Choroni. He particularly wanted David to see the village because it was one of the few settlements that had survived the succession of earthquakes and civil wars that had destroyed nearly all the colonial architecture in the country.

'I enjoyed seeing the farm. Thank you.'

'Come again then,' said Alberto. 'Safe drive.'

He climbed into the back seat of Jordi's white Mercedes and within a few minutes he had dozed off to sleep. He awoke with a start as the car bounced through a large pothole.

'Where are we?' he asked.

'Just past El Castano, the water bottling plant,' said Jordi. 'How are you feeling?'

'Better for the sleep.'

The road, part paved, part dirt, rose steeply.

'I wanted to talk to you,' said Jordi, 'to tell you what our plans are in the University, and how you fit into the picture.'

'Yes?'

'Manuel wants us to do the modelling on the Capital Region.'

'My Spanish isn't very good!'

'You'll be working with Alejandro—you'll be programming and he can handle the rest of it. I'm relying on you to help get the unit established now the contract's signed.'

'Contract?' asked David.

'The work for the Ministry. We can do some of the theoretical work in England, but we'll need you to help to collect the data and run the programme. It's important that the unit is seen to be operational, and that's why your role is so important.'

'Is that the research you told me about in England?

'Not exactly,' said Jordi. 'The priorities have changed.'

David felt like saying that it wasn't fair; it wasn't what he had envisaged. But he responded to Jordi's trust. Jordi had the gift of making people feel they could do anything. He felt, irrationally, a growing confidence that he would be able to cope.

Jordi had been driving fast, sounding his horn on the blind bends. Now he had to slow. From bright sunlight they were plunged into shade and mist. The road levelled out and David realised they must be at the top of the pass. Through the mist they could see the dim outline of looming trees, grey in the half light: forest giants leaning under the weight of trailing vines, propped by the stumps of their rotting neighbours;

trunks covered in ferns, hanging curtains of Spanish moss like tangled worms, lianas, vines with leaves the size of umbrellas, pitcher plants and bromeliads designed to collect water, as if there wasn't enough running in abundance from the dripping sodden foliage. Everywhere there seemed an explosion of plant life in the midst of death and decay; a kind of desperate, devil take the hindmost, clawing for light and life.

He jumped at the sound of an unearthly shriek. Mariella giggled and said, 'I always feel spooky here too.'

'What's that?' A candle shone brightly from a small shrine by the side of the road.

'It marks where a car went over the edge. Relatives build them, you find them all over the place. There is a shrine by the waterfall, a grotto where people come to worship and pray. It's dedicated to the Virgin, but all these things go back before Christianity.' Half hidden, they could see hundreds of tiny lights.

They came out of the mist into the soft warm light of the setting sun. David recognised the livid flowers of morning glory, vibrant trumpets at first light, hanging now like deflated balloons after a party. In the distance there were crumbling, vegetated cliffs and he wondered whether he would find any solid rock in all the decaying compost. The road dropped steeply. He saw tree ferns and a bright red spike of flowers bursting through the forest canopy like a firework.

Finally there were signs of cultivation. They passed mud houses with thatched roofs. On the small plots of land he could see bananas, corn and pineapples and everywhere the wild colour of tropical flowers. Next to a bar a lorry laden with beer and soft drinks was stuck in a ditch.

On the outskirts of the village, the road narrowed,

funnelled by the houses. They swept through the plaza and parked outside the massive door of one of the old houses on the square.

'We're here,' shouted Jordi, fishing a long iron key from under the dashboard. 'Welcome to our colonial past.'

The dark entrance lead through to a courtyard of trees and flowers and formed a black cube of shadow next to the light filled space. A roofed veranda ran round the patio, and the many doors suggested suites of rooms beyond. The walls were painted the colour of primroses and the grey-green woodwork was peeling in places to reveal a brown tone beneath. The general impression was of a home that had been used for generations but was now a little unloved through lack of use. David asked if the house had been in the family a long time, imagining they'd had it since the Spanish *Colonia*. Jordi said they'd bought it only a couple of years ago. A professor in the school had persuaded a dozen or more students and colleagues to buy houses in the village as an investment to stop them falling into decay. Jordi told him to leave his bag, and, when Mariella was ready, they went in search of food.

'It must be a fiesta,' said Jordi.

Groups of men stood outside bars drinking, and in the gutter, where the road widened, young boys were burning piles of newspapers at the mouths of hollowed out tree trunks, the biggest the diameter of a car wheel. They were drums and Jordi said that they were heating the air inside to made them resonate properly.

A mountainous black woman came to the table to take their order. Jordi took charge, saying something that made her laugh. Tears rolled down her face and she slapped her thighs, rocking the rickety table and threatening to upset their drinks. The others joined in the laughter.

'He's asking her for the first dance,' whispered Christina.

'What are you going to have? There's merluza, red snapper, grouper, bonito,' said Jordi.

'What's merluza?' asked David.

'Hake.'

'I'll have that,' said David, feeling unadventurous. The others ordered red snapper which arrived whole, their jaws bristling with teeth. David enjoyed the meal, listening to the surf and the drums as the young boys warmed up. The conversation buzzed round him, he felt relaxed and happy for the first time since his arrival.

Outside, the boys were sitting astride the drums and beating the hide covered ends with short sticks. Children were dancing—the boys in white shirts, their hair slicked with oil, girls in their Sunday best: cotton dresses and shiny black shoes. The beat was insistent, each drum overlaying its fellows, combining to produce a rhythm that was totally foreign yet as familiar as his own heartbeat.

One of the children, a little boy of seven or eight, was a particularly good dancer. Each time the music halted he chose a different girl, saying nothing as he took her hand and whisked her on to the dance floor. He wondered if the children were conscious of the sensuality and suggestiveness in their movements or whether they were just imitating the adults. He saw two old women look at the boy and shake their heads.

'Let's join in,' said Jordi, finally dislodging a fish bone with his toothpick. It was dark now and the square was crowded with people. Jordi pushed to the front and invited one of the young women to dance. He led with his usual confidence, guiding her with his hand in the small of her back; dancing with abandon and surprising grace for such a heavy man. The girl feigned disinterest. Other couples took the floor, leaving a wide space for Jordi and his partner in the centre. David noticed a man on the other side of the circle looking darkly at Jordi. As Jordi danced near the man he suddenly stepped in, bouncing Jordi to one side like a pinball. Jordi pushed back through the crowd unperturbed, delighted with himself. Older men took the drums from the young boys and the rhythm at once became more complex and assured.

Christina asked David to dance and led him on to the floor. He felt awkward and lumpy, as if he were seventeen again at the Friday night dance in the church hall.

'You have to relax the hips, you're much too stiff,' said Christina. They danced a while and it got better. A group of musicians were playing maracas and small ukulele-like instruments accompanying a woman singing irresistible wailing songs.

Much later, lying in his hammock, he heard Julio and Christina whispering at the other end of the patio and was surprised to feel a sharp pang of jealousy. He was getting involved. This wasn't a holiday, he had come to live here. By the light of the moon he could see the waxy flowers of the Eucharist lilies. The still air was laden with the scent of jasmine, flowing over his body like water.

The next morning, while the others were having breakfast, he went out to look round the village. Most of the houses had wrought-iron grills over painted shutters and heavy studded doors with ancient hinges and locks. The walls were white or pale yellow and the windows painted pastel tints of green and blue or shades of ochre and burnt sienna. Only one house was in disrepair—crumbling plaster revealed baked mud on wickerwork, and through the open doorway he saw the charred roof timbers were open to the sky.

In the plaza David examined the bronze head in Napoleonic uniform and the plaque that read 'Simon Bolivar, Libertador'. Liberator of a continent and died forgotten in Cartegena. Liberty, equality, fraternity? Was liberty the only one of the three worth dying for? Sitting on a bench, watching children as they played with spinning tops under the mango trees, he wondered if he was prepared to die for something he believed in.

He remembered Jordi talking about Bolivar in England, and how romantic and improbable it had sounded. What a sheltered life he'd led in England. Here ordinary things, like going to work in the university, could be a matter of life and death. He couldn't imagine being prepared to die for a cause; he was more likely to risk his life for a friend. He took risks rock climbing and there had been times when he had almost gone over the fine line between life and death. But that was different, somehow, because he felt in control.

In the last year before he came out here he hadn't cared much whether he lived or died. But there was something in his nature that rebelled against the idea of throwing his life away. It was just too melodramatic.

The sandy bay was enclosed by low cliffs and backed by a grove of coconut palms. Julio and Jordi were surfing in the breakers. He and Christina walked in the hard sand left by the retreating tide.

'How do you feel now you have been here nearly a week?'

'I felt good last night, I'm not so sure this morning.'

'What do you think of Aurora?'

'I don't know her,' he said.

'But what's your first impression?' she persisted, wanting to see what effect Aurora had on him. She knew that some men found Aurora's childlike body and knowing nature irresistible.

David glanced back to where Aurora and Mariella were sunbathing. 'I suppose I find her superficial, coquettish and a bit dim.'

Christina smiled at his directness. 'Would it surprise you to learn that she was a lawyer? She married Angel and hasn't practised since.'

'Why?'

'She doesn't have to work, Angel earns a huge salary. Anyway, most men dislike the idea of their wives working.'

'What do you do for a living? I never asked you.'

'I'm a lawyer too. I work with a firm that specialises in human rights issues; we defend political detainees.'

'Including terrorists?'

'Yes, of course, the ones that come to trial!'

'Does Jordi have to leave?' he asked.

She hesitated a moment before saying, 'Not really, but it gets him off the hook. People were looking to him to lead them—going to England saves his pride. Revolution was the name of the game Jordi used to play, but times have changed and he's working with the system now.'

He wanted to ask her more but Julio caught them up and suggested they climb round the rocks at the end of the beach. A shelf of rock, exposed by the tide, ran round the base of the cliffs. The rocks were sharp and covered in barnacles and they clambered slowly and carefully, having to use their hands. It took over an hour to reach the point. Spray was breaking over the half submerged reef which formed a breakwater between the ocean and calm water of the bay.

They dived from the rock shelf. At the reef they ducked beneath the surface and swam down the vertical wall of coral. It was like swimming in an aquarium; the coral cliff was teeming with brightly coloured fish.

'We need masks and snorkels,' shouted Julio, above the surf. 'Let's swim back, the ledges will be covered now and it's not far.'

David looked back. They had come a long way scrambling along the ledges and he estimated it was at least a mile, perhaps more, back to the beach. He paced himself, swimming a slow, economical stroke. At one point he thought he saw a black fin out to sea and asked if there were shark.

'Yes, there are plenty of shark,' said Julio. Involuntarily David lifted his legs up to his body and swallowed seawater. He came back to the surface coughing and spluttering.

'I'm glad it makes you happy,' David said, and began to swim for the shore with a strong vigorous crawl.

He had learnt to swim when he was eight, on holiday in Llandudno. His father walked beside him in the water, chest deep, holding him up. Suddenly he had removed his supporting hand. David sank. The salty water went up his nose, then down his throat and he felt he was about to drown. His father yanked him out, laughing, and said that would teach him not to trust anyone. From then on he had taught himself.

'How serious were you about the sharks?' David asked. They were sitting in the shade of a large palm, sipping cold beer from the ice cooler and eating chicken and avocado.

'There are sharks and occasionally they attack,' said Julio.

'Tell him about Alberto and the shark,' Christina asked Jordi.

'We were fishing near Los Roques, they're small islands due north of here,' said Jordi, reaching for another can of beer. 'Alberto had just landed a blue marlin, and was leaning over the side to gaff it, when his wallet fell out of the top pocket of his shirt. Without stopping he hopped over the side, practically straight into the jaws of a shark. He came out of the water and back on deck like a jack-in-the-box, clutching the wallet. It was unbelievable, we all laughed. Mildred called him a fool, and what the devil did he think he was playing at. He opened the wallet and showed us it contained two thousand bolivars. That was a lot of money in those days.'

In the port, men were unloading boxes from a fishing boat beached in the sandy creek at the mouth of the river. Jordi stopped the car.

'We'll stop here for a swim to wash the salt off.' The river flowed over large smooth rocks into a deep clear pool. There was a clearing in the tall cotton trees and the sandy bank was lined with sweet smelling ginger lilies. Children were sliding down the rocks and they scampered off giggling round a bend in the river.

'Where's Christina?' asked David.

'She's gone back to the house,' said Aurora, arranging her towel in the sun.

'What do people live off here?' he asked, sitting next to her on the rock and dangling his feet in the stream.

'Fishing, tourism and 'Black Label' whiskey. You saw the cartons? They bring them over from the Dutch islands.'

'Christina said you were a lawyer.'

'Trained as, but not practising,' said Aurora.

'Why not?'

'You wouldn't understand.'

'Try me.'

'Did your mother go out to work?'

'I see your point,' said David. 'But you have a maid?'

'We have a cook, a maid who helps with Carlitos, a chauffeur who also does the garden and someone who comes in once a week to help with the washing,' said Aurora, her voice challenging.

'What the devil do you do all day?'

'It's none of your damn business.'

'I'm sorry.'

'Are you offering to make my life more interesting?' she sneered.

'No,' he flustered, 'I'm sorry.'

'All right, I'm sorry too,' said Aurora, softening. 'How are you going to make out at the University?'

'Hopefully better than just now,' laughed David.

'You seem confident.'

'I'm worried stiff actually.'

'He'll be fine—Chelo and Alejandro will look after him,' said Mariella, putting her book down.

'Who is Chelo?' asked David.

Neither of them answered. Why not, he wondered. He was intrigued. Jordi came back and sat down. 'I've arranged for you to meet the group in the University at ten,' he said, 'and we have a meeting with Americo Faillace at twelve.'

'Who?'

'The dean. We have to convince him that your expertise is indispensable.'

'I'm not sure we shall be able to do that,' said David.

'It's a bureaucratic formality. He has to have a story.'

'What do you want me to say?'

'I'll do most of the talking. Tell him about your job in England. He's not very intellectual, just astute. Don't burden him with too many ideas, give him a phrase or two to take to his committee and he'll be happy. And don't forget there is a leaving party for us at Manuel's tomorrow night. I'll write the address for you. You can take a taxi.'

'We want to show you off, don't we Aurora,' said Mariella.

'I'm not sure he wants to be shown off, do you David?' said Aurora.

'I'll try not to be too churlish,' he said, smiling.

'Grandfather may come. He managed the national baseball team that won the World Series,' said Christina.

'He's incorrigible,' said Mariella. 'Mildred won't let him out, he has a bad heart, so his girlfriends come to the house when she's out. Last week a redhead came round. She stayed in her car, a convertible with the top down, and sounded her horn. He was hanging over the balcony in his dressing gown chatting to her when Mildred caught him.'

'The man I told you spent three years in manacles,' said Jordi.

On the drive back, cocooned in darkness in the back of the Mercedes, half listening to Jordi and Mariella talk, David took stock. Six days since he left England—so much in one week. The weekend, he realised, had been organised around him, so he could meet people. Jordi had gone to a lot of trouble. Perhaps they did not come to the farm very often. But he did not like Jordi as much here: he was cock-sure and the energy he had admired in England now seemed overbearing.

6

The University was a garden: trees and plants everywhere, filling the open spaces between the buildings. David joined the young students hurrying to lectures and smiled back at a group of girls who waved at him. It was early and he paused to browse at a second-hand bookstall. Further on he stopped at a coffee stand to watch the passers-by: confident and light-hearted, just like students in England on a summer's morning.

The School of Architecture occupied a tall blue and grey building and David took the lift to the fifth floor. Through an open office door he saw Jordi dictating a letter.

'Olá, How d'you like the building?' asked Jordi. 'The construction is clever, but cheap. The rooms have high ceilings, like colonial buildings and the open corridor means that, even on still days, the air circulates.' A woman quietly entered the room and Jordi broke off what he had been saying.

'Chelo! This is David. David meet Chelo. I'll see if the others are here yet,' said Jordi, leaving the room.

'¿Cómo estas? ¿Cuándo veniste?' said Chelo.

'I'm sorry?' said David.

'How are you? When did you get here?'

'I'm fine,' said David, feeling foolish. 'I got here last week.'

She spoke with a throaty accent, which he liked, and was taller than Jordi by a good two inches. He liked her face: there were laugh lines round her eyes. David thought she must be twenty-seven or eight. She seemed to regard him with amused curiosity. She asked him if he was still trying to find somewhere to live and added that she had time free that afternoon if he wanted some help. He said yes, he'd like that.

She showed him round the department and took him to meet Alejandro. He was a soft-spoken man, greying at the temples. He explained that he was co-ordinating the unit while Jordi and Luis Carlos were away. He'd be working closely with David and Chelo, but managed to convey the impression that they would be doing all the interesting work, while he went to the departmental meetings and did the boring admin. David did not mind, in fact he preferred it like that and was glad it was clear from the beginning.

It was just after ten when the members of the unit arrived from the coffee bar downstairs. He was introduced and Jordi took the chair at the head of the table. The meeting was in English and David listened carefully while Jordi outlined the ideas for the modelling work.

They switched to Spanish and the words 'Cambridge' and 'Londres' were used frequently. David spent the time watching people and trying to remember their names. Jordi had stood and was writing on the blackboard. Why did he always wear that massive belt with the buckle to one side, David wondered. It gave him a sort of piratical-military air, like a comic opera general, and went with his moustache and the pacing about.

There was a knock at the door and an urchin came in. 'Café?' he asked, pulling a stack of tiny plastic cups from a shoulder bag. He had two thermos flasks of coffee, one with milk, the other black. The boy's arrival was obviously a regular feature of the day. Julio offered to pay, and the lad said something that made everyone laugh. Taking advantage of the interruption, Luis Carlos spoke. Again David couldn't follow the discussion, but from the looks on people's faces he gathered they were talking about something serious.

Later, in the corridor on their way to the dean's office, David asked what Luis Carlos had been saying, but Jordi refused to be drawn. David had gathered it was something to do with the work for Manuel—he had understood the words contrato and ministerio. Jordi's voice had stayed calm and persuasive and he had kept smiling, but he had been unable to hide his anxiety, constantly getting up and pacing about, while Luis Carlos, in contrast, had kept dead still. Alejandro had rescued the situation by what looked, to David, like a compromise. Whatever it was Jordi had grasped it with both hands.

They reached the top floor. Jordi greeted the dean's secretary with a kiss. 'Americo's on the phone,' said Jordi, picking up the documents in her filing tray. He read through them systematically, commenting now and then, and asking her to clarify the things he didn't understand.

The door to Americo's office opened and out came a man with popping eyes and thin lank hair. Jordi was completely unabashed, replacing the papers and greeting Americo with a backslapping embrace. Americo ushered them into his office. After David had said his piece about his research in Manchester and his computing experience, Americo and Jordi settled down to a long intimate discussion in Spanish, leaving David feeling like a spare part.

'What about my contract?' he asked as they left.

'It isn't ready yet. It's still with the rector.'

'What does that mean?'

'It means, like everything else in this country, that there is a hold-up.'

'I've got to start work now; I've almost run out of money.'

'So has the University, unfortunately,' said Jordi. 'Let's go and have a coffee.'

They got the lift down to the ground floor. The coffee bar was crowded but, on the far side, they could see Chelo and Alejandro.

'Go and sit down, while I get the coffee,' said Jordi, going off to chat to someone near the front of the queue.

'What happened?' asked Chelo.

'I'm not sure,' said David. 'The contract is not ready and I don't think there is any money to pay me.'

'Don't worry. That is normal. You will just start work, and you will get paid next month and then you will sign your contract. Some of the others had been here over a year, in fact, one had just resigned, when their contracts came through,' said Alejandro.

When it looked as though Jordi had forgotten the coffees, Chelo suggested that the three of them go out for an early lunch. 'Let's go to that Italian restaurant in Los Chaguaramos. If we take your car, David and I can walk back.'

Walking behind her on the way to the car park he noticed the way her dress swung as she walked. It was navy blue with a pattern of magnolia flowers that he liked. Her shoulders were broad, her legs long and lithe and she gave an impression of vitality.

The coffee boy stood next to Alejandro's car, as if putting the finishing touches to a wax polish. Alejandro handed him a note and he saluted with his rag.

'It's a kind of protection racket,' said Alejandro, 'his gang cleans the cars and stops them getting vandalised.'

During lunch David asked about a statue he had seen on the autopista of a naked woman astride an animal the shape of a pig with a trunk and long spindly legs. 'She's holding a horn of plenty above her head like a football trophy,' he said.

Chelo said that the animal was a danta—a tapir. There were supposed to be some on the mountains above the city, but they were very shy and rarely seen. The woman was Maria Lionza. She was a warrior priest who, it was said, used to live in the mountains of Falcon. There was a cult that worshipped her and believed she was still alive.

'We are a very superstitious race,' said Alejandro. 'Spanish fervour and Indian fatalism ... you must have seen pictures of Dr Gregorio, the little saint, in the taxis.'

'The man in the trilby?' said David.

'He was a doctor working in the poor barrios. He died of tuberculosis and has been canonised by popular acclaim. There's a whole industry producing portraits and statues of him.'

As Alejandro and Chelo began to talk in Spanish about a meeting that afternoon, David observed the people walking past in the street. This was an area of small traders: immigrants from the Canarios, Italy, Spain, Germany. From the cafe he could see an ebanista at work in his open fronted shop gluing the legs on a table he had just made. He could smell a bakery nearby. There was a window full of bolts of gaudy material, a ferratería selling ironmongery and, on the corner, a mimbrista weaving cane into a tubby chair. Middle-aged women shopped, thick bodies held in tight by bulging cotton print dresses.

Why, he wondered, of all the images he had seen since arriving had he homed in on Maria Lionza? An Amazon, an earth goddess with a stupendous figure, a champion. And Gregorio, the saint in a trilby—a do-gooding idealist, over-dressed for the tropics. He looked across the table at Chelo, animatedly conversing with Alejandro, who sat head cocked on one side listening to her. Maria Lionza—natural, exuberant, vital.

He noticed that she had high cheek bones and that her brown eyes were set wide, giving her face a frank open look. Her hair was a thick mass of wavy brown, bleached auburn in streaks by the sun and her complexion was brown, rather than olive like Jordi's. She had stuck sunglasses in her thick curly hair and her only jewellery was a thin gold necklace.

After Alejandro had gone Chelo asked him if he any addresses of flats he was interested in. He fished the newspaper pages out of his jacket and handed them to her.

'Have you any idea where you want to look?' she asked.

'Round here would do, it's near the university.'

Have you a pen?' she asked and began to tick the ones worth seeing. But the ones they tried were unsuitable or had already been let. After a couple of hours tramping round they passed a pavement cafe and stopped for a rest.

'I had a dream last night,' Chelo said, when they'd been served. 'I was given a small, beautifully wrapped present— pearled paper and a white bow. But before I could open it I woke up.'

David looked at her for a moment and then said, 'I'll tell you what it was.'

'Yes?' she said, intrigued.

'It's a box … with a lid.' She asked him what it was made of, smiling with anticipation. 'Wood … ebony, matt black, warm to the touch … inlaid with thin line of ivory or silver.'

'What's in the box?' she asked.

He didn't know. He had never done anything like this before, taking an idea from someone else and turning it in his own mind. He had just plunged in without thinking and did not know what to say next. He looked at her face, searching for inspiration. She looked disappointed.

'Can you open it?' she prompted.

'The lid is very tight,' he said, smiling. Then it came to him and, hesitatingly, he described that inside there was a ring—a gold band with a stone setting. She asked what kind of stone. He didn't know and said the first thing that came into his head. 'It's a stone that has never been used before to make a ring.'

'What colour is it?' she asked, smiling with delight.

Knowing that it was all right, that he had not failed her, he let his imagination soar and told her that in one light the ring was green, in another blue, and if she looked at it long enough she would see all the colours imaginable. She clapped her hands and thanked him for finishing her dream. 'I hope I find my ring,' she said with a sigh.

'Your name … Chelo?'

'It's short for Consuela … after my mother.'

They walked back towards the University and Chelo said: 'Don't give up, you'll find somewhere sooner or later.'

'Christina has offered to drive me round on Thursday, but I haven't got much time, I can't stay in the hotel any longer.'

She told him to try La Florida, near where Alberto lived, and added that he could walk to the mountains from there.

'Will you be at Jordi's leaving party tonight?' he asked as they said goodbye.

'I'm not invited,' she said simply.

'You American?' asked the taxi-driver.

'English.'

'I was in England. In Newcastle—with the merchant navy. English! they're all left handed. Ha, Ha. English women: they love a Latin. ¡Carajo! I was doing them a favour.'

National stereotypes. Maybe the Latin macho was as much a cliché as the standard Englishman, thought David.

The guard must have been told to expect him because he was allowed through the gates without fuss. A group of chauffeurs stood smoking and they stopped chatting as he squeezed past the parked cars.

'Great, you made it,' shouted Jordi, pushing his way through. The garden was lit by hundreds of hanging lanterns and light flooded from the tall windows on the ground floor. White coated waiters hurried about with trays of drinks and food. David felt intimidated and almost wished he hadn't come. It was important he meet these people; important that he make a good impression. It was not that he was awed by the affluence, but more that he distrusted his own outspokenness.

David thought people in the West should consume less and nowhere was that more evident than in this oil rich state with its spend now, hang tomorrow' mentality. An economy based on constantly increasing consumption. Progress and prosperity: an expanding economy, a developing nation. And he was part of it, earning a good salary, if he ever got paid. At least, as an architect in a unit advising the government, he might be able to move things in the right direction.

'Come, Mildred wants to meet you.' Jordi grabbed his arm and guided him through the press of people. Between the terrace and the house they were waylaid by a dozen people who shook his hand and fired questions at him.

Mildred was a small vigorous woman . She was dressed in a cream and chocolate linen suit and David had the impression of stylish self-confidence.

'I've heard a great deal about you,' she said. 'What happened at the University? what did Americo have to say?'

'I'll leave you,' said Jordi.

'There is some delay. They seem to have spent the budget.'

'So I understand. But that is not uncommon. Well, never mind, you must start work and get on with things. You are working with Chelo and Alejandro Galvis. You will be fine.' She spoke of Chelo with tenderness and a touch of regret, but her manner recovered immediately and she said: 'Have you met Manuel?'

'No, not yet.'

'He's my little brother, the baby of the family—Armando and Diogenes are much older. Funny to think of him as Minister of Planning.'

Manuel was a baby-faced man with dark rimmed spectacles and a sweet mouth that old aunts must have loved to kiss. His manner of greeting was both direct and charming. 'David! Jordi has told me so much about you. And now your here to help with the project … wonderful! We were just talking about the difficulties …'

'It's a crisis, Manuel,' cut in one of the women. 'What are you going to do?'

'We shall be developing other centres,' said Manuel.

'But in the meantime the capital is out of control,' insisted the woman. 'You must do something.'

'We are doing everything we can, there is some debate about the best strategy,' he replied.

'You mean there is disagreement about whether you should develop a new city in the Tuy,' said Christina, joining them.

'The Tuy valley will develop whether we designate it a new city or not. It is too near the city to pretend that development there can be halted. And as to a disagreement, I still believe the Minister and the cabinet have the last word on these decisions,' said Manuel suavely. 'You are too intelligent for you own good Christina, but I love you. It has been a great pleasure meeting you, David. I look forward to working with you. As soon as you are settled we must arrange a meeting at the Ministry. Now if you would excuse me.' With affectionate kisses to his sister, Manuel moved away to join the men in the drawing room.

'What did you think of him?' asked Christina, drawing David away from the women.

'I rather liked him,' said David, a little surprised at his positive reaction.

'He's sly, but he knows his job.' They walked into the garden. A man threw his arms round Christina and gave her a bear hug. He said something and guffawed.

'Really Armando, you're impossible,' she said, tucking his shirt back into the top of his bulging waistline. 'David, this is my uncle Armando.'

'Mira, David have a drink,' said Armando, stopping a waiter. 'But I've already got one,' said David, beginning to feel a little light-headed after his third drink on an empty stomach.

'Petróleo!' shouted Armando, grabbing David's glass and pouring the contents into the flowerbed.

'I'll leave you two together,' he said, grinning.

'We drink more whisky than any other nation on earth.'

'Why did he throw my drink away?'

'You're not drinking fast enough, the ice had melted.'

'I prefer it without ice.'

'Without Coca-Cola maybe, but never without ice!' she laughed. Chivas Regal, ten-year-old Scotch, there must be a small fortune lined up on that table, he thought.

'I think I'd better eat something.' He felt light-headed, confused by the strange names, wondering which of them he would see again or would be important in his own life-story.

He watched the guests on the lawn, moving in shoals like two distinct species, one bejewelled and colourful, the other drab, opening their mouths in unison. Their conversation was a babble of noise he did not try to differentiate. He could imagine what they were saying: 'bla-bla, money, cars, money, scandal, bla-bla'. The sentences were so ponderous any meaning was lost to him.

'Let's go back inside and find grandfather,' said Christina.

They got a plate of assorted tapas and went through into a living room where an old man sat on a sofa surrounded by three or four young women.

'Christina!' he growled, his voice like shingle in surf. He staggered to his feet, embraced Christina warmly and shooed away the women.

'Who's this then?'

'I told you grandfather, David! David meet my grandfather, Jorge Manuel.'

'Come and sit with me, I'm too old to stand,' he said, pulling their hands and seating them either side of him on the sofa.

'And what interests you David?'

'Mountains … and designing things,' said David, after a moment.

'An interesting combination. I'm interested in sex. I used to like deep sea fishing and baseball, but now I'm too old.'

'You're a wicked old man,' said Christina.'

'A fine woman, eh!' he said, leering at David.

'Grandfather!'

'Yes, all right my dear,' he said, winking at David. 'What do you think of Latin women, eh!'

David was slightly appalled, but found his enthusiasm compelling.

'Tell me, you've got more experience than me,' he said.

'Ha! It's the pinta! Not just the war paint though, they've got fire—fuego. ¡Es el tropico!'

'When are you going to grow up, grandfather. Why are you always chasing women?'

'Because they're irresistible and because they make me feel alive!' he spluttered, coughing and choking with laughter.

So this was how the family had inherited their boundless energy, thought David. The directness, the intellect and the family nose! On the grandfather the nose had risen to a magnificent cadenza.

Jorge Manuel cadged a cigarette off Christina. She lit it for him with a gold lighter from her purse and he took one long drag, went red in the face and coughed so hard David's lungs hurt in sympathy. His dad used to cough like that, first thing in the morning, in the upstairs toilet when he lit his first cigarette and opened the *Daily Express*. He used to pretend it was the newspaper that made him cough. When he was five or six David asked him why he read it if it made him sick and he'd said he liked to feel indignant.

The young women had returned and the grandfather was telling them stories, making them laugh. David wished he had that easy manner with women. His dad used to hold the floor in the same way, leaning with one elbow on the mantelpiece, the other cocked on his hip, with a cigarette, telling stories. It's the way you tell them that counts, he used to say. David remembered the one about the man who went into a cafe and ordered a cup of coffee without cream. The waiter said we have no cream sir, but you can have it without milk.

'What are you smiling at?' whispered Christina.

'I was thinking about a story my father used to tell.' He wanted to tell her more, but this wasn't the right time.

'Let's go back to the party,' said Christina, after a moment, kissing her grandfather goodbye.

'See you around,' shouted the grandfather. David waved.

On the terrace she asked him if he wanted to join the men sitting round the big polished table in the dining room. He could see Jordi talking, wheeler dealing. He hesitated. His attitude to Jordi was increasingly ambivalent. He remembered one evening in England. A guitar was propped against Jordi's armchair and David had asked him if he played. He said he was learning, that he was teaching himself and planned, within four years, to be as good as John Williams. Ever since there had been no sign of the guitar and David had never heard him play. David suspected Jordi still believed he could be the best guitarist in the world, it was just that classical guitar demanded too much effort for too little return.

'Olá, Christina! David!' shouted Aurora.

'Oh lord, do you want to join them?' asked Christina.

'Yes, why not?'

'This is Manuel's brother, Diogenes,' said Aurora, kissing David enthusiastically. David shook hands with a man who had the smooth expensive look of handmade shoes.

'Would you excuse me, I have to get home. I'll expect you for lunch about twelve,' said Christina, striding away.

'David is going to work with Jordi's group at the Central,' said Aurora.

'How much are you getting paid?' asked Diogenes.

'I don't know,' said David, discomfited.

'You must have some idea.'

'Yes, the contract isn't signed yet, but thirty-six thousand a year.' It was over three times what he had earned in England. He was interested to see Diogenes' reaction to know what it was worth here.

'That's very good,' said Diogenes. 'Of course you'd earn more in the private sector. By the way, where did you get that shirt?'

'My shirt! In London,' said David, astonished.

'Ah Londres!' intoned Diogenes, moving off to join another group.

'Don't mind him,' said Aurora. 'You English are so reserved. Here money is crucial. It can literally be a matter of life and death—the clinics won't treat you, they won't touch you, even if you're dying on the doorstep, until they've checked your credit worthiness.'

His father taught him about money. On Saturday mornings the two of them drove to the bank and, regardless of which queue was shortest, his father would always go to the same cashier, a big man with an RAF moustache. They used to swop stories and then his dad would meticulously recount the pound notes, all except the bottom one, in case the cashier had made a mistake. Finally the man got a sub-branch of his own. It was in a Portakabin on the dock road—just what he had been waiting for. Two years later there was a piece in the Echo saying he had been arrested on his way to Brazil with £350,000. David never really knew whether his father disapproved of the theft or that he had been stupid enough to get caught.

His mother valued honesty. When he was four or five he had taken a half-crown from her purse after convincing himself she owed it him. When he denied having taken it she burst into tears and said she did not mind him stealing but it was his lying to her that hurt.

Other men joined them and soon Aurora was surrounded. She wore a tailored suit, which might have been demure but for the hem of the skirt which was a couple of inches shorter on one side. She was elf-like, with short cropped dark hair and a figure like a young boy's. David stood at the edge of the group and saw how the men fawned on her. They obviously found her sexy, but she aroused protective feelings in him. Aurora noticed him watching and eyed him with an ironic twinkle.

David eased his way to the edge of the group and waved goodbye.

'How are you going to get back? Do you want a lift?' she shouted, seeing him leaving.

'No, thank you, but I'd prefer to walk, and it's downhill,' said David, wondering why she had offered.

7

Mariella was in the bedroom with Aurora pulling clothes out of her wardrobe. The two maids, were rushing from the bedroom to laundry and getting in each other's way. All the available surfaces in the living room were heaped with clothes and the desk and floor in Jordi's office was strewn with papers and books.

'The problem with going to England is that you have to cater for all weathers,' said Mariella.

'Are you two fucking ready yet!' shouted Jordi over the noise of the shower. Mariella raised her eyebrows at Aurora. A few moments later he appeared, dressed in a pair of underpants, walked through to the kitchen and asked the maids to make him a toasted cheese sandwich. In the bedroom, he gave Aurora a kiss, switched on the television, pushed the clothes over to one side of the bed and lay face down like a baby ready to have its bottom powdered.

What with friends and relatives, half the city seemed to be there to see them off. Jordi was striding about the crowded concourse, directing the porters carrying their cases, greeting friends, enjoying the attention. Moments of consequence debased by bogus sophistication. Goodbyes were hard enough without all this, thought David, wondering, not for the first time, why he felt such a keen sense of abandonment when people left.

'I've forgotten my mink coat!' shrieked Mariella, and asked her father to go and fetch it from the car.

'She won't need that, it won't be cold,' David said to no one in particular.

'It's the only chance she's got to flaunt it,' said Aurora, mischievously. He hadn't noticed her standing right next to him. Jordi was checking in and the airline staff were weighing the luggage. There seemed to be some argument and David went closer to see.

'I'm afraid the scales are correct sir,' said the young man. 'The baggage allowance is 40 kilos per person and you and your wife have 240! There will be an excess baggage charge of 3200 bolivars.'

'That's scandalous!' said Aurora. David grinned.

'This would never happen with Viasa!' said Mariella.

The queue stretched as far as the doors of the terminal and anxious passengers began to shout. Jordi looked completely unperturbed, as though he could stand there all night. The officer looked at Jordi, and back at the queue and said: 'I'll halve the excess; that's 1600 bolivars.' Jordi reached into the breast pocket of his suit, took out a leather wallet and counted sixteen notes onto the counter.

'I'll give your love to England,' said Jordi, giving David a hug.

'Take care, and write!' said David.

When they had disappeared into the departure lounge, Aurora asked, 'How are you getting back?'

'I came with Christina, but I don't know where she is.'

'Come with me then.'

'No, I'd better find her, I'll see if her car's still there.' He crossed the road to the car park and found her Renault empty, but looking back to the terminal saw her waving from the roof.

She was standing with Mildred and Alberto when David reached the viewing gallery. Jordi's plane was about to take off. The fuselage flashed like a mirror as the plane gathered speed. It lifted into the air, tilted back on its tail and powered into the sky. They heard the roar of the engines, and saw the plane level, turn and set course.

The next morning Alejandro called a meeting. 'The contract's been signed and Manuel wants us to get cracking,' he began.

'How does this model work?' asked David.

'Population is determined by birth, deaths and migration. Births and deaths can be predicted quite easily. Migration is more difficult. The model assumes it is a function of employment. The more employment, the more migration; and employment depends on investment, and here that means government investment. That's the theory.'

'That's it!' said David, incredulous.

'At the regional level, yes.'

'Where do we come in?' he asked.

Alejandro explained that Jordi needed data to run the model in England. David looked at the list Jordi had left, and, although it would be a lot of work, it was straightforward. But he also wanted David to write a computer program to evaluate different strategies.

'Is that all!' said David.

Alejandro was unabashed. He said he might find time to help later but he was up to his eyes at the moment. '... and Manuel's expecting you at a meeting this afternoon,' he said offhandedly. 'Jordi particularly wants you to liaise with the Ministry.'

'Why me!' David objected.

'That way you'll learn quicker,' said Alejandro. 'Anyway, Chelo can't go and I'm too busy.'

'What's wrong?' Chelo asked later in the coffee bar.

'Why won't you go and see Manuel with me?'

'It's not as simple as that,' she said, refusing to say any more.

'I seem to be doing all the work,' said David, angrily. 'What the hell's Alejandro doing?'

'Quite a lot.'

'Yes?'

'Alejandro provides the cover, he's a political trapeze artist, looking after our interests here in the University. How else do you think we keep people off our backs? He's also stool pigeon—he keeps Jordi informed what's happening here. What Jordi doesn't know is that he writes to Luis Carlos as well.'

'What!'

'He's playing both sides.'

'What sides?'

'Jordi and Luis Carlos disagree about the direction of government investment. Luis Carlos wants to develop the regions to take pressure off the centre. Jordi thinks we should advise the Ministry to develop a new city near the capital.'

'And that's what this model is supposed to do?'

'Yes. You've got to devise an unbiased method of comparing the various alternatives.'

'Jordi is good at figuring what people can do for him.'

With a rueful smile Chelo said Jordi had a gift for spotting what people had to offer, what they were good at, and making use of it. Jordi had sold the idea of computer modelling to Manuel as the answer to all his planning problems. But, she added, lowering her voice, it was political—Manuel wanted to break the logjam on development in the Tuy.

'Why me?' asked David.

'They needed someone to work on the Tuy—someone independent, someone good at the things you do.'

'But we didn't talk about the Tuy in England; it wasn't on the agenda.'

'Jordi thinks ahead. He could have used you in all sorts of scenarios. You're a very adaptable person.'

'Great!' he said, getting angry.

'I told you … he loves that, talent-spotting, and you were a gift. Don't kid yourself though … you popped up and he fitted you in. He's like that—it makes him feel good. Maybe he asked other people, but you took him up on it.'

§

On the twenty-sixth floor of the south tower of the Ministry of Public Works two porters guarded the door to Manuel's office. The walls of the lobby were lined with dark cork, there were no windows. They might have been in the basement for all David knew. The porters sweated in their suits; the air tasted second-hand.

He had been waiting forty minutes when a porter told him to go through. Two women were typing, one of them offered him coffee. They tried to entertain him with small talk, and then went back to their work. After another hour he was shown in.

'David! Good to see you,' said Manuel, his smile opening like an umbrella. He was dressed in a white shirt and wore a black knitted tie. His jacket hung on the back of his chair and his sleeves were rolled up over hairy arms. He waved David to a seat in front of his desk which was cluttered with papers as though he was working on a dozen things at once.

David glanced round. It was a large office with a view along the length of the city. A large table running the length of the room was piled with magazines, books and reports and papers. David imagined Manuel had been using them like children's building blocks to model the view out of the window. The piles were skyscrapers and the spaces between them avenues. It was a high-rise chaos and the slightest tremor threatened to slide the whole tottering paper city onto the floor.

'Let me tell you what we do here at the Ministry of Public Works,' said Manuel, eyeing David over the rim of his thick spectacles. 'The Division of Urban Planning is responsible for all towns and cities outside the capital. The Engineering Division builds the infrastructure and our local offices control building permission. And I, for my sins, am in charge of it all.' A man came in from the adjoining office and whispered something to Manuel.

'Tell him no, not unless they can bring the density down,' said Manuel. 'Grimaldi, this is David Anthony. He's going to help implement Jordi's modelling.'

'Enchanted,' said Grimaldi, leaving noiselessly.

'What do you want me to do?' asked David.

'We want you to run Jordi's model. We need to demonstrate that development should go ahead in the Tuy. It is unrealistic to expect the regions to absorb the growth—people want to locate near the capital. But we need to test the model first.

'Jordi and I have chosen a small city called Cumaná as the test site. My department is in the process of preparing a plan for the city and I want you to go there and collect the data you need. You can go with Joselyn Calderón. She's in charge of research and information and I want you to liaise with her.' He lifted the phone and asked someone to fetch her.

He took David to the large table and showed him a plan of the metropolitan region.

'There is five times more flat land in the Tuy valley than in the capital and, if the proposed autopista is built, it will be less than half an hour away.'

'Why hasn't it been developed already?' asked David.

'There are various reasons. Ah! Joselyn.'

A dark-haired woman was shown in. She might have been very beautiful, but her hair was pulled back in a severe bun and her bright lipstick and pale skin gave her a clown like appearance. David sensed that she resented having to work with him.

She took him to a large drawing office. People turned and

stared at him. In that first unguarded instant their faces, like a frozen snapshot, registered alarm. Joselyn introduced him with a torrent of colloquial Spanish. He heard 'paracaidista'— parachutist! what the hell did that mean? He saw scorn replace uncertainty.

He was introduced, shook hands, failed to catch their names. Clearly they had met foreign consultants before. Joselyn took him to her own office and introduced him to her staff. He was talking to one of them, when a man put his head round the door. Joselyn introduced him. His name was Keith, he was English, and also an architect. David was about to ask him how long he'd been in the country and what he was doing, but he'd started talking to Joselyn in Spanish.

He seemed to be telling her a funny story. She giggled, then reddened and looked round. Then she laughed, tears running down her cheeks. They both looked at him and Keith said something and Joselyn burst out laughing. Was he imagining it or was Keith now ridiculing his attempts to speak Spanish? People near enough to hear were sniggering. David felt his ears burning. He was being paranoid. No, Keith was mimicking Spanish spoken with a plummy English accent. Then, perhaps because Keith was a fellow countryman, David got angry.

'I think I've had enough for one day. Is tomorrow at ten in the University convenient?'

'Yes,' she said, her eyes wide.

'We're on the sixth floor.'

'How about a drink?' asked Keith.

'All right,' said David, surprised at himself for not refusing. He heard Keith shout goodbye to Joselyn and follow him out of the office.

The restaurant was in one of the oldest surviving parts of the city. The crisp table linen and dark woodwork, the old-fashioned courtesy of the headwaiter calmed David and soothed his anger. He leant back in the heavy chair and took a sip from a glass of iced beer.

'How long have you been here?' he asked, settling back.

'Three years,' said Keith.

'What's it like?'

'What? Work? Life in general?'

'Everything. Tell me about it?'

'It's like swimming in treacle.'

'What is?'

'Working here in the ministry. It's frustrating. You do your work and pass it on and there is no reaction. Nothing!'

'Why?'

'Nobody knows what they're supposed to be doing. There's tremendous uncertainty.'

'Yes?' He wondered whether Keith would get to the point. 'Let's have something to eat shall we,' he suggested, catching the waiter's eye.

'I saw Manuel this morning,' he said.

'It's almost impossible to see Manuel,' said Keith. 'Did you meet the terrible twins?'

'Who?'

'Grimaldi and Osuña.'

'I met Grimaldi.'

'And?'

'He looks like an undertaker.'

Keith laughed and said, 'They write the fairy stories Manuel needs. Information has to be immediate or it's useless. Joselyn's unit is no use: it takes them months to produce a report. Grimaldi and Osuña guesstimate—population, traffic flows, you name it.'

The waiter brought their meal.

'The office is divided into sections each responsible for a region. The problem is it takes too long to produce a plan for a city and we are hopelessly behind schedule. Only Manuel can take decisions. Everything gets passed up the hierarchy, nobody will take responsibility. You saw how his office is defended. It's the only way he can cope with the daily crises.'

'I thought that was to make people feel small,' said David. Keith smiled and nodded. David asked him what he did.

'Damn all most of the time. Nobody does anything. We clock on at eight and clock off at six, and try to avoid dying of boredom in between. I read the paper, but that's frowned on. The important thing is to be seen to be doing something. Every now and again there's a flap on and I have to get my finger out—my speciality is perspectives.'

'What do you mean?'

'You know, the sexy bits—the artist's impression of the final scheme, the aerial view of the city centre, the drawing of the shopping centre, complete with trees and fountains. It's the only part of the plan most people look at, apart from the zoning ordinance which defines what can be built where.'

'Why do you stay?'

'Difficult to get back. I'm tropicalised now.'

'Why don't all the redundant people get sacked?'

'Each time the two main parties swop power everyone above a certain level is replaced. But they aren't sacked—they just get pushed sideways.'

'I see,' said David.

Keith sensed he hadn't grasped it. 'During the election both parties make a lot of pledges. That means jobs. Nobody wants to upset the system. Those in power know the balance could swing back in three or four years. It's in no one's interest to kick people out. Anyway, all the revenue comes from oil and it's a way of distributing the wealth and creating a middle class.'

'But what a waste!' said David.

'Acción Demócratica took over from Copei last year. Funny thing is, Manuel's a Copeyano, but he stayed in power; no one's sure why. He's good at his job, or at least people think he is, which is what matters. But he also has lots of *palanca*—pull.'

'He talked about the Tuy Valley. Any idea why it hasn't been built yet?'

'The land was expropriated by presidential decree in 1959. The owners resisted the purchase and there is still no agreement about what price should be paid for the land.' David understood the crux was whether the government should pay the value of cow pasture in 1959 or of urban land now, in 1970. It was the age-old problem of who should benefit from planning decisions—a few property owners or the whole society.

'Who owns the land?'

Keith lowered his voice and said, 'Important people; there are rumours.' He asked about what and Keith mouthed, 'Manuel'.

David sat back in his chair, incredulous. He didn't want to believe that a Minister of State could be involved in a land deal like this. It was unthinkable that someone in his position could get away with it, there would be rules governing ministers' behaviour, he would have had to declare an interest. Manuel would never have survived politically— at the first hint of corruption the opposition would have demanded his head. He was tempted to pursue the argument and challenge Keith to justify his assertion. But David hated gossip, besides Manuel was Jordi's uncle. So he fiddled with his knife and said nothing. Keith looked uncomfortable and made a show of calling for the waiter to order another drink.

David remembered them talking about him, he could see Keith sniggering, assuming he would not understand, and Joselyn laughing, right in front of him. It was so insulting and he felt himself getting angry again. How preposterous!

Keith obviously loved intrigue. This kind of thing— stabbing people in the back—happened in all the other places he had worked, it was a feature of bureaucracies, and one of the things he most hated about working in institutions. People were charming and friendly to your face and assassinated you behind your back. That's all this is, scandal-mongering, he decided, suppressing the nagging doubt that there was something more, that Keith's accusation was of a different order.

Where would this kind of speculation lead? Was Jordi involved? What about Luis Carlos, Alejandro or Chelo even? If you couldn't trust the people you worked with, who could you trust? Alberto and Mildred were treating him like one of the family. Talking about Manuel like this, surreptitiously, was cowardly. It made David feel implicated, like a cheap crook, or a sordid conspirator, as though merely talking about the alleged corruption meant they were unavoidably tainted. It was like the smell that lingered in the nostrils after you encountered a dead sheep on the fells. It was something you gave a wide berth; only dogs enjoyed rolling in carrion. Consequently he dismissed the allegation as baseless, drawing conclusions about Keith's character, rather than Manuel's.

The waiter brought more drinks. Keith seemed to recover easily from David's obvious disapproval and described how a firm of English planning consultants had done a structure plan for the Tuy five years ago. He had come out to work for them and had stayed on when the work was finished. 'It's a carbon copy of Milton Keynes,' said Keith, entirely recovering his self-assurance and good humour.

David could hardly believe it. The low density of Milton Keynes, which assumed high car usage, had resulted in a soulless city without identifiable centre or coherent structure. Keith looked at him quizzically.

'Isn't that rather inappropriate,' said David.

'All right for people with cars, not so good if you walk to work,' said Keith, laughing.

'Surely you can't just plonk a city down anywhere,' he said, finding Keith's flippant attitude irritating. A city had to develop gradually in response to millions of different pulls and pressures. It couldn't be the dream of one individual or even the vision of a team of planners.

'What about Brazilia? or Letchworth for that matter?'

'What's the site like?' asked David, feeling he had to find out more.

'Hot as hell! Imagine a deep bowl, fifty kilometres across, surrounded by hills and mountains. There's no wind to speak of and the only water is a stinking river that dries up half the year. Thank God I won't have to live there. I just hope they never build it.'

'Why?'

'It has a funny feel. Maybe it's the atmosphere, I don't know. We only went there once. The small villages on the edge of the bowl are fine, but in the middle, where we planned the new centre, there are bad vibes.'

'What's she like?' asked Chelo.
'Crabby!' said David.
Chelo ripped open a new packet of Marlboro and lit up belligerently. They sat in silence, waiting for Joselyn to turn up.

Deep moody eyes, furrowed brow, white complexion, and a black skullcap hair-do. Maybe she was a witch, he mused. Her clothes were old-fashioned: he imagined her wearing a mantilla to church on Sundays. Keith had said she was from an old Spanish family.

Spanish colonization in America, David thought, was based on cities. Wherever an expedition conquered a new territory its leaders founded a city, with a municipal council, chosen from amongst the conquerors.

'What time did you tell her the meeting started?' asked Alejandro, looking at his watch.

'Half-an-hour ago.' He felt uneasy. Maybe they were paying for his brusqueness. Brusque! He was bloody rude. Why didn't he grow up! He should have given her clear instructions, gone through the social conventions: how important she was to the work, how they couldn't manage without her. Was she late, or had she decided not to come? Maybe she'd forgotten.

Ah, at last! Alejandro leapt to his feet. How could he be so effusive? Such a meaningless stream of words. She was apologising for being late: the traffic! the parking! Chelo's joined in. They've found a link, the bridge was firming up.

'Let's make a start,' said Alejandro, once they were seated with coffee. He turned to David. My God! they're all waiting for me to tell them what to do. He hadn't bargained for this. He came to work in a group, not have to do the leading.

'Let's begin with how the model works...' David started. Alejandro yawned. There were two deep furrows in Joselyn's brow which ran vertically from either side of her nose. 'We can't stop cities growing.' He had their attention now. 'Planning is about seeing the ways things are moving, and giving them a shove or a brake. The problem is that we are uncertain about the form growth is likely to take. There is a fundamental difference between planning in Britain and planning here.' He could see Joselyn bristle. No, I'm not going to make some odious comparison, he thought.

'Planning in Europe is negative. Its purpose is to contain, to preserve the sharp distinction between town and country. Britain is crowded. We plan because there is a finite amount of land and we believe it better to regulate its use rather than allow a free-for-all.

'Here it's different. Why are vast tracts virtually empty? Because people want to live where there are jobs and services, manufacturers want to locate near markets. So people move to the city. The purpose of the model is to predict the shape of this growth.

'We don't begin with a clean sheet. The buildings and spaces, the people and activities which form the city aren't random. They form patterns. The model replicates this process ...'

He didn't believe in any of this. Planning was a control system to preserve inequality. It was a profession like any other: hypocrisy and restrictive practices. Nevertheless, he carried on. 'The nice thing about the model is that we can try alternative plans,' he said, controlling his scepticism.

'That's where the evaluation comes in,' said Alejandro, perking up.

'I've just started working on it, but the idea is ...'

'What information do we need to run the model?' asked Chelo.

'Right. We need population and employment data for 1960 and '70. But totals won't do, we need figures for zones.'

'That's impossible,' said Joselyn.

'Not necessarily.' Here it gets tricky, he thought. Careful.

'The important thing is the zoning.'

'What do you mean?' said Chelo.

'The commercial centre, government offices, industry ... they're all fairly straightforward. And we need to distinguish residential areas in terms of indicators like income and size of dwelling.'

'I'm against building in social division,' said Joselyn sharply.

She's got a point, he thought. The model is biased by the zoning you choose.

'That's why you need to visit these places; to do the zoning properly,' said Alejandro.

Joselyn looked unconvinced. It was wrong, she argued, to define social class a priori. Society was divided enough without him compounding the injustice. Her approach, David realised, was to try and make him feel guilty.

'I have to go there anyway,' she said. 'I need to interview the fuerzas vivas...'

So she'd been planning to go all along, he thought. And

what the devil does fuerzas vivas mean!

'Local government, the Chamber of Commerce ...'

The movers and shakers, thought David. She had a nerve, blaming him, when she planned to interview the power lobby.

'What are the arrangements?' asked Chelo.

'Manuel wants us to go next Monday,' said Joselyn. 'I'll book the flight and the local office can provide a car.'

'Excellent,' said Alejandro. 'I think that about wraps it up.'

8

Alberto's was the last house in the road, just below the Cota Mil, the autopista which followed the thousand metre contour, dividing the city from the mountain. There were no apartment blocks this high, and sprinklers kept the lawns green in front of the houses. Beyond the house he could see the tall dry grass and a trail leading up. The house was beautiful: architecturally elegant, formed by simple rectangular shapes and balconies from which foliage spilled like waterfalls.

He had walked the three miles up hill from the University and was feeling hot and tired. But it was cool inside after the street. The walls were lined with bookshelves, and the well-worn leather chairs made the house feel as comfortable as slippers.

Christina called from the kitchen. 'Everyone is out. Would

you like a drink?' When he said water she came through and guessed he had walked up the hill in the sun.

'You're crazy,' she said.

'I like your house,' he said.

'Alberto helped design it soon after they were married. I've lived here all my life.'

David sat at the table and watched her cooking and it struck him what a remarkably independent woman she was. It was the way she moved about the kitchen, beating the eggs, making the omelette. She knew in which cupboard to find a bowl, in which drawer to find the whisk, and she cracked the eggs one-handed, she had obviously done it before. None of this would have been remarkable in England, but here, living with her parents who had a cook and two maids, it was significant. David suspected Mariella would not know how to boil an egg never mind make an omelette.

Christina's freethinking struck him as singular in this male dominated society. But then Mildred had the same strong character. Maybe the women he had met here were exceptional or perhaps male dominance was overrated.

'Tell me about your work.'

'There's nothing much to tell really, I'm a lawyer. At the moment we're defending two young men charged with terrorism. They were involved in demonstrations in the university. Then weapons were found where they live, but the boys don't know how they got there. They face the death penalty.'

'What's likely to happen with all this terrorist activity?'

'In Cuba armed insurrection changed everything.'

'But here?'

'Cuba was very influential—the idea of a rural nucleus

challenging the state—it appealed to young middle class intellectuals. It promised action and there was a time, in the early sixties, when it looked like succeeding. I was in Paris, during the demonstrations; it was so exciting. For a while you believed things would change, you could imagine a new world without injustice.'

'And now?'

'It'll probably fizzle out.'

'Why's Jordi involved?'

'My family have always been subversives. My grandfather spent five years in jail for opposing Goméz … and my uncles helped overthrow Perez Jimenez, the last military dictator.'

She described how her uncles, Armando and Diogenes, had stormed the presidential palace at Miraflores. The cadets from the military academy launched a counter attack down the hill from their barracks in Catia. Most of the young cadets had been killed but Perez Jimenez had escaped in the confusion.

Armando and the others chased him to the airport but were held up at the gate by a platoon of paratroops. By the time they got into the airport the plane was already taxiing down the runway. Armando had got abreast of the plane in his jeep and could actually see Perez Jimenez looking out through the cockpit window. They fired at him but the jeep was bouncing so much they missed. To try and stop him taking off Armando cut in front of the plane as it left the ground. Its wheels took the canvas off the top of the jeep, but Perez Jimenez got away.

But Romulo Betancourt, the leader of the revolution, formed a government which was as ruthless in dealing with opposition and the remaining guerrilla units operating in

Falcon were tracked down and eliminated.

Five or six years ago young tigers like Jordi and Luis Carlos were calling for a new revolution. Although their families were amongst the richest in the country they had seen no contradiction in becoming Marxists and student leaders. What they wanted at bottom was power and influence. 'But things have changed over the last couple of years. They've seen the writing on the wall and are busily extricating themselves.

'Luis Carlos is still idealistic. He wants to restrict the growth of the capital and direct development to the poorer regions. Jordi plays along with him, but I suspect he's more opportunistic. He's looking to the future.'

'In what way?' asked David.

She laughed. 'That's why he's gone to England—he's sold on the power computer modelling appears to offer. He loves computers and the wonders of modern technology.'

'So nothing's changed?'

'There is something in the Latin American character that responds to authoritarianism. Many people see dictatorship as the best way of maintaining a stable economy. That's why the United States supports undemocratic regimes. Maybe it's all to do with the Spanish character,' she suggested laughing.

'Do you believe in national stereotypes?' he asked her.

'Don't you?' she said.

In a way he did. He found the pressure to conform to the stereotypic Englishman particularly onerous. 'People expect me to play some Edwardian, stiff-upper-lip, midday-sun character.'

'I do too,' she said, laughing.

'How did you get into defending terrorists?'

'Alleged terrorists!' she said. The young men were friends of the family, she explained, and Alberto was paying for their defence. David marvelled at their generosity.

Christina parked her tiny Renault at the supermarket in La Florida and they walked up the hill until they reached a small green filled with trees. The flat they had come to view was an oldish house on the Avenida Los Mangos owned by an English couple named Jardine. While his wife made tea, the man told them he had retired and that they were planning to return to England. He had been a safety officer with an American oil company and began to tell stories about his travels in the interior.

'They don't want to hear all your tales, Henry,' said Mrs Jardine, returning with a tray of tea things. 'Milk, my dears?'

'We shall be taking most of the furniture, I'm afraid.'

'That's fine,' said David, noticing the patterned chair cushions and the floral curtaining. The furniture was the ubiquitous dark colonial-style he had seen in most homes and restaurants, but somehow the Jardines had created a thoroughly English feel to the room. Maybe it was the chintz fabric or the prints of Norfolk fens and the Lake District; or maybe it was the Englishness of the Jardines that created the illusion.

'Is it for you both, my dears,' asked Mrs Jardine, touching her handkerchief to her lips as she spoke.

'No, just for me,' said David, grinning at Christina.

'We don't want to rent it on a long lease; we haven't decided whether to sell or not,' said Mr Jardine. 'This place may be too big for one, on the other hand it could be ideal renting it to someone like yourself. How long do you intend to stay?'

'I'm not sure, I came with the intention of staying two years and seeing what happens.'

'Who are you working for?'

'The Central University, in the School of Architecture.'

'When would you want to move in, dear?'

'As soon as possible.'

'We're leaving on Friday. The removers are coming in tomorrow to pack up. You'd better see round the place.'

Apart from the main living room, there were two bedrooms, a bathroom, a kitchen and a dining room. On the flat roof there was a small room that might have been used as a maid's quarters. The garden at the back was shaded by a giant mango tree but there was a corner near the house that caught the evening sun, and from the roof David could see the mountains. Along the high brick wall there were dozens of orchids.

'I'm afraid we shall be giving away our orchid collection to friends.'

'Yes, we shall miss it here,' said his wife, 'but it's not what it was—so many people have left: the tennis club is full of nationals now.'

Jardine asked him if he had registered with the embassy. It was good form—important in case of evacuation. 'Anyway you'll want to join the Commonwealth club otherwise you won't know what's happening—it's the Queen's Birthday Party in June!'

David asked what it entailed and Mrs Jardine said that there was a party at the embassy, it was the high spot of the year. Jardine said he could get tickets from the British Council and they had a good library.

'Yes, we'll miss it here,' said Mrs Jardine, vaguely. She reminded David of his mother. The same abstracted concern, as though she was drifting far away in some happier land.

'Well, what do you think?' asked Jardine, when they were back in the living room.

David liked the house and thought he could afford it out of his salary. 'It's ideal,' he said, 'I'd like to take it. Will you need references?'

'A letter from your department or someone who knows you and is prepared to act as guarantor. We will also need a deposit of one month's rent in advance. Can you manage that? I know how things are when you take a job with the government here.'

'I must tell you that I haven't signed my contract at the university and there does seem to be some delay in paying my salary.'

'Oh!' said Mrs Jardine.

'That's not unusual,' said Jardine.

'My father has agreed to help,' said Christina. 'We live just round the corner.'

'We'll hold the house until mid-day tomorrow. Come by tomorrow morning and I'll have the contract ready,' said Jardine, holding out his hand as he showed them to the door.

Alberto was in when they got back. Christina explained the problem and he went straight to his desk and wrote David a letter of guarantee and put it in an envelope together with some bills from the desk drawer.

'Here are three thousand bolivars,' he said, handing the envelope to David. 'It's a loan until you get paid by the university. It's in cash, the banks wouldn't open an account and clear a cheque in time. Pay me back when you can.'

'That is very kind of you. I don't know how to thank you,' said David.

They were both a little embarrassed. It was something he would never have done in England. But he didn't know what else to do and, the way Alberto had offered, it seemed insulting to have refused.

Christina came with him to the door. It was dark already and she asked him where he was going and if he wanted a lift. He said he planned to go to the Instituto Latino-Americano to register for Spanish classes and no, he didn't need a lift, it was downhill all the way and he liked walking in the night. She looked disappointed.

He twirled his jacket round his head as he walked down the middle of the road. He turned round and skipped backwards looking up at the stars and the black outline of the mountain against the night sky. Then he remembered the money in his inside pocket and realised why Christina had offered him a lift. He checked that the envelope was still there and put his jacket on.

On the hill down to Las Mercedes, the wide pavement thronged with pedestrians. At the lights, men and boys jinked between the cars selling newspapers, flowers, cigarettes, hot pasties and tray-loads of cheap knick-knacks. A beggar, his right arm dislocated behind his head, his legless torso perched on a rustic trolley, thrust his one good limb at David. His singlet and shorts were grimy and streaked with oil, his hair matted with filth. David wanted to run, to get away from the sight of the man and the stench of his urine. But he forced himself to stop, to take out the coins from his pocket and, worst of all, to look the man in the eye as he put the money into his outstretched hand.

The foyer of the Institute was crowded with students, mainly young Venezuelans there to learn English. Although he had only come to find out about courses and register the receptionist said a beginners' course started that evening at eight, in less than half an hour.

'How much does it cost?' he asked. He needed to be careful with the money Alberto had lent him. He didn't know how long it would have to last.

'For the term, eight hundred bolivars,' she said. It was much more than he could afford. He explained that he had just arrived and hadn't been paid yet and was turning away when she said, 'Would you like a word with the director of studies? Perhaps he can help.'

The director was a young American who listened to David's story and suggested he pay a deposit of a hundred bolivars, with the balance deferred until the end of term. Surprised and pleased David readily agreed and was given a note for the receptionist. After he had filled in the registration forms she told where to find his classroom and sent him to the little shop in the foyer to buy the textbook he needed.

Other people had arrived already and David found a seat near the front. The desk was too small for his long legs and, looking round the room, he relived his nervousness at starting secondary school.

The teacher was squat, dressed in a pin-stripe suit and had the face of an Inca. 'Me llamo Jaimé Martinez. Soy su professor. I speak no English!,' he announced, his face breaking into an infectious grin.

They went round the room introducing themselves.'

'Soy abogado—I am a lawyer,' said Jaimé. 'Soy de los

Andes.'

Most of the class were American, with a couple of West Indians, a Japanese. David began to enjoy himself: the lack of self-consciousness in the Americans' pronunciation made him feel easier with his own poor accent. Jaimé wind milled his arms, lost in the joy of teaching.

After the class, Jerry, one of the Americans, invited David for a beer in the supermarket across the road. He had been an insurance salesman in a small mid-Western town. 'I wasn't making hardly enough to keep the wife and baby and pay for the car. I came down here to work for my uncle—he's got a company selling catering equipment. He had a heart attack and he's had to slow down. He's not actually an uncle, he's an old friend of the wife's parents. Anyway the pay's not so hot, but the prospects look all right. I'm on commission and he says he'll cut me in on a share in the business if things work out.'

David ordered two beers.

'How did you get here?' Jerry asked him.

'Nepotism. I've always been interested in South America and one of my students got me a job here in the university paid for by his uncle.'

'What's the job?'

'This friend and I were planning to work together, but he's had to go back to England for a while,' said David, surprised again at how abandoned he felt. 'I'm not sure how it's going to work out.'

'Do you like walking?' asked Jerry suddenly.

'Sure,' said David, studying him with new interest. He was a beanpole of a man with a habit of bobbing his head as he spoke, stabbing the air with his long pointed nose.

'Want to climb Cachimbo?'

'Where?' asked David.

'The ridge up Pico Oriental … you know, the big pointed mountain you can see from all over the place.'

David knew where he meant immediately. 'Climb?' you mean rock climb, with ropes and stuff?'

'Not my scene,' said Jerry. 'It's a hike.'

David felt disappointed that Jerry wasn't a climber, he badly needed to find someone who knew about climbing here. But Jerry was better than nothing and they fixed up to hiking on Sunday.

§

On Friday David left work early and returned to the hotel to collect his things. He had warned the manager that he would be leaving and the bill was ready. The manager called his wife and she cried a little and pressed his hands as she said goodbye. In the taxi he wondered, when neither spoke the other's language with any certitude, how they had got to know each other. He would probably never see them again.

The Jardines had left a note on the table, it read: Sorry we missed you. Would be most grateful if you could redirect any mail to above address. Best of luck, Jardine. There was a P.S. in another hand which read: We left you tea things.

David looked round. The place had the sad, dingy look of a vacant house. There were patches of different coloured wall where the furniture and pictures had been removed. At first David thought they must have painted round things and then realised the walls were dirty. In the kitchen there were two cups, one chipped, a teaspoon, Lipton's tea bags in a battered caddy with a picture of the Queen and, on the greasy stove, a pan with a broken handle. There were mouse droppings in the cupboard under the sink and a cockroach skittered across the floor. The room had the musty, slightly fetid smell—a combination of burnt-on fat and rotten food.

Opening the back door, David went out into the garden and climbed the stairs to the roof. The sun was still warm, and the light had the soft warm tone of sunset. The long shadows hadn't yet reached the sunny corner of the garden and he filled his lungs with the sweet evening air. Strange how the house looked so different without the Jardines and the little world they had created.

Inside the maid's room there was a rustic chair, encrusted with dirt. David thought of burning it along with some of the other things and then decided that, washed and polished, it could be his first piece of furniture. He fetched a broom from the kitchen, swept the room and systematically carried or dragged all the furniture the Jardines had left and stored it there. Then he swept out the rest of the house and scrubbed the floor tiles in the bedroom. By now it was nearly dark and he was dirty and tired. There was gas, but no electricity. He put a pan of water on to boil, undressed and showered in cold water in the dark.

I'll buy paint and brushes and work on it over the weekend, he thought. Maybe I'll use one of the bedrooms as a workshop if my tools arrive. And the dining room? Leave it empty. So that's only three rooms to paint.

There were two candles in the sink cupboard and he lit one to dress by. The water boiled and he threw in a tea bag. He was hungry but there would be no time to find somewhere to eat before his Spanish class. He swallowed some of the tea, locked the door and ran down the hill to catch a por puesto.

It was 10 o'clock by the time he got back. The bedroom window was open and the room smelt fresh and clean. He lit the candle and rolled his sleeping bag out on the floor and, almost immediately, fell asleep.

At eight the following morning David went to the hardware store and bought three cans of white emulsion, a roller, a two inch brush, a kilo of sugar soap to wash the old paint work and more candles. At the bakers on the corner, he bought bread rolls, still warm from the oven, and, holding the brown paper bag to his chest he drank in the smell of the fresh bread. The shops had only just opened and, being Saturday, there were few people about as he crossed the road to the supermarket to buy coffee, butter and jam. Laden like a Sherpa, the groceries perched on top of the box of paint, he climbed the hill to his new home.

While the water heated up, he sharpened the old knife the Jardines had left, by rubbing it on the stone step in the garden. He buttered two rolls and spread one with jam. When the water had boiled, he turned off the flame and spooned a generous measure of coffee on to the surface of the water. The grounds settled and he carefully poured a cup. The coffee was strong and delicious. He bit into the fresh buttered roll and wandered into the garden, the roll in one hand, the coffee in the other. He stopped, the roll half-raised to his mouth. In front of him, not more than five paces away, there was a bird, a bright jewel-like thing, a humming-bird, hovering, its wings moving so fast they were a blur, its body an iridescent blue. He kept absolutely still and the tiny bird hovered from one hibiscus to another, its long curved beak pushing deep into the flower. In an instant it disappeared over the wall.

A wren used to visit him in England, until the old lady's cat got it. But then David liked the cat too. He was called Smirnoff: the old lady liked a drink or two. Sometimes Smirnoff would stay the night, usually in the winter when David's flat was warmer than downstairs. He would wake David in the morning by pushing things off his desk, his rubber, then his pencils.

David took another bite of his roll and looked round the garden. He would buy a hammock and hang it across the corner between the wall and the house, or maybe from the mango. He finished the roll, put the empty cup down and went and fetched an old pair of men's pyjamas he'd seen in the room on the roof. He ripped them into rags, filled a bucket with water from the tap, added boiling water from the stove and stirred in some of the sugar soap. Working steadily he washed the metal skirting boards, architraves and window frames in each of the rooms. They were pale orange brown and despite the chips and scratches, he decided not to bother painting them.

The bell rang and he stood up and straightened his back.

'I thought I'd come and see how you were getting on,' said Christina. 'I brought you some lunch.'

'Come in, see for yourself.'

'It looks totally different!'

'It looks bare, but I'm going to put up some shelves for my books and things.'

'What things?'

'There's a box coming by sea.'

'So you burnt your boats then, like Cortés.'

'I could get a plane home, but yes I suppose I did. I imagine I might be here for the rest of my life, while, at the same time, thinking I can go back whenever I like.'

'A clever trick!'

'Can you stay for lunch?'

'I can't stay long, I've got a meeting.'

They sat on the grass in the warm shade and ate the ham and cheese.

'What's your meeting?'

'We're going to visit our client, and after that we're hoping to interview one of the witnesses who can corroborate his alibi. The case is due for trial next week.'

'What are your chances?'

'They should be good,' she said, shrugging her shoulders.

After Christina left, he opened one of the cans and, standing on the chair, began to paint the bedroom ceiling. By seven o'clock he'd finished the first coat. He was tired, his right arm ached and he felt a little light-headed. He looked round the living room. The furniture marks still showed, but they were much fainter. He scrubbed his hands and, not bothering to change, walked down to the cafe he'd seen near the bakers.

Back home, with food inside him, he worked till midnight and finished the second coat. He had been painting by candlelight and it remained to be seen in the morning whether he'd missed bits. The bedroom smelt strongly even though he'd left the window wide open. He stripped off his clothes, washed, and carried the sleeping bag onto the terrace in the garden.

David woke at four, for a moment unsure why he'd woken so early, then he remembered he had arranged to meet Jerry. His back felt stiff, and his right shoulder ached with the work and the hard ground. Showered and dressed in a clean shirt and the jeans he'd worn for painting, he walked up to the autopista and, keeping to the gutter on the hard shoulder, jogged the half-mile to where he could see a figure on the other side of the empty road.

'Hello, been waiting long?'

'No. Where are your boots and pack?'

He looked down at his trainers. Jerry wore knee high leather boots, a wide-brimmed hat and had a rucksack on his back.

'I'll be all right in these, we're only going for a walk.'

'I told you there are snakes,' said Jerry, looking alarmed.

'We'll keep to the path, don't worry. Does it go up here? You lead the way.'

The road was so steep he was astonished a vehicle could drive up it. He felt sick from lack of sleep. It was only with the greatest effort that he forced his legs to keep moving. Just keep going, don't think. One, two, three, four. He would get a second wind soon, he told himself. For a moment he looked up from the path immediately in front of him. Some kind of tropical pine had been planted next to the track, pine needles crunched under foot and he caught a whiff of turpentine from the resinous bark. But Jerry was getting ahead and there was no time to stop.

Jerry waited for him at the fire-break, a broad track, cleared to stop fire spreading to the city, which contoured round the mountain and disappeared in dense vegetation.

David stopped, his hands on his knees and took deep gulps of air. He was just thinking what a pleasant walk this level track would make when Jerry set off upwards.

This path was made to be walked. Unlike the road, which tackled the incline head-on, the trail followed the contours, zigzagging up the slope. He noticed signs of cultivation—flowering shrubs had been planted and a little further on the coarse grass had been cut. Through the trees he could see a green cabin and, standing outside, a man in khaki uniform.

'It's the park ranger. I usually stop for a chat and time myself from there to the top.'

Time yourself? thought David.

The metal cabin was oval in shape and had a dome roof. The ranger asked them inside to sign the book. There were two small rooms, the far one had a hammock and was obviously his bedroom.

'They had the National Guard up here on exercises last week. It's the trouble in the university,' said Jerry. They walked to a water tank a few hundred feet above the cabin and Jerry stopped to fill his water bottle.

'Does he live here all the time?'

'Yes. There are six stations spread out along the skirt of the mountain.'

'All like this?'

'No, his twin brother has a proper house at Sebucan. It causes a lot of bad feeling.'

'What do they do all day?'

'They watch for fires or any other trouble. We'd better get moving,' said Jerry, setting his stopwatch.

'What are you timing?'

'I'll tell you later,' said Jerry, marching off.

He felt much better—he'd woken up, the path was less steep and he had no difficulty keeping up. They reached Loma Serrano, a grassy knoll surrounded by tall eucalyptus whispering in the breeze. Birds sang and the grass looked soft and inviting. Jerry pressed on. The ridge fell away steeply on both sides and as it steepened sharply, he found himself panting to keep up. They climbed onto a large rock sticking out of the mountain side like the prow of a ship and looked back. The valley was hidden by a uniform white blanket, like a huge closed eye.

Jerry allowed a moment's rest and then was off again. They had left the tree line far below and the path was reduced to the width of a sheep track.

'This is the bit I hate!' said Jerry.

'Why?'

'Snakes, man!'

David wondered if they'd lost the way. The path kept disappearing where the coarse dry grass had grown over, but, by looking far ahead into the distance and squinting, he could see a faint path leading towards a deep gorge. Satisfied they were going the right way, he was surprised when Jerry suddenly turned left up what he had thought was just an erosion scar. It was so steep he was forced to use his hands. His knees and calves screamed in protest and he imagined the tendons ripping with the effort. The blood was pounding so strongly in the veins of his neck that his head spun. Above in the distance he could see the top and gritted his teeth.

'How about a rest?' he shouted.

'Keep going!' said Jerry.

Over a rise, they could see two small figures ahead of them. Soon they overhauled them. The man said Hi! The woman smiled. Her face was bright red and they were both gasping for breath. The top he had seen was false—the ridge levelled and he could see a cross on the true summit at least a thousand feet higher. He blanked out the pain and his mind entered a trance-like state which he was able to maintain by concentrating on the tiny detail of each footstep.

The vegetation changed to a kind of gnarled bush, like monstrous heather. They had to clamber over large black rocks and finally reached the top, where a latticework of aluminium formed a huge cross. Almost too tired to sit, he looked down the great sweep of green to the blue ocean and the thin line of surf.

'You're pretty fit, man,' said Jerry, gasping for breath. 'This is my best time yet—an hour and fifty-three minutes. That's the first time I've broken two hours.'

'I'm glad,' David said, his legs suddenly giving way beneath him as he tried to sit. The morning haze had cleared and they could see the city spread below them like a sleeping dragon.

Smoke curled from the municipal dump at the end of the valley where the ranchos on the hills above Petare rose like a scaly head. The great body of the valley lay in repose, sinuous, following the contours of the foothills to the south and subsidiary ridges of the coastal chain to the north. Tree-lined avenues radiated out from the autopista as ribs, tall apartment blocks poked up a horny crest and, in the distance, the valley flowed round the hill of Calvario like a forked tail.

It felt good to have woken early, stiff as he was from all the painting, and made the climb. Without these mountains it might be impossible for him to live in this crowded, noisy city. Whenever it got too much—when the traffic became unbearable and the concrete caved in over his head—he could come up here where the air was pure and find peace and quiet in the way some people found solace in Sunday morning church or meditation or maybe even in jogging.

But it had always been difficult to come back to earth. And, the longer the time away in the mountains, the more difficult the transition back into everyday life. When he first started climbing at sixteen his mother used to ask him how it had been. She wanted to know what he had done, to share a little in his adventures. He tried to tell her about it but because she had not been there herself he found it impossible. It was impossible for him to put into words the sights, smells and sounds he had experienced: the feel of warm incut holds in the evening sun, the spring of heather under his feet or the smell of herbs released as he walked through meadow grass after rain.

He wished he could talk about some of this with Jerry, but he could see Jerry wanted to make a move, to hurry back to the enveloping security of the city. Jerry was a nuts-and-bolts man. He liked to talk about complicated moves in American football or how he had unblocked the fuel line on his Chevvy. On the other hand he seemed genuinely interested in David's work and wanted to know all about the unit: about Jordi and Luis Carlos and who made the decisions. But there was something intriguing about Jerry—he could speak good Spanish, yet they had met at beginners' Spanish.

He wondered if he was being stupid. Jerry was just Jerry. You had to accept friends as you found them, and anyway David knew no one else who would want to climb a mountain with him this early on a Sunday morning.

There was nothing like moving fast, covering the ground

126

and letting rip. David felt unfit, but already his muscles were responding. At some inner level that was beyond thinking and feeling, walking fast, climbing hard, was satisfying.

'We're over 9,000 feet above sea level. That other peak is higher,' said Jerry. Strangely it looked lower and, wondering at his own bravado, he asked if Jerry wanted to climb it. 'I'm not sure, man. I like this route, it's nice and open, less snakes, and I've been timing it.'

'How many times have you been up here?' asked David.

'Seven or eight.'

'And nowhere else?'

'Sure, I've been up to the hotel on the teleferico.' He pointed far along the ridge.

'Have you got any food in that sack?'

'No—rain gear, a flashlight, stuff like that. I've got water, here have some. We'll be back in time for lunch, it only takes about half an hour to get down.'

What was the point of rushing back as soon as they'd reached the top, David thought.

'Are you ready?'

He forced himself to stand, his legs felt weary but Jerry was bounding ahead. Once moving he began to enjoy running down such a steep slope. If you didn't think about falling and looked two or three strides ahead you could, surprisingly, stay on your feet.

The two Americans were stretched out on the ground with a picnic laid.

'Let's stop,' said David firmly, and sat down. Jerry stood for a moment or two and then gave in.

'Hi, I'm Bob and this is Diane. Where are you from?'

Jerry introduced them both while David looked at the

food. There was pâté, smoked ham, salami, cheese, fruit, grapes, bread and a bottle of wine.

'Would you like some?' she asked. She said they were supposed to be on a diet, that she guessed they had been living too well. David sat down and helped himself. He was just feeling like a sleep when Jerry was on his feet consulting his watch.

'Where're you rushing to?' Diane asked.

'He's timing us,' said David.

'You guys are crazy,' she said.

Near the motorway, almost back in the city, they crossed a stream. By the side of the path, under a tall stand of bamboo, there was a patch of dappled shade and he felt an intense desire to lie down and rest.

'I think I'll stop here for a while, you go on,' he said.

'I wouldn't sit there,' said Jerry.

'Why not?'

'It's a bad place for snakes under bamboo,' said Jerry, who looked, now that they were nearly back, as if nothing would budge him from the path. 'You think I'm making a fuss about nothing don't you?'

'I'll be all right. See you in class,' he said firmly. He lay in the dry leaves and looked at the sky. The bamboo moved in the wind, the thick stems creaked and the leaves rustled metallically like tiny bells. There was nothing to feel frightened of in the wild. He was sure that if there were snakes they wouldn't attack him while he slept.

He woke feeling cold but refreshed. The sun had gone and he looked at his watch and saw it was after five. There was much more traffic on the autopista. Half-way back he passed a deep bowl, like a natural amphitheatre with a steep cliff. He stopped and sat on the crash barrier to study the rock. It was much more solid than anything else he had seen and well over a hundred feet high. It was divided halfway up by a small overhang which crossed the cliff from left to right in the form of a great arch. He could traverse from one side to the other under the overhang, and in the centre of the rock, at its highest point, there was a step in the overhang where it turned an angle. When his things arrived from England, he'd come back and have a look.

9

His legs refused to respond and he had to clutch the garden wall to avoid pitching over. It was as if his legs had become paralysed from the waist down but, by leaning forward until he was about to fall, he found that he could force them work and in this way managed to reach the taxi rank near the supermarket.

'You're burnt,' said Chelo, when she met him at the airport. She laughed when he told her about Jerry and the excursion and how he could hardly walk. Her laughter was unrestrained and joyous as though her good spirits had too long been bottled up.

The car was waiting for them at the airport in Cumaná: an orange Beetle with *MOP—Ministerio de Obras Publicas* painted in blue letters on the sides.

'We'll go to the hotel,' Joselyn said, handing David the

keys. 'If you drive, we can talk.' David opened the door and Chelo and Joselyn climbed into the back seat. He loaded the luggage.

'Turn left and drive straight through town,' said Joselyn. He felt like a chauffeur.

The hotel was on the edge of the sea and their rooms, which were on the ground floor, had glass doors opening to a pool. The women were to share; David had the adjoining room. They agreed to meet in the restaurant.

At seven he was sitting at a table watching the waves break gently on the shallow beach. The sun was fast disappearing and the hills across the gulf turned to sombre shadow. Within a few minutes the sea slid from blue and gold to silver and purple. The waiter brought the menu; David was his only customer. He ordered a drink and bit into a bread roll to stave off hunger.

It was suddenly dark and the lights came on. Chelo and Joselyn were escorted to the table by the waiter. Joselyn had let down her hair, which was luxuriant and black. Her lips were less vivid, the scowl lines on her forehead had softened but she still had the same challenging smile.

'Have you ordered?'

'No,' said David.

'Let's. We're hungry!' said Chelo.

They waited to be served in silence. David watched the moths circling the lanterns. Above the bar there was a strip of blue neon. It attracted the insects. Every few seconds there was a sharp fizz and a charred body plopped into the metal tray.

'I went swimming,' said David. Neither of the women seemed interested. David chewed his fish. 'This is good!'

They must have caught it today, fresh and succulent. He wondered what Joselyn looked like in a bikini, she was so pale.

They ate in silence until the waiter brought coffee. Chelo offered Joselyn a cigarette and lit it for her. David hadn't smoked since his father got ill, but he didn't mind them smoking, especially outside, although the initial whiff as they lit up reawakened the old desire momentarily.

'We'd like to go into town this evening, to the cinema,' said Chelo.

'Is there anything worth watching? I'd thought we might stop here and have a drink and watch the sea.'

'That doesn't sound very exciting,' said Joselyn.

'Okay, see you in the morning,' he said.

'Don't be obtuse. We can't go alone, you have to come,' said Chelo.

'All right then, I'll come.'

The film was a story of teenage love in a mid-west town. Joselyn complained that the plot was fatuous, the women empty-headed, the men chauvinist.

I didn't want to come anyway, he thought, but I'm too tired to move. The picture's all right, in a mindless kind of way. His mind wandered. It was a man's world— they needed him to accompany them.

Chelo nudged him. 'We want to leave, this is awful.'

'Fine,' he said, not moving.

'Let's go!' said Chelo.

David passed her the car keys. 'I'll walk,' he said. They whispered. Why was he so unco-operative, the picture was lousy. He was tired, daydreaming happily to himself, he didn't want to be bossed around.

Walking out at the end Joselyn looked thunderous.

'Why are you so Turk!' Chelo yelled at him. They got in the car. He drove with his foot hard down on the accelerator. He realised he was furious when he went through a set of traffic lights at red. He hated being saddled with Joselyn as a working partner. They reached the hotel and the two women got out and walked to their room without a word.

Showering, the following morning, David sang a medley of half remembered songs. He hoped they could hear through the wall.

The local office was just off the main street in the old part of town. It was a small colonial style house with a bright yellow door. The shutters were closed over the front windows to keep out the dust and fumes from the street, but the shade was welcome after the heat and the corridor fed a cooling breath of air from the courtyard.

Joselyn spent the whole time on the telephone. He studied the maps on the walls—brightly coloured plans of the city. He traced the ones he thought would be useful.

He was still busy when Chelo asked, 'David! What questions do you think we should include in the interviews?'

'I don't know,' he replied, still unclear why they needed to speak to these people—the vital forces. 'To test the model we should ask them to help us devise different alternatives.'

'It's our job in MOP to decide that,' said Joselyn. 'We can't give people the idea that they can dictate terms to planners.'

'Then I'm not sure how useful it is to speak to these people.'

'It's vital,' said Joselyn, slapping the edge of the table. David smiled and looked at Chelo to see if she had appreciated the irony.

'We can ask them about their aspirations for future development,' said Chelo. David raised his eyebrows.

'Joselyn has to write a socio-economic report!' said Chelo.

'Yes,' said David. What with? he wondered, a crystal ball! The only up-to-date survey was MERCAVI, funded by an American bank interested in family purchasing power, and although Joselyn had a magnetic tape of the data, she was not using it and was being difficult about letting him have it. The deal he had offered her was to write the computer program and get her useful information in return for the data he needed for Jordi. Manuel had told her to help, but Joselyn was still playing games with him.

He felt irritated. He was there to collect information for the model, not help Joselyn write fairy stories. What would she write? People here lived in sewers right next to people in palaces. But that wouldn't be what the 'vital forces' told her. How could social scientists keep their integrity in a country like this and not lose their jobs?

Their first interview was with the alcade, the mayor. They'd arrived on time and had been waiting half-an-hour. David could feel the anxiety in the pit of his stomach as he visualised being late for the following appointments. Joselyn and Chelo chatted, unconcerned. David sat with his legs crossed, trying to be patient, his foot keeping time as he hummed Leonard Cohen's 'Sisters of Mercy' to himself.

When he was eighteen, he remembered, he had gone climbing in the Dolomites with a friend from school. David's dad drove them to the station. As they heaved their rucksacks onto the luggage rack and sat down in the window seats, a man in a bowler hat said, Hadn't they seen that the seats were booked. David savoured the moment and said yes, he had noticed because he had booked them. He was feeling smug when his friend remembered that they had forgotten their brand new climbing rope.

They had half-an-hour to departure time and his dad, who was still on the platform waiting to wave them off, offered to race back and get it. He arrived back in the nick of time, panting heavily. David had been worried that he might have had a heart attack. He loved him, not just for helping, but also for not making a meal of their incompetence. Ever since then he'd liked to get to stations and airports with plenty of time to spare and got very anxious if he was late for an appointment.

Eventually they were shown into a panelled office. Guido Bermudez, the mayor, seemed to pop out of his leather chair and waddle round the desk. His ample stomach slumped forward over his belt as his piggy eyes ravished the two women. He was fat and wore an open-necked shirt tucked haphazardly into his trousers.

'Come, sit down. What a pleasant surprise!' he said. 'You're both from MOP? Ah, no, you work at the Central. How nice. Where have you been hiding, and both unmarried? Yes? *Caramba!* So beautiful and delectable.'

David looked at the women and was shocked to discover they seemed to be enjoying this performance.

'How long are you here?'

'Three days,' said Joselyn.

'Such adorable creatures … You are booked every night of your short stay?'

'No, we haven't anything planned,' said Chelo.

'Then I must insist that you are my guests. Tonight ... yes? I will show you the night-life!'

Not a disco! thought David.

'And you Senor Anthony ...'

'Yes?' said David.

'What are you thinking of, neglecting these angels? You English ... so reserved! Now Latinos,' he said, brushing his thick black moustache, 'the most virile ... '

I've had this from taxi-drivers, thought David. Myths!

' ... famous for witchcraft. You want a horoscope, or an aphrodisiac maybe? ... Doña Luisa ... she's infallible,' intoned Bermudez.

I don't believe this, thought David. We're supposed to be discussing the development, not love potions.

David have you anything you'd like to ask Senor Bermudez,' Chelo prompted.

David explained briefly about the model and its capability to test alternatives. Sr Bermudez interrupted: 'It's all quite clear—a question of communication.' He tilted his head back and gazed into the middle distance, visualising the projects that would bring prosperity. ' ... the airport terminal, a new bridge over the Manzanares, an autopista link to Barcelona ... The perspectives for the whole region have never been more favourable,' he intoned. 'Tourism, petroleum ... remodel the central area ... develop the coastline with a string of beach complexes ... thousands of tourists ... declare the city a free port ...' The list was endless.

David had given up making notes and looked across at Chelo in desperation.

'Most valuable,' said Chelo. 'Just what we needed.'

'Perfect! I shall collect you at nine. You're staying at the

Cumanagoto?'

'Yes,' said Joselyn, offering him her hand.

'I'd like to look round the town,' said David as they paused at the bottom of the steps.

'We have other interviews with the Chamber of Commerce,' said Chelo.

'I know. Look, why don't you go? You don't need me. I'll meet you back at the car at one and we can go back for lunch together.' He could see Chelo was furious. What do they expect, I'm not going to suffer any more meetings like that. 'It's important that I look round, get a feel for the place. We only have another full day.'

'Come on,' said Chelo, taking Joselyn's arm and marching off.

At lunch they were all tired and irritable.

'Have you anything planned for the afternoon?' asked David.

'No,' said Chelo.

'Let's go swimming.'

'We went this morning, before you were up,' said Joselyn.

'I think we'll have a long siesta,' said Chelo.

David felt disappointed. He had hoped things might be friendlier if they spent time together at the pool. He had looked forward to this trip with Chelo, but she was behaving so distantly.

She asked him what he'd done that morning.

'I got a feel for the town. How about you?'

'We talked to people in the Chamber of Commerce, they're quite optimistic,' said Joselyn, with little attempt at disguising her disdain.

People with energy and enterprise, he wondered, planning to stay and invest in the town: sons and daughters coming back home after graduating, people starting new businesses. Almost in defiance of fortune, an air of expectancy and buoyancy.

On his walk round the town he had paused on a bridge and watched the eddies in the muddy river as it quietly flowed to the sea. The river, the Manzanares, was why Cumaná, the first city in South America, had been founded here.

On his third voyage Columbus had sailed along the coast of the Guyana, past the mouth of the Orinoco, the immense volume of fresh water flowing far out into the ocean convincing him he had discovered terra firma, the mainland of a great continent. He landed at a place the Indians called Paria, then rounding the point, had sailed up this river to find shelter, water and fodder for the horses. He would probably have anchored in deep water just downstream from where David stood.

A year later, after a period of bitter fighting, Cumaná was founded, the first colonial municipality on the mainland.

David had seen the sun glint on the dome of the cathedral over the tops of the tall trees. The church was the key to the conquest. It provided the moral justification. Every expedition had its priests – Dominican friars and, later, Jesuits. And these men of God wielded a sword as well as the cross. But it was gold, like that glittering on the cathedral dome, that provided the impetus for conquest.

And he had watched a man sitting in dappled shade reading a newspaper outside his house. The city was on the brink of inevitable and cataclysmic change and yet here was someone sitting peacefully, outside his home, in the very centre. It lent the town a sleepy civilised quality that David found attractive and admirable.

David had a part to play in this drama and his evaluation would, by influencing government investment, have an impact on this city and how quickly it grew. David liked the place, he was tempted to make sure it did not get chosen, no matter what the *fuerzas vivas* might have told Joselyn.

In his room David studied the coloured tracings he'd made while walking around the city. Then, taking a fresh plan of the city, quickly, and without too much thought, he drew his first attempt at a zoning. It was like a jigsaw puzzle, and, for a while at least, totally absorbing. Satisfied for the moment, he drew a cross in each zone at random. His idea was to go and talk to the people living in the nearest house.

What did he need to ask them? He didn't need a questionnaire, he could get survey data from Joselyn. He wanted to know what people thought of the place, their hopes for the future, and whether their priorities were the same as the notables Chelo and Joselyn had spoken to.

He stopped the car at a standpipe to ask directions of the smiling women and children: bare feet on beaten earth. Dry watercourses made the dirt roads almost impassable and there was no mains drainage. But the place was well ordered and clean and every plot had a garden, covering the shacks in dense foliage.

By six o'clock he'd managed to visit six homes. He felt tired, but pleased with his day. Allowing half-an-hour for each zone he could do another twelve or so tomorrow.

At dinner Chelo and Joselyn seemed less hostile.

'What did people say?' asked Chelo.

'Oh! you know the obvious things. They want drains, a better water supply, and they're worried about strikes in the schools. They're worried about the lack of jobs and the cost of living. People aren't that interested in expansion.'

'Is that all,' said Joselyn.

'An old man complained that his roof leaked.'

'What old man?' asked Chelo.

'Just a little old man in a one-roomed shack.'

The farm, inland in Monagas, where the man had lived all his life, had dismissed him because he was too old to work and he had come to the city to be near his daughter. He was dressed in the clothes of the farm: a short-sleeved shirt and cut-off pants which may once have been white cotton but were now a sweaty khaki, a wide brimmed straw hat and, on his feet, the habitual footwear of the peasant, a hemp sandal with a sole fashioned from recycled car tyres.

He ignored David's questions, insisting on telling his own story, interspersed with a catalogue of complaints about his house. It was too hot in the day and too cold at night and when it rained the little old man said the noise deafened him so he could hardly think. Zinc sheeting was hardly the best building material, but it was quick and cheap.

The room was about ten foot square and contained a wooden cot, on which the man slept, a crudely made table and chair, a paraffin stove for cooking and a small cabinet with wire mesh doors containing a couple of tins of food. Pinned to the wall above his bed there was a coloured print of the Virgin of Coromoto and a black and white photograph of President Rafael Caldera.

It seemed to David as though the little old man had decided his visit was providential, that David was his saviour.

If David came from MOP, the ministry of public works, he could build him a new house, and quick about it.

The disco was dark and half-empty. It was mid-week and business was slack. But Bermudez, the mayor, and his friend Danilo, who ran a furniture factory, were doing their best to entertain the two women. David was bored.

'Would you like to dance?' Chelo asked him.

He felt stiff. 'The beat—I don't understand it.'

'Come on, I'll show you,' she said.

'I can't.'

She grabbed Danilo's arm and dragged him chortling to the dance floor. Despite his bulk, he was a good dancer. David looked on; chagrined.

'Danilo has some zinc sheeting,' Chelo announced as they quit the dance floor and reached the table.

'So!'

'For your old man!'

'It's insulated with bitumen; double thickness,' said Danilo. 'It's off the old factory, I was keeping it to roof the timber shed, but I can spare enough sheets for a shack.'

So the old man was right after all, thought David.

'Do you think he'll want them?' asked Chelo, excited.

'If you can deliver, he'll be delighted.'

She gave him a delightful smile. Her heart seemed have softened to him. Maybe it was the pleasure of helping. Despite his taciturnity, he must have communicated his concern, and she had discovered someone to help. Millions of people lived in shacks, but they had concentrated on the needs of one old man. David thought, with a sad smile, that this might to be his only contribution to rancho development, and he was glad Chelo had created the chance.

Danilo asked David where the old man lived and, since David only knew it was in El Rosario, they arranged to meet early the following morning, at the factory, so David could show him the way.

When he got back, Chelo and Joselyn had decided they wanted to spend the rest of the day visiting the witch Bermudez had mentioned.

It was a long dusty journey and they had to walk a mile or so along the beach. They could see the house from a long way away—a simple wooden building, the clapboarding bleached by the sun and salt. A canvas screen hung across the door and there were square openings without glass on either side like two black eyes. As they drew near a head appeared momentarily in the left hand window and a tall dark woman appeared, dressed in a long caftan—Doña Luisa, the witch of Paria.

She said she was expecting them and asked them to sit on the wooden crates outside her house. She served them tamarind juice from a green glass pitcher and they drank out of cups that looked as if they had been fashioned from goat's horn. She asked them where they had come from. David thought she was just making conversation until, without preamble, she said: 'When three travel together one drops out. When you journey alone you find a companion.'

David went for a walk, leaving the two women to have their fortune's told. He had no intention of going in himself. He felt angry: with the hot drive and the waste of time when they were supposed to be working. How was he going to find time to visit to the rest of the zones?

He felt over-dressed in his office trousers and good shirt,

which hung round him like a wet dishcloth. His shoulders felt tight as if his skin were a wet suit that was a size too small. He picked up a handful of pebbles and began throwing them out to sea as far as he could. The sun was bright and it hurt his eyes. Far out there was a tanker heading east and fishing boats at anchor and men with nets. Across the gulf he could just make out Trinidad in the blue haze.

He sat on a stump buried in the sand and took off his shoes and socks. He felt angry and upset, yet didn't understand quite why. He loved exploring, he would have enjoyed the trip on his own. Maybe it just because it wasn't his own idea, because it had been initiated by Joselyn. Or perhaps he was afraid to go in, of what the witch might say to him.

He started back. The three women were waiting and he expected them to complain about being kept waiting, but they said nothing and just looked at him patiently. Then Doña Luisa stood and lifted the curtain across the doorway and said 'Ven!' David followed her, curious and half glad he had not been given the opportunity to protest.

Inside the walls were unlined and the wooden boards retained some of their original richness. Bright light from outside penetrated through the cracks and knot holes and the air seemed to dance with colour as if it had been separated by a crystal. Without speaking she indicated he should sit. There were two leather stools facing each other on the dirt floor.

For a while she sat absolutely still with her head bowed and her caftan spread wide across her knees. He could see her hair was straight and black under the scarf she had wound round her head like a turban. A curtain of purple plush hung from a tie-rod which ran from one side of the shed to the other, concealing her living space. Hanging from hooks in the rafters there were strings of dried fish and baskets of fruit: oranges, guavas, tamarind and bananas.

Doña Luisa looked up and said: 'You can control anger by keeping still.'

David didn't know whether to be amazed or offended at this comment about how he had been feeling. Maybe Chelo had told her, then he realised his annoyance must have been written all over his face. He wondered about getting up and leaving when she took something out of a pocket in her skirt and, opening her palm, showed him three flat stones. They were oval pebbles of a dull sandy colour and each had a depression in the middle as though someone had imprinted them when the rock was still liquid. Without speaking she put her hands together and dropped the stones on the ground. She repeated the action three times and then sat in silence again. It made him uncomfortable, this woman, so close, staring at him. The stool was too low, his back hurt, and he wanted to get up and run along the beach.

Then she smiled, radiating warmth. He relaxed.

'I will tell you three things,' she said. 'Su suerte, su amor y su viaje.' Luck, love and a journey.

She told him that he faced conflict with his masters and that he would be placed in a dangerous position. He should not yield immediately to those he served but should bide his time. 'Wait until you are impelled to act, then you will not be injured.' David was intrigued by her insight into the growing pressure he felt at work and wondered if Joselyn or Chelo had said anything to her.

In love, he should not run after the women he wanted, but should hold back. 'The impulse that springs from the

144

heart,' she said, 'is the most important of all, but you will dine at another's table for some time.' Finally she said it would favour him to cross the ocean. David sat bemused, thinking through the significance of what she had said, suddenly realising the interview was over.

Outside Chelo asked Doña Luisa if they could give her some money. She replied that she did not charge for soothsaying, that wisdom was not for sale, but that they could make her a present of three hundred bolivars if they wished. David got out his wallet and paid.

They walked back along the beach in silence, all three of them feeling subdued. David asked what she had meant, as they were leaving by, mala fortuna. Chelo said she didn't mean bad luck, she'd said they were in for a storm. David looked up at the blue sky and the clear horizon and wondered if she had been referring to the weather or some impending row.

Their plane was delayed. They had confirmed their bookings, but it was still unclear whether they would fly. He'd spent a trying morning driving from one home to another in a frantic rush to finish in time, but at least he had managed to cover all the zones. He forced his way to the front at the airline desk. Self-important businessmen were cajoling, threatening, bribing their way onto the plane. Middle-aged matrons were being hysterical, as if a disaster of epic proportions had hit the nation. He could feel himself succumbing and had to fight to resist the hysteria all around him.

'The previous flight was cancelled,' he reported back to the two women who had found a relatively quiet seat away from the mêlée. 'There are storms along the coast and they don't know whether we'll get away.'

This was the rainy season: the time of tropical storms and hurricanes.

'Have we places?' asked Chelo.

'I'm not sure. I did my best. There seems to be a lot of horse-trading.'

The wait lengthened from one hour to four. Although still only afternoon, it was pitch dark outside as the storm approached. He fetched coffee and sandwiches and went to investigate car rentals. Chelo was enthusiastic and they had just decided to drive back in a hire-car when the flight was announced.

They fought their way to the barrier and, to David's surprise, boarded and found their seats. The plane took off and turned west for the quick hop along the coast.

The stewardess brought round coffee and Chelo lit a cigarette. The flight got bumpier and bumpier. They could feel the wind raging outside, lifting and shaking the big plane as if it weighed no more than an autumn leaf. Chelo looked pale and put her hand on his arm.

The pilot's voice announced they might have to turn back. There were groans of protest from some of the passengers. They had resigned themselves to returning and finding a hotel for the night when the pilot said that they would be landing in the next few minutes and they should fasten safety-belts and extinguish cigarettes. The stewardess appeared from the cockpit looking pale and anxious. She went down the aisle checking their belts.

'This is your captain speaking, we're going to land!' came over the intercom.

'Our valiant captain is going to attempt to land,' repeated

the stewardess. I wish he wouldn't, thought David. Chelo gripped his hand.

'Are you all right?' he asked.

'No, I'm terrified.'

He wasn't afraid of dying, it was just being trapped in this flying sardine tin unable to do anything. Any moment the plane might plunge into the sea and drown them all or crash into a mountain and incinerate them. He looked for the nearest emergency exit and told himself that the life jackets were under the seat. He realised he was still holding her hand tightly.

There was a flash of lightening and he could see the white wave crests. We can't be more than a hundred feet up, he thought. There was a deathly hush as the plane swept over the low hill at the end of the airport at full power. The left wing lifted and he felt the pilot fighting with the controls.

The wheels touched, settled, rolled, and they were down. The cabin erupted in spontaneous applause. The stewardess remained strapped in; she looked sick. As they filed off the plane into the lashing rain, both women and men, some in tears, embraced the pilot, who stood at the exit like a blonde god.

10

On Sunday Christina invited him to the beach. They could borrow Alberto's jeep and explore the dirt road past the tourist areas. She asked if he'd like to drive.

There were lots of families making the pilgrimage to the coast, but they were early and the traffic was moving freely. He pointed out the fish restaurant Jordi had taken him to on his first night in the country. The coast here was a narrow strip, blasted from the cliffs, the width of the carriageway. There were men with long rods fishing from rocky promontories.

They drove through Macuto and past the entrance to the Sheraton. There were shops in the village selling beach balls, straw hats and buckets and spades. It reminded him of holidays on the sands. The tiny paper flags for sandcastles, lemonade and comics on wet days, the boating lake and pitch and putt. The family snaps of him in grey flannel shirt and long wool socks.

'How's work. How did the case go on Friday?'

'He got eleven years.'

'I'm sorry.'

'No, congratulate us. We did well. They dropped the manslaughter charge.'

'I admire what you're doing.'

'I wonder sometimes. We just manipulate the law. We got the sentence reduced on a technicality, not on the evidence.'

'Was he guilty?'

'Not as guilty as some,' she said enigmatically. When he asked her what she meant she said she couldn't tell him.

The hard top finished. The national guard at the checkpoint asked to see their papers. The road led inland over a headland. Descending the far side they could see a white sand cove and the turquoise blue of shallow calm water. The track down to the beach was steep and narrow. It had been cut along the side of a ravine which dropped sharply on one side. There was another car already parked at the bottom and the driver warned them not to drive on to the beach because of the soft sand.

They walked down to the beach, found a patch of shade under a sea grape and spread out their things. The sea was a cold shock after the heat of the drive. They swam through the shallows and dived into the breaking surf.

'Let me put some oil on you or you'll burn,' she said. 'Relax!' She slapped him between the shoulder blades and gradually he felt himself unwinding and began to drift.

'I'll do you—if you want?' he said.

Christina lay on her front, on a thick towel. He poured

some of the oil on his palms and started to massage her shoulders.

'What is this?' he asked. The oil was thick, with slightly coarse texture.

'Pure coconut oil,' she said, lifting her head. He noticed that the towel brought out the green of her eyes. She reached behind her back and unfastened her top. 'Don't be shy, rub harder. No! you're not basting meat! Firm yet smooth. Yes, that's better.'

He began to enjoy the rhythm. The oil let his hands move fluently.

'Keep going, that's nice,' she said.

He lay back on his mat and dozed. He woke feeling too hot, and went to cool off in the sea. After a swim he fetched the paperback he brought and stretched out on the wet sand near the waters edge, his head on a half-buried log.

It was impossible to concentrate on the novel. He looked across to where Christina was lying, face down, her head in the shadow of the palm. The sun hurt his eyes and he had difficulty focusing on the book.

She turned over and came and lay next to him in the shallows. 'What are you reading?'

'Struggling to read! The book Mildred recommended, the Garcia Marquez. I've started it eight times now. Each time I get a little further. Last week it started to flow, you know like the first time you realise the book is telling a story and not just stringing words together.'

'Do you like it.'

'I'm lost in it. The pace is fantastic, it leaves me breathless. I still don't know what half the words mean, but I sound them as I read and they're like poetry. The meaning of a new word jumps out and it's like finding a beautiful pebble on the beach.'

Quite suddenly, without preamble, she said: 'I'm going to marry Julio!' It came as a complete surprise. She reached for his hand but he pulled away. Why was he reacting like this, he thought. She was only being friendly.

She had been engaged to Julio for ages, she said. Their mothers were making plans: a date had been set, the church arranged. Even the hotel had been booked, in Acapulco, where Julio's sister had been for her honeymoon. It had been understood for years that they would marry. Having made up her mind, she felt she had to tell David, so that there were no misunderstandings. She wanted them to go on being friends. She said she assumed he would have heard from someone else, knowing he hadn't.

She doesn't owe me an explanation, he thought, feeling miserable. He asked if he was invited to the wedding. She felt discomfited, unable to explain that the reason she had not included him on the guest list was because she had been keeping him in a separate place in her mind, a place where she was not marrying Julio.

David was hurt. He felt she had allowed an unspoken understanding to develop between them when she knew she was spoken for. From the start he had felt easy with her. It might have developed into something, he reasoned. She hasn't much in common with Julio, he thought. Amazing, even someone as independent as Christina has to go along with the social conventions.

It was still early but he did not feel like stopping at the beach any longer. If they left now they would avoid the heavy traffic. A dozen or more cars were parked up the track and it was difficult to reverse. There was hardly room for two cars abreast and he was worried about scraping. They cleared the last car and he relaxed. Then there was a heavy thump and the jeep tipped sideways.

'Get out!' he yelled. The rear wheel was hanging in space over the ravine, the jeep perched on the back bumper. He felt the drowning sensation of panic. He climbed down the slope and tried to shift a boulder under the axle. The jeep rocked alarmingly when he pushed the rock under the wheel. If it fell, he'd be crushed. A car reversed up to them but the jeep was blocking the way. As the driver tried to squeeze past, his fender nudged the jeep's front wheel. Christina yelled at him and he stopped. He was angry at being held up, furious he'd been shouted at.

'I'll go up to the road and get help,' she shouted, as David climbed back onto the road.

'Where from?'

'There are some shacks on the other side. Just hang on.'

Other families wanted to leave, everyone was talking, offering advice. David sat on the front bumper, using his weight as a counterbalance, and ignored them.

Christina returned with three men carrying spades. One of them said something he couldn't understand and together they grasped the rear bumper and lifted the jeep. The sinews stood out on their forearms and David could see the strain in their bare calves.

'Get in and drive forward,' shouted Christina.

'What!'

'Drive! They'll hold it.'

David looked in the mirror and saw the men's faces

through the back window, straining with the effort, one of them had his eyes closed, his forehead pressed against the glass. He put it into gear and let out the clutch, but the jeep moved backwards. He saw the shock in the men's faces and rammed it into first and the jeep leapt forward. He parked well away from the edge and got out. His legs were shaky and he felt embarrassed. The men look relieved: one of them made a joke and they started laughing.

'They say they thought you were trying to kill them,' said Christina.

'It's the damn gears. I'm not used to them.'

'Give them some money.'

When he got home he took a chair out on to the patio and stared at the mountain until it was quite dark.

He worked steadily all morning. After coffee a boy came into the office and asked to clean his shoes. He was about to say no, when he noticed the look of longing in the boy's eyes. He had always cleaned his own shoes, the heels as well as the toes, like his mum told him. How old is this boy? David wondered, seven, eight? He should be in school.

'Okay,' he said, realising that he needed the business.

The boy sat at his feet on an upturned powdered milk tin. He wound a strip of rag round his fingers and wiped a liberal coating of brown polish over the shoes. He used another rag stretched between his hands to polish off, spitting on the leather to produce a high gloss. He could feel the boy's fingers massaging through the leather of the shoe. Relax, he told himself, it's only the same as having your hair cut. Nevertheless it felt odd, demeaning even.

Where did the little boy live? In a rancho? Was it nearby? He must have walked here. David asked him and he said St Agustin, up the hill.

He'd been reading about ranchos. Despite Jordi's loss of interest he wanted to see them for himself. Working at his desk all day long was no good. Chelo suggested he contact a friend at Banco Obrero, the agency that built low-cost housing. The man said he was working in Valencia but suggested he might take David when he got back.

'23 de Enero is an estate of super-blocks, and San Agustin del Sur, is a rancho. They're both on fantastic sites overlooking the city and you'll see the contrast between state provision and self-help,' the man said.

Alejandro had gone home when David told Chelo what her friend had said. He didn't want to have to wait though and said he might go on his own. She was dead against it, saying it was dangerous and almost pleading with him to talk to Alejandro first. David assumed she was exaggerating, she had never been to a rancho herself, and he wanted the chance to get out of the office and away from his books. After all, he argued, both areas were near the city centre and he was used to looking after himself. Chelo was so upset she shouted it would be his own stupid fault if anything happened to him. The vehemence of her opposition surprised him.

'I didn't know you cared,' he joked. Chelo called him arrogant and slammed out of the room.

The following morning he took a por puesto to Silencio and walked up the long hill called Calvario to 23 de Enero. The blocks had been built on a vast scale. The staircases and walkways were daubed with political slogans and the open spaces, conceived as a communal park, were spoiled with car wrecks and heaps of refuse. He talked to a woman and was told the police had arrested a dozen or more youths that morning.

He walked to Silencio, past the two massive towers where Manuel's Ministry had its offices. There were great holes in the sidewalks, as though the ground had been churned up by an earthquake. His ankle hurt where he had caught his foot on a twisted steel bar poking out of the paving. In the Plaza Bolivar he bought a sandwich and found a bench in the shade where, for over half-an-hour, he watched a sloth transfer its weight, almost imperceptibly, from one branch to another.

On the way to San Agustin he stopped to watch men working like ants at the bottom of a deep hole. They were constructing inverted egg-boxes on stilts. He realised they were building the shuttering to support the concrete for the underground car park.

Looking down from a bridge of a wide avenue he watched people in the rancho below and took photographs with his pocket camera. Getting out of the office was a good idea.

His mood changed as he climbed the concrete steps into San Agustin. It was all very well to hang over the bridge and watch from a safe distance, but here, at close quarters, he was out-of-place—too well dressed, too rich—asking for trouble. The path was steep and narrow and he was shoved aside by the press of people descending. He felt conspicuous, as if he'd gatecrashed the wrong party.

The path levelled and he tried to go slowly and look around. People stared, some of them with hostility, and only the children smiled or showed any friendly interest. He shut out his discomfort and forced himself to take his camera out of his pocket.

Three youths stopped and asked to have their photograph taken. Their breath smelt of drink, and one of them staggered. They made him feel uncomfortable and embarrassed. They were fooling around; they weren't doing any harm, he reasoned. When they asked for some money, for bus fares, he gave them the few coins he had in his pocket. In his wallet there was a ten bolivar note to get him back to the university.

He stopped at a widening in the pathway near a standpipe. Some women were walking away with red Saltina biscuit tins on their heads. There was a low parapet above a drop and he stopped to take a picture. He was aware the youths had come back and pretended to ignore them.

One of them grabbed his wrist, another stuck a knife at his throat, the camera was ripped out of his hands. He heard himself shouting with rage.

People appeared from nowhere—the woman opposite ran out of her house and the men who had been drinking in the tiny cantina came out with bottles in their hands to see what all the noise was about. Suddenly the empty street was crowded.

He heard his own voice—loud and harsh. He saw the people, afraid to interfere, watching a tall well-dressed foreigner about to get badly hurt.

Two boys held his arms and a bigger youth in a yellow shirt waved the knife, as if he was going to stab. One of the boys grabbed his father's gold watch and ran off. David chased the lad and caught him by the sleeve and half the jacket came away in his hand. Despite all the noise, the ripping sound, as the stitching parted down the back seam, seemed to shock the lads into immobility. David twisted the boy's wrist and took the watch back and put it in his pocket.

Then they had him surrounded again, like dogs baiting a bear. In Spanish, he shouted: 'Give me the camera!' He took out his wallet and held up the money in return for the camera. The youth in yellow tried to grab it and David pulled it away.

Surrounded by a tide of frightened faces, inside, David was deadly calm. Things happened fast but his mind observed the action in slow motion, like a replay. He knew he could get hurt—he could get killed! Yet he felt he had been through this before. He felt in command, yet completely out of control; terrified of what might happen, yet resigned to any outcome.

The one in yellow slashed at him, screaming, spit coming out his mouth like a mad dog—he was going to charge. David stared into the young man's eyes and saw he was tired of playing, that he could no longer bear the ambiguity of the situation and had to push the drama to some resolution. David saw that he wanted to hurt and lash out and cause pain. He knew he could turn the blade away, that all he had to do was think the blade out of the youth's hand.

David moved forwards and the youth struck. People screamed, seeing the knife sink into his stomach. But David had stepped sideways and the lad dropped the knife. It clattered on the concrete and David kicked it away, turning his back on the youth as if saying: you can't touch me, you're nothing. The young man looked lost—like the bull when the matador turns his back—he looked as though he could cry.

One of the boys fetched the knife and the youth grabbed it. He wanted to kill now, to bury the knife and see the blood spurt. He ran at David, screaming with rage and the people

157

fell back out of the way. David sensing him charge, whipped round and produced a great roar from deep inside himself.

The youth halted in mid-charge and turned away. All three of them ran off down the hill. David was breathing heavily, his head back, chest out. He loved it, the danger, it made him feel totally alive. Like a fighting cock after a spurring—he looked as if he might crow. Then, as he saw the crowd's reaction, the film inside his head returned to normal speed. He saw peoples' faces, ordinary people, men and women looking concerned and shocked. He felt ashamed and crest-fallen.

He asked questions. '¿Quién era? ¿Los conocen? ¿Dondé viven?' Who were they? do you know them? where do they live? He was rattled. Nobody would answer. He felt himself getting angry as he grabbed a man and asked him if he knew the youths. The man just shook his head. People moved off—they did not want to be involved. David realised he was interrogating them and stopped and waited, quietly. Someone said the youths lived two levels down. He wanted to chase after them. People tried to stop him. They said he must be crazy, they would get him next time, he would run into the rest of the gang and get killed for sure. A woman said they were bad boys, that they had hit her on the head with a rock and stolen her purse.

'¿Dondé esta la policía? he asked. Why were the police never there when you wanted them? a woman complained. People were talking about it, breaking up into groups. The men were drifting back to the bar for more beer. He heard people say he was pavoso—like a cock; others thought he was bloody fool! Everyone agreed something should be done about these youths terrorising the neighbourhood.

In the police station they laughed when he told them where he'd been and what had happened. He realised that he had seen the last of his camera.

'San Agustin? Not up on the hill?' said the sergeant on the desk. 'Hey this man went up in San Agustin! But it's really dangerous up there, those youths have the brothers in the secondary school terrorised.'

Back at work, in the lift, he put his father's watch back on his wrist. He was amazed to see how little time had passed—it felt like a lifetime. Chelo asked him where he'd been and he told her about the attack. He wanted sympathy, and to sit down and rest.

She was furious: 'You men are all the same—you think life is a game, like cowboys and Indians. You make me sick! I thought you were different—you're worse than Jordi!'

She grabbed her bag and ran out of the office. David chased after her.

'It's not how you think … don't leave.'

She stopped, toying with her car keys, finally saying, 'I'm going to an exhibition at the Athenaeum … of Zapata, a political cartoonist.'

'Can I come with you?' he asked.

'All right … yes, if you want.'

They drove to Parque Los Caobos. They were early and the place wasn't open for another hour. Chelo parked the car and they walked without talking as far as the cafe near the fountain. They sat at a table and ordered cold drinks.

'Tell me what happened? Why you're so upset?' she asked.

'I'm all churned up,' he sighed. 'The great thing was that I was living for the moment, it was marvellous.' All the doubt, all the analysing, had been suspended and he had felt free.

'Is that why you took such a stupid risk?' she asked, getting upset again,

'I'm a fool! I don't know what's going on. I must be naive—pretending that I could change society—rebuild the ranchos. I must have been mad! I shouldn't have been there.'

Chelo didn't say anything.

He told her that he felt out of touch, out of tune. 'Like when you're driving and it feels you're in a goldfish bowl, watching the world on television,' he said. 'Jordi seems to know what life is all about and gets on with it. I feel as though I'm waiting for something to happen, but don't know what it is. Do you know what I mean, am I making any sense.'

'Yes, perfect sense.'

On one of his school reports his headmaster had written: 'Promises much, but achieves less.' Perhaps he wrote it on everyone's report, but maybe he's right, thought David.

'What am I supposed to be doing; what's it all about?'

Chelo thought for a moment and said, 'The people I love are the most important thing in my life. For men it's their career.'

David suddenly felt shy. 'I'm sorry, that was inexcusable, I don't usually indulge in bouts of self-analysis.'

'You should try it more often, it will do you good.'

They left the cafe and walked back through the park. David felt better, as if he had been absolved. They strolled beneath the mahogany trees, the boles like the flying buttresses of a cathedral.

'I want to explore—I don't mean dash about to the most exciting places, I want to really get to know this country. You know, I never thought I'd like the tropics, that I would only feel affinity for bare moors and arctic winds. But when I was on the mountain with Jerry I felt completely relaxed. Cities are threatening and dangerous; I feel at home in wild places, regardless of whether they're hot or cold.'

'The city is very fast. If people take a siesta it's because they have another job at lunchtime. It's as though everyone in the city gets up, gets in their car and drives around all day long.'

There was a small queue waiting to enter the Athenaeum. Huge canvases divided the room into a maze and mobiles hung from the ceiling, further heightening the sense of enclosure. The paintings depicted grotesque creatures, part human, part beast. He felt enveloped, as though he and Chelo were figures in a weird comic strip, rather than outside, coolly appraising.

The figures reminded him of Hieronymus Bosch's torments of hell. Then he began to see more. Scaly fish faced politicians in frock coats threw men and women into a municipal incinerator. Money dripped like candle grease off mitred clerics with bats' wings. There was a banquet of the middle classes—medics, bankers, architects, writers—gobbling ragged little children, as if they were sucking pigs. And David felt part of it, as though he were there in the cartoon, eating with the rest of them.

This was how most people experienced life—like a comic strip. The cartoons were full of life—bold colours, red, yellow and black—and David's reaction to them was to want to shout that there was beauty and love in the world too. He felt a great upsurge of joy at being truly alive and with this feeling came the knowledge that the hell depicted on the canvases was in his heart, and in the hearts of all human beings, and the heaven he desired was there too. The only solution, the only meaning, was to take part, to get stuck in. It was no use waiting for eternity; if eternity was timeless, eternity was here and now.

§

One morning David received a brown envelope in the internal mail – his first pay slip. Three months salary; even when he'd paid Alberto back he'd be rich. Last week he'd rung Mildred to tell her his money had run out and she'd promised to talk to Manuel.

The boxes he had sent by sea had finally arrived with all his climbing gear and he felt like exploring. He could afford to buy a car, he realised and decided to get a jeep like Alberto's.

The sales manager was a tall man with a crew cut and the trace of a German accent. David thought he was making a meal of it. He decided he'd have the yellow jeep in the showroom after sitting in the driving seat and finding it comfortable. He hadn't wanted to see the engine, admire the wheel hubs or go for a test drive. The salesman didn't take him seriously.

'How much discount is there?' In England he'd have been too embarrassed to ask, it was wonderful how the Spanish made him bold. By offering to pay a third in cash David negotiated a twenty per cent discount and felt delighted with himself.

He felt excited and nervous driving the new car to work. He'd timed it during the pause in traffic before the midday rush. There was space in the staff car park. The young entrepreneur and his gang were impressed.

'Here's a bolivar,' said David, 'to watch it! Don't wash it!' Chelo came down to admire.

11

David forced his way through the long grass and under-growth to the rock he'd seen from the autopista. The dust tickled his nose; grass seeds stuck to his skin and made him itch. At the bottom of the cliff he took off his rucksack, sat on the path and changed into his rock boots, methodically tight-ening the laces, the same automatic ritual he'd been through hundreds of times. For weeks he had been anticipating this moment, but now felt sluggish and a bit queasy.

His stomach contracted and he had to hurry and run for the trees. Well away from the path he dropped his trousers and squatted. There was an immediate eruption and looking down he saw, between his feet, a pyramid of white worms glistening like intestines. The mound subsided to a flat seething pancake. He retched and stepped back. He felt violated and empty as after vomiting. He went back to his sack and, still shaking, took a drink from his water bottle.

So that was it—he had felt bloated that morning—he'd got worms. He was going have to take more care. Maybe it was an arepa he bought from a street stall, or maybe he hadn't washed some fruit properly. Worms he could cure by going to a chemist and getting a powder. But if he got amoebic dysentery, that would be serious. Mildred had told him that once you got it you could never get rid of it.

After a short rest he started up the steep wall, reaching a point about sixty feet above the ground. Looking down it seemed further because the ground continued to drop away steeply below the path at the base of the rock.

The tiny shale flakes on which he was standing were almost too small to see and there was nothing substantial for his hands to grasp, the friable rock tending to crumble under his fingertips. He blinked to clear the sweat from his eyes, wiped his fingers on his trousers and tried again, only to have to retreat to the tiny footholds. The move was hard and if he managed it there would be no possibility of climbing back down. With an effort he concentrated on the move ahead.

He tried the next move at least seven or eight times and the hold was slippery with his sweat. He reached far left to a tuft of grass and rubbed his left hand in the sandy soil in an attempt to dry it.

Afterwards, when he thought about the next few moments, he could remember no difference between this attempt and any of his others, except perhaps that for a moment he stopped thinking and in one smooth flowing movement climbed to a neat square foothold below the roof.

There were handholds under the overhang where chunks of rock had broken away and by using one of these he was able to lean right back and reach round the lip of the roof. Above there was another sixty feet of steeper rock. He decided to come back and attempt it with a rope. The problem now though was how to get down.

He found the hold he had used under the roof and gingerly lowered his body. He would have to traverse under the roof to the side. There was no alternative. Slowly and carefully, testing the dubious holds, he inched leftwards.

He'd gone about thirty feet when he spotted the wasps. A slender wax comb about a foot long and the width of a rolled umbrella hung inverted from the roof. It was stuck to the rock by a brown stalk and five or six large black wasps were clinging to its surface. They had been disturbed and he could hear them buzzing menacingly. If he traversed back in the opposite direction he would likely encounter other nests. He tried stepping down below them, but there were no holds. He would have to try and climb past them without arousing them to attack.

He moved nearer and one of the wasps opened its long wings and flew towards his face. He locked his fingers on the holds and held himself as still as possible. The wasp buzzed within inches of his eyes, it flew round his head, dived towards his fingers and then, as if satisfied, flew back to the comb. He reached past and found a hold; his right hand was within a foot of the nest. He could see the wasps moving more aggressively. Two of them left the comb and he turned his head away and made the next two moves quickly. He kept moving until he could no longer hear the buzzing.

As the ground grew nearer and nearer, the rock seemed to get easier and he reached the end of the traverse without difficulty. He went back to take a look at his worms. They had disappeared.

On Wednesday nights, after class, Jerry usually came back for a drink. They watched baseball on television and made Cuba libres—rum, coke and gin, with lemon and lots of ice. Although David never managed to grasp the finer details of the play, and Jerry had given up trying to explain, he enjoyed Wednesday nights and they had become something of a ritual.

'You've fixed this place real well.'

He'd put up shelves for his books and bits of carving, and built a desk in the alcove. He'd bought a low table in a second-hand shop and Christina had given him a chair as a house-warming present. In the kitchen two wall cabinets held his cooking pots and crockery. He'd made them from thin wide planks of saman. It was a dark, almost black wood, with violent cream slashes. It was sopping when he'd bought it from the timber yard, and, not daring to let it dry, he'd cut the dovetails wet and the planks now twisted against each other and held the shape true. Below them he'd built a counter from solid mahogany, gluing the strips to make a wide slab. The hammock, in which Jerry now lay, did double duty in the living room and garden.

'How's work?' asked David.

'The old man's worse. You know he had a bad cardiac a month ago; well he still isn't recovered. I'm having to carry the business.'

'What happens if he dies?'

'Bad news! His old lady doesn't like us. She's got a son back home—she'll probably sell up and go and join him.'

'And what about you?'

'We'd get nothing. He's said all along he'd cut me in for a share of the business but when I suggested he might change his will, he stalled me. Here, forget it, let's play darts.'

The baseball had finished, they'd had three or four drinks. To give the evening some purpose, he had bought a board and two sets of darts in a store in Chacaito. Perhaps it was nostalgia—after work, on long summer evenings, he and three friends used to go climbing in Derbyshire and later they'd play darts in a tiny country pub.

Rather unsteadily they carried their drinks to the patio. Jerry hurled the darts. The piece of plywood David had hung behind the board was peppered with holes.

'What do you miss most?' asked Jerry.

'The same thing as Ben Gun?'

'What's that?'

'Cheese!'

'But they've got cheese here.'

'Yes, but it's not the same.'

'I miss Hershey bars and clean fast-food.'

'What about Marta?' Marta, Jerry's wife, made a fuss of David and the two small children both liked him. He had started to go round most weeks, usually on Saturday afternoon. The first time he had been to their house, Sebastian, a five-year-old, had been uncontrollable, kicking and screaming, and Marta had asked David to bath him. Sebastian kept pulling the plug and letting the water out. David held him down, dragged a shoe off and tossed it into the bath. By the time the rest of his clothes were floating in the muddy water Sebastian was rolling round the bathroom floor in hysterics and was quite happy to be lifted in. His sister watched, wide-eyed, and then insisted he do the same for her. Bath time since then had become a very damp ritual.

'She misses her folks,' said Jerry. 'It's not so great being a woman here.' Jerry said she was having problems at work. The staff were trying to negotiate a new contract and the management were putting the squeeze on. If things didn't work out they might move to Merida and start a business of their own. The plan was for her to pack in her teaching job and help. David wondered where they would get the money.

He realised he would miss them both. They were his only English-speaking friends. He enjoyed doing things with Jerry and he liked talking to Marta. She was a quiet, lovable sort of person. David could talk to her about his feelings—something he found impossible to do with Jerry.

§

At El Paraiso the river was a placid stream and it was cool in the green shade under the trees. The sun, filtering through the foliage, made the pebbles shine and it felt good, standing on the bank, looking at the clear water and the bright leaves and the sunshine.

He'd got tired of climbing Pico Oriental—they'd done it five times—and he was in the shower when he had the idea of spending all day climbing down the Quebrada los Chorros, the gorge he and Jerry had seen from the path. From a distance they'd glimpsed a waterfall, a vertical ribbon of light in a clearing in the forest. At first, Jerry hadn't been keen. But David had argued it was worth the trouble: the gorge looked inaccessible, probably no one had ever been there, yet it was so close to the city. Suddenly Jerry had changed his mind and agreed to come.

Now they were there, all they had to do was step into the water; yet they hesitated. The path, which crossed the river at this point, seemed to exercise an almost palpable restraint. Maybe he'd been right when he'd told Jerry that nobody had ever been down it. Once they had started, after they had gone over the first big waterfall, they would be unable to turn back. They would have to keep going until they reached the city, where the river flowed under the autopista. David had a momentary panic wondering whether his ropes were long enough. What if they only reached part way down the big falls they'd seen? Then he put his fears aside and, stepping lightly from one boulder to the next, shouted, 'Let's go.'

The scene changed suddenly—clouds passed across the sun and a gloom descended on the forest. Maybe this was the start of the rainy season David worried. There was a splash and when he turned round he could see Jerry had slipped off a rock into the water. 'Shit! my boots are soaked.' That's not all that's going to get wet, David thought. Dimly he could hear the sound of a waterfall. 'What the hell!' he laughed and stepped into the stream.

They had gone perhaps half a mile when they came to the first fall. The gorge narrowed and the river was forced through jammed boulders. They clambered between the rocks. They were wet to the waist, but the sun kept them warm. A fallen tree was wedged and they slid down its steep trunk across a deep pool.

The valley floor levelled and they moved more easily along the sandy banks through the vegetation at the side of the stream. Pulling on saplings on a steep bank David grasped a tree trunk and felt an acute pain in his right hand. Three long black needles stuck in his flesh: the trunk of the palm bristled with spines.

The banks steepened and they were forced back to the river. On a flat rock, within a foot of his hand, he saw a snake. It was mottled grey, like the rock, and coiled in a tight spiral. Its knurled tail gave a threatening rasp.

'What are you doing?'

'I'm coming,' he said. They could go back, it wasn't too late to turn round, but he wanted to keep going.

Jerry was sitting on a rock when he reached him: thirty feet below there was a pool.

'What now?'

The water was black and deep. David pushed off with his hands and slid down the rock, gathering speed as it steepened, and splashed into the water. He sank deep and didn't reach bottom.

'Come on, its fantastic. What's wrong?'

'I can't swim!'

This is a fine time to tell me, David thought.

'Tie the rope round your waist and I'll pull you across.'

Jerry threw down one end of the rope and, letting out a great whoop, slid down. He sank beneath the surface, popped up and then disappeared. His rucksack had twisted and floated over his head. David pulled on the rope and watched the trail of bubbles as he hauled Jerry across. He landed like a great fish, coughing and choking.

'I nearly drowned! You bastard—stop laughing! What are we going to do now.'

'I'll swim with you. Tie your waist-strap, the rucksack will help keep you afloat.'

The gorge narrowed and steepened. There were high rock

walls on either side and ahead they could hear the thunder of falling water. David thought this might be the main falls but, when they reached the edge, they were in a deep ravine quite unlike the open space they'd seen from the ridge. The water poured over the lip in a great spout.

David retreated from the edge: looking down at the crashing water had made him dizzy. If they descended this fall there would be no going back. Ten feet from the edge there was a stout tree.

'This tree is just what we want for a belay,' he said, making a play of taking the rope from his sack. For a moment he wondered if he'd been wise. Jerry had said he knew how to abseil, but he had next to no experience of rock climbing. It would be fine, he decided, feeling confident. Working methodically he uncoiled the rope onto the rock, careful to keep it out of the torrent. He passed one end round the trunk, knotted the two ropes, went back to the edge and threw the coiled ends one after another into the void.

'I'll go first. You know how these descenders work?' Jerry nodded. 'The rope goes through this ring which acts as a brake. Yes? Then you clip it to the sling round your thighs.'

He stepped to the edge, allowing the rope to take his weight as he leaned backwards. The rope came taut and he stepped over the edge. His right foot slipped and he fell sideways. His knees smashed into the rock. He let the rope run and slid down under the overhang. A great weight crashed on his head and shoulders and he could hardly see. He was falling faster and faster. He felt his hip glance the wall and, in the split instant before shooting into the pool, wondered quite dispassionately whether he would get mangled on the rocks. The water pushed him down and the long trailing ends of the rope wound round his legs and thighs entangling him. He tried to swim to the surface, but the weight of the ropes in the strong current held him under. He was drowning. He was going to die. Who would look after Jerry?

Using all his strength he heaved on the rope and, hand over hand, pulled himself up to the air. Hanging by one hand in the whirling torrent, he managed to free the coils from his legs, and struck out for the bank.

After sitting on the sand a moment or two to catch his breath, he waved for Jerry to start.

As Jerry slipped on the same green rock, he yanked the ropes taut and Jerry slid clear of the falls and fell into the middle of the pool. David waded in and, grabbing his rucksack, hauled him to the bank.

'What next!'

'Keep going,' he said, worried about the time.

The terrain was easier now and they made good progress, wading the sandy floor of the stream. The trees opened out ahead of them; it was like emerging from a tunnel into the light. They had reached the falls they had seen from the ridge. The forest widened into a bowl, rising in tiers from thick forest to shrub and then grass slopes before reaching the thin line of eucalyptus on the ridge.

They took off their wet clothes and spread them on the rocks. Jerry was wearing an identity disk just like Jordi's and David asked him about it. Jerry said it was something he got while doing national service. David was surprised he still wore it.

They got out the bit of food they had brought and, while eating an apple, David began to prospect for a belay to fix the rope. Inching down the sloping rocks in bare feet he reached a tree and, clearing the undergrowth, uncovered a trunk which looked strong enough to hold his weight. He uncoiled the ropes and carefully cast them over the edge. It was impossible to see whether they had reached the bottom of the waterfall.

Their clothes were clinging and cold and the sun had gone in. He felt surprisingly nervous as he tested his weight on the ropes but, once started, he began to enjoy the descent. He'd tied a big knot in the end of the rope so that at least he wouldn't shoot off the end if it didn't reach the bottom. The water fell in a silver cascade and beyond there was the great sweep of the hillside. His foot slipped, he recovered his balance and saw he had strayed from clean rock into the green slime of moss and algae growing in the middle of the falls. Step by step, he descended.

He reached the end of the rope and gained a footing on a ledge near the bottom. When Jerry was down safely they had only to retrieve the ropes. But when he climbed back up to reach them, they wouldn't move. Around them, the walls of the canyon were vertical and David knew there were more falls ahead. If they could not get the ropes down, they were stuck.

'Did they run all right when I tested them?' he shouted.

'Yeh,' said Jerry.

He tugged with all his strength and swung on one end but they wouldn't budge.

'We'll have to try together,' he said, 'When I pull in the slack, you take the strain.'

Together they hauled and the rope moved. They continued heaving and the free end came tumbling down the cliff and landed in the water. David coiled the two ropes. It was now five-thirty—they had two hours to get down before dark.

They were able to traverse around the next falls along a ledge and then descend the steep slope by clinging to the saplings. David stung his hand again, this time on a plant that looked like rhubarb. He cursed and braked his wild descent and clung to a branch to suck his injured hand. The trees ended in a steep corner and, unable to stop, they slid the last twenty feet into a pool. They were covered in soil and stinking slime and rolled in the water to wash off the muck.

Fortunately, for a while, the obstacles were relatively small and they were able to avoid getting out the ropes and thus wasting time. They were making good progress, but by now it was getting dark. The gorge had narrowed and they were enclosed by steep rock walls. They reached a square platform over which the water poured and fell free. There was a strong wind blowing up the gorge. He couldn't see the bottom of the falls. Nearby there was a tree round which they could fix the ropes and faintly, on the wind, David could hear the sound of traffic on the autopista.

'What do you want to do?' he asked Jerry. 'We either stop here until morning or take a chance and hope these are the last falls.'

'Let's keep going. I'm cold and we must be nearly down. I can hear the cars.'

'I'm not sure, it could be a long way still.'

Leaning over the edge of the overhang he looked down into a black well. He dropped the end of the ropes. They billowed up in the strong up draught and dropped out of sight.

Jerry sat against the tree. He seemed to have fallen asleep. David touched his shoulder gently.

'If the ropes feel slack, come!' he shouted to make himself heard over the crashing water.

David lowered himself over the overhang. He was hanging free, totally reliant on the ropes, his side against wet rock. Then there was nothing, just the thundering sound that stopped his mind and the crash of icy water over his head, forcing him down. He was turning in a black void. He had no way of knowing how far this free fall would continue or if he was about to slide off the end of the rope into space. He wrapped the rope round his thigh ready to brake.

His feet touched ground, slid off and his knees hit. He stopped and felt around with his hands. He appeared to be in a steep chute about three or four feet wide. The rock was smooth and there was no ledge on which to stop. He lay on his side in the rushing water and tried to think. He levered himself up and, by bracing his legs either side, was able to stand. Very slowly, a step at a time, he moved down. Please don't start Jerry, he prayed to himself.

At the very end of the ropes he found himself standing in a tiny rock pool where the chute levelled before plunging down again. The ropes were pulled out of his grasp and he knew Jerry must be descending. He shouted a warning but it was drowned by the wind and the crashing water. Because he had taken so long Jerry must have thought he had reached a safe place when he felt the rope go slack.

Frantically David grappled in the bed of the pool, feeling with his hands in the blackness for some block or spike to wrap the ropes round. There were only loose stones. Then he had an idea. He pulled a tape sling from the top of his sack, and, feeling for the largest boulder he could find, he threaded the sling round it and jammed it where the side walls narrowed at the lip of the pond. The boulder moved, but it was all he could find. He held the jammed sling like a lifeline.

What seemed a long time later, Jerry arrived and David had to grab hold of him to stop him sliding past. He pushed him into the back of the chute and started pulling down the ropes. In the din and the dark he had to feel for Jerry and put his mouth close to his ear. Hunched in the freezing cold water, Jerry was fast asleep! After ten at night Jerry always got sleepy, but this was unbelievable. David's whole body was shaking, his face stretched taut, his head jumping so hard his teeth clashed terrifyingly. He wanted to shake Jerry, make him share the terror. All the time he had been climbing he had never been so frightened, so near letting go. He screwed his eyes tight shut against the blackness and fought to regain control.

He didn't trust the boulder— he had to find a tree. The side of the ravine was steep and wet but there were small ledges and he managed to climb fifteen feet or so. His fingers found a thick root. He threaded a sling round it, clipped the rope in the snap-link and gingerly lowered himself back down. Now he had two anchors, both dubious. He tied knots in the ropes and let them slip away down the watercourse. Just let there be a flat area at the bottom and we'll stop, he thought, shaking Jerry awake.

In the dark, as he descended the ropes, he felt leaves and branches and then, miraculously, his feet reached flat earth. After what seemed an age, he heard Jerry crashing through the trees and then he too was down safely and they were hugging each other with relief, slapping each other on the back to try and warm themselves.

Leaving the ropes hanging in space, David took the two nylon hammocks from the sacks. He tied them, one above the other, between two trees. There was a cold wind and he shivered in his wet clothes. He could hear Jerry snoring, but his mind refused to rest. Why do it? he cursed, he didn't like feeling terrified. But he hadn't known it was going to be that bad. It had gone well—it was fantastic! It only got out of control at the end. You were bloody lucky, he thought. If the boulder had slipped, the root would have ripped and you would have fallen. True, but it hadn't. And he would do it again, but not tomorrow.

He woke to a piercing shriek. A ginger ape swung between the trees and, taking a last look at them, disappeared over the rim of the canyon.

'Howler monkey,' said Jerry. 'I didn't know they lived so close, he was as big as a chimp!'

The gorge looked almost benign in the morning light. A shocking blue butterfly flew down the river, as large as a blackbird, its wings beating in slow lazy time like a manta ray. He let his eyes travel up and up to the overhang and realised how fortunate they had been. The chute appeared as a slight depression in the near vertical rock wall and the tiny perch, where David had found the loose block, was impossible to discern.

There was a long deep pool like a sheep dip and David had to swim with Jerry clinging to his back. He spotted a great tree on the wall of the pool, its roots fanning out sixty feet or more. He dragged Jerry to the side and they clambered out of the water and along the tree to the bank.

There was a small concrete dam with an iron wheel and a faint path through the trees. A deer was browsing on new leaves. Seeing them it bounded away. They could smell smoke and soon reached a timber shack. A man emerged and asked them what they were doing. They told him they had come down the river. At first he didn't believe them, then told them they shouldn't swim in the pool because it was drinking water. Finally he asked them to stop and have coffee. They sat on the crude bench outside his shack, sipping strong sweet coffee while they watched the river flow by in the sunlight.

It was still early when they crossed under the autopista and walked to Jerry's house. They passed a bread shop and the smell of fresh baked bread was irresistible. David went in. The shop was crowded with women waiting to be served but, since David's clothes were wet and smelly, the crowd parted ahead of him and he found himself at the front of the queue.

Outside the sound of crashing water had been exchanged for the noise of traffic. David bit into a bread roll and handed the warm bag to Jerry. His muscles felt tired and he looked forward to sitting down and resting, but it was a pleasurable sensation. With food inside him and his clothes nearly dry, he was already forgetting the terror. Jerry had done well, he had kept going and not cracked up. They'd survived.

12

The rainy season finally broke the following week. The sky was dark, obliging them to switch on the lights at midday, and there was a heaviness in the air. Chelo had left an hour ago, warning him the traffic would be bad. David worked on, wanting to finish. Despite opening all the windows the air refused to stir. Flashes of lightening momentarily lit the corridor through the concrete lattice wall. Rumbling from the east, each pause from flash to roll marked the advancing storm.

They had arranged to meet at ten, after his Spanish class. There was a season of Cuban films showing and Chelo had invited him. Five hours of propaganda, what had he let himself in for? She'd been insistent, said he would be interested. There was only one performance and it was unlikely to be repeated.

Outside an unexpectedly cold wind blew his jacket open and he had to clutch his papers to prevent them blowing away. The first drops of rain plopped on the hot concrete, spreading as large as saucers before disappearing. The line of traffic was moving at walking pace and David hopped onto the platform of a passing bus, hoping it was going in his direction. The bus was already full, but other people pressed on behind, pushing him forward into the cabin. A deafening crack, seemingly directly overhead, rattled the windows of the old bus and the woman next to him opened her mouth to scream but only whispered '¡Dios mio!'.

Stooping David could see out of the window. The rain looked like steel rods. It drummed on the roof of the single-decker bus and the passengers seemed to huddle and crouch under the weight. It was as dark as night and within minutes the road had flooded, the water clear at first and then rich brown as the rain leached the red earth from the land. The bus felt like a submarine, submerged. The driver hunched forward in his seat, his face close to the windscreen trying to see the road and the vehicle in front, the wiper blades having no effect on the downpour.

Abandoned cars jammed the road, some with their front wheels buried to the axle in manholes where the torrent had lifted the covers. The bus took an hour to crawl a distance he could have walked in ten minutes. The deluge eased and people skipped across the road, running for shelter, trousers soaked to the knees, newspapers opened over their heads like capes. It was hot on the bus. The woman pressed against him and he could feel her soft outline under her damp cotton dress, see the slick on the black hairs in her armpit as she grasped the strap. He turned round and the sharp foxy smell from the man next to him made him blink. He squeezed past people and got off the bus. He hadn't paid, there had been no one to pay, nobody minded.

At Chacaito he heard children's laughter and, looking over the railings, saw that the sunken restaurant had flooded. The ragged children had piled chairs on the tables and were diving from them into the muddy water.

As he crossed the bridge to Las Mercedes he stopped to look at the river. The surface was covered with dry sticks and plastic bags. Orange rents had appeared in the western sky and in the failing light David was shocked to see a tidal wave approaching. His first instinct was to run, the wave seemed so huge, but then he realised that the bridge would be well above the flood. Within moments the river doubled in breadth and was covered in a spume of rubbish, debris from the dry gullies and ranchos on the hillsides: bloated bodies of dogs, crates and boxes, mattresses and whole trees, undulating in the brick-red torrent.

A sudden squall, the last of the storm, scattered late-night shoppers and obliged David to run for shelter under the awning of a roadside cafe. He ordered coffee and a cheese sandwich eating them standing at the bar while the rain passed over.

He was late for his class but less than half the other students were there. There was a mood of fiesta in the classroom—it was nearly Christmas. The exercise they were doing was a scene at an airport.

He thought about Jordi and wondered how he was spending Christmas. He'd been gone three months. The elections would be over soon and then Chelo said he'd be able to come back.

The lesson moved on. When it was his turn to answer he did all right, he had progressed.

Outside the theatre, waiting for Chelo to arrive, the road was littered with branches broken in the storm. Bastard! He jumped back as a taxi roared by and threw up a plume of water. It was after ten. Had she gone in already? he worried.

Chelo arrived, gave him a kiss and took his arm. Why was he feeling anxious? His legs felt shaky and there was a slight fluttering sensation in his guts. He was glad she had come. Apart from the trip to the art gallery, this was the first time they had been out together.

They sat down halfway through a film about sugar production. Films about the revolutionary war and Batista's overthrow followed. It was after midnight and David fell asleep during a film about rural education.

Chelo nudged him. The trailer announced 'Memorias de Sub-desarrollo'. It was about a rich and successful architect. His wife took the children and fled to Florida but for some reason the architect decided to stay on. In a scene reminiscent of the French revolution, a neighbourhood committee arrived to requisition his flat. What impressed David was that such a subtle and complex film could follow such simple propaganda. The man lost all his beautiful things: his car, his paintings, his furniture. His flat was wrecked. He stopped working, stopped shaving. His clothes got dirty, then tattered. He fell in love with a young woman. His perspective changed, he pulled through and started working again.

There were two more pictures but Chelo suggested they leave. It was after two in the morning. He said yes automatically when Chelo offered him a lift, then wondered whether he would have preferred to walk home alone. He didn't want to spoil the evening by talking about the film.

'Would you like to come to my place?' she said.

'It's late.'

'Yes. But I won't sleep. Have a drink and I'll run you home.'

'Thank you, yes fine.'

She drove fast, there was little traffic, and he could feel the turmoil the film had produced begin to settle as the jigsaw pieces rearranged themselves in his head. He identified with the hero: they were both architects. He imagined what he would have done in the same situation, and realised that he would have stayed too.

Good films always had a strong effect on him. Some pictures made him feel physically ill. After watching Peter O'Toole in Lord Jim, he'd had to lie down. He joked about being seasick but it was abandoning the pilgrims to the storm that had made him feel ill.

The best picture house was the Continental in Birkenhead where they showed foreign films with sub-titles. There were double seats on the back row and the manager used to serve tea in the interval. There was only just time to catch the last ferry home and if the tide was out the slope down to the floating landing stage was so steep you had to run to keep your balance and could jump on at the last minute as they were casting off. David liked to sit on the top deck on the hard wooden benches that doubled as life rafts and watch the reflections of harbour lights on the oily river. Gulls soared above the wheelhouse on the dark night wind which brought the sharp salt smell of the Irish Sea.

It was the anarchy and chaos in this film from Cuba that

184

frightened him—his fear of letting go, of literally letting himself go like the hero in the film. His mother had kept up standards: ironing towels, washing his father's ashtrays. He remembered her in a headscarf, on her knees, her brawny arms scrubbing the back drain with hot disinfectant.

Chelo parked in an underground car park and they walked to the lift. 'Where are we?' he asked.

'Altamira.' She unlocked the door. It was a little like a smart hotel room. There was a low shelf running the length of the room with some pottery sculptures and a large record collection. She noticed his confusion.

'Not what you expected? Let me show you round.' She opened a door into a small room next to the entrance. 'This is the kitchen. And there's a bathroom.'

'It's nice. How long have you been here?'

'A couple of years. I lived with my aunt before.' She shook her head and gave a momentary smile.

David went out on to the balcony. 'There's a beautiful view, we must be near Jerry's.'

'Why?'

'The mountain looks the same, only we're a bit lower.'

'It's dark, you can't see anything.'

'Look,' he said, drawing her out into the night air, 'the mountain is black against the sky, you can see the outline.'

'It's just a mountain,' she laughed.

'Yes … of course. But I don't think I could stay here without it.'

'You obviously navigate by it!'

'I knew a Japanese who was just as crazy about Mount Fuji. His name was Ichiro.'

He designed the crockery for hospitals in Tokyo—it fitted

together on a tray like airline meals. David could hardly believe anything made out of plastic could be so perfect.

'Come and sit on the sofa,' said Chelo.

He told her about the meal Ichiro had cooked for him: fish soup and seaweed rolls. He cracked a whole egg into the bowl and laughed when David couldn't eat it with chopsticks. His flat was a six by eight back bedroom in which he cooked, washed, worked. Everything was within reach of the bed. He had taken the room because it had a basin—for his photography. But he also did his washing in the sink and hung it out on a line he'd rigged through the window on a pulley. He cooked on a tiny gas stove.

'His wife had sent the stuff over—it was a special treat, to say goodbye to me.'

His wife had stayed in Tokyo with the two children, living with her parents in a two-room flat. He was celebrating. He'd had a letter from his wife saying they'd won a flat in a raffle. He showed David a picture—one tiny window had been ringed in a massive block. He said it was three hours from his office, very close.

'A bit like this place? What would you like to drink?'

He laughed and said he would have tea. While she made it he looked round. A swatch of woven material hung down one wall into which she had pinned her earrings and necklaces. He got up to examine the ceramic figures.

'What do you think?'

'They look like Chimu pottery I've seen in books'.

'Close. They're beautiful aren't they.' She told him that they were over a thousand years old, Colombian mainly. 'That's from here, near Barquisimeto.' She pointed to a squat female figure about six inches high. 'China or herb?'

'China, please.'

'There's no milk, I'm afraid. You English always drink it with milk. How did you like the film?'

'I liked it. Interesting that a picture critical of the revolution could be made in Cuba.'

'Complex rather than critical.'

'Why did he stay?' he asked her. It fascinated him—a sensitive individualist, an intellectual; there was nothing for him working in the fields? His motivation had seemed personal rather than political, emotional, rather than rational.

'It was the most exciting thing that had ever happened to him' she said. He felt imprisoned by his old life. He wanted to find out how he'd respond to chaos.'

'You mean take his chance to be part of it.'

'Yes. And you? how are you coping with chaos?'

He didn't reply immediately, realising that he'd been holding back, and she knew this and wanted to help. 'I need to loosen up, take part more,' he said finally, 'maybe not worry about changing it all to fit me.'

'I thought you wanted to change the world,' she said smiling.

He laughed.

'What is the first thing you can remember,' she asked.

He said the first thing that came into his head. It was of a railway station, at night, going to see his nanna in St Helen's. He remembered the noise and blackness, the smell of oil, steam and smoke and the fear as he was handed up to the driver to look into the firebox. He remembered a terraced house on a steep street, the kitchen table with a green cloth and a drawer full of treasures and his grand-dad in bed, with a moustache like all the kings and generals in the pictorial encyclopedia he read lying on the floor in front of the stove.

He had been happiest sitting stirring the pedal of his tricycle in the back yard, pretending to make ice cream. His dad came home one day with a wigwam; it was summertime. David had watched him bang in the wooden pegs with the coal hammer. It wasn't anyone's birthday and he didn't know why he'd been brought a present.

But he couldn't remember his mother's arms or the smell of her skin.

'What was your mother like?' asked Chelo.

Suddenly he wanted to tell her about finding his mother. 'I was adopted,' he replied. 'It wasn't that I didn't love my adoptive parents ... but after they died I wanted to find her. I couldn't remember anything about her. I was only six months old when I was adopted. But I searched and found her.' Then he found he was talking about his feelings. About how joyful it had been to meet her and then how devastating when she wouldn't see him again.

Chelo stared at him as he spoke, distressed. Then tears came to her eyes and she said very quietly, 'I lost my mother too ... when I was eight.' She said she could remember her mother screaming, in the big bedroom at the hacienda in the country. It was the end of the *sequía*, the dry season, just before the rains came, and the plains were all dust and the beasts hid under the tiny islands of shade. Chelo had been allowed in to see her. The shutters were closed and the air was heavy and moist like wet flannel and smelt of rotting flesh. 'Mother was propped up on the pillows, her all hair tangled and damp. I stood next to my father, too frightened to run to her. The pain came again and she was tossed from side to side. I wanted to scream: Why can't you lie still.

'*Zamuros* – you know the black turkey buzzards – they sat in rows on the fences round the house. The smell was awful. It followed you everywhere, even down to the dried up creek a mile away. It permeated everything, so that for days we were unable to eat for the taint of death in the food.

'I wasn't allowed to see her again and she had died three days later. I seemed to have to grow up overnight. We lived on at the ranch, but father seemed to lose all interest and finally we moved to the capital.'

They sat together in silence, holding each other tightly.

§

It was David's birthday. He had invited Chelo to dinner and took the afternoon off work to shop, cook and clean the house. He didn't cook much for himself and hadn't had much practice so chose something simple: guacamole, sliced potatoes in wine and milk and thinly sliced pork fried in herbs. There were two bottles of white Rioja in the fridge. He hoped they'd had time to chill.

Chelo arrived. She'd brought flowers and a silk tie.

'I thought we'd eat outside.'

'How your plants have grown! That wall was bare when you moved here. And the scent!'

Jasmin covered the wall where the Jardines had grown orchids, and hibiscus filled the corner, the scarlet flowers blatantly sensuous.

'This is lovely. Did you make the table and benches?' she asked, stroking the smooth surface.

'Yes. Would you like some wine?'

They sat facing each other, dipping the carrot and celery and the hot tortilla chips into soft green mess. Chelo sucked her fingers: 'I like to feel the food when I eat.'

'I noticed!' he said.

'The nicest things in life are messy—food, sex …'

He grinned and said nothing.

Seeing his reserve she asked, 'How's work?'

'I've been thinking,' said David, after a moment or two. 'This modelling, it's like the emperor's new clothes.'

'Why?'

'It's so crude, too simple. But people are seduced by the computer output.'

'It works.'

'Because we fix what happens by defining the zoning. The paper I was reading today: the author claims that the model increases the information about the city; that you get more out than you put in. That's nonsense. It suggests the model's magical, when in fact it's just a way of organising the data.'

'But the theory underpinning the model?'

'It ignores the complex processes that affect growth. The model jumps to the end and paints an instant city. The problem I've found is that no amount of tweaking improves the fit in some zones. In some parts of the city the model is just unable to match reality. Now, to me, that's interesting! For example, some zones are obviously more desirable than others, more desirable than one would expect from the model. They have status. The wealthy locate there and, consequently, densities are much lower than the model predicts.'

'So!'

'The author of this paper writes as though these differences—between what the model predicts and what the city is actually like—are errors. He implies there is something wrong with the city, not the model; that the model is optimum and reality imperfect.'

'And you think they should be explored.'

'Yes, exactly.'

'Jordi's advanced model will take care of that.'

'But there is still no theory.'

'How's the other work?'

'Yes. Well I've been writing to a professor in the Hague. He's been developing social indicators.'

'But you don't agree with him!'

'I've been trying to define how people judge a city. The main problem is that the model only allows you to work with a small number of the important variables.'

'And this professor?'

'Oh, yes. Well, he's wrong. I think, when we try and evaluate the quality of our lives, we compare what we experience with some ideas about what would be ideal, or at least acceptable. Just as a doctor has an idea of how a healthy body should function when he diagnoses a patient.'

'Are all variables weighted equally?'

'Not necessarily. But you would need to justify weighting one thing more than another.'

'What do you get at the end?'

'A quality of life score. It also gives a very rough indication of costs.'

'Jordi will like that.'

'It's a far cry from reality though.'

'Why.'

'It has built-in social justice.'

'How?'

'Each person in the city carries the same clout. Young or old, rich or poor. The more people benefit from an alternative the better.'

'So!'

'That clearly doesn't happen, or why would Joselyn have wanted to interview the fuerzas vivas so badly.'

'Because if anything is going to happen here you have to convince those with the power.'

'Hell! I forgot the dinner!'

David rushed to the kitchen. He'd left the meal in the oven to keep warm. The sauce round the meat had boiled away and the bottom of the dish was beginning to burn.

Shit! it's ruined—what else can I serve her? Don't panic, he told himself.

He poured on some wine from the second bottle, stirred in the burnt juices and heated the resulting gravy on the hob; hoping for the best.

'This is delicious,' said Chelo, 'I didn't know you could cook.'

'Ha! Ha!'

'No really, it's good,' she said. 'The potato is perfect— crisp on top and soft underneath.'

'Good.'

He watched as she mopped up the juice with her bread. Her silver earrings glimmered in the candle light and her eyes shone when she looked up.

'I love the night,' she said, looking out at the dark shadows in the garden. 'And you …?'

'I miss the long evenings in England in summer, after rain, when the sun comes out and the light is mellow and everything is clear and well-defined.'

'No, I prefer the dark. The world changes—it becomes more mysterious, more feminine. I like walking in the night, but you can't here! When I was growing up, at my father's farm in the llanos, I'd walk in the pastures, alone, with the cool stars and the warm friendly moon.'

He nodded, understanding.

David cleared the dishes and put the coffee on.

'Why were you so hard on me when we were away?' he asked her, pouring the last of the wine.

'I didn't know I had been.'

'Maybe I was imagining it then. But I found you very distant. I felt you were siding with Joselyn, that you were angry with me, and I didn't know what for.'

'No, you weren't imagining it,' she said, relenting. 'Sometimes you can be so infuriating … we need her co-operation with the model.'

He nodded and said he was sorry for being obtuse.

'What about your climbing?' she asked, changing the subject.

He felt awkward and didn't want to talk about climbing. It was impossible to explain to someone who had never done it.

'Fine' he said, 'I've been exploring San Juan de los Morros.' The Morros were limestone towers in the shape of bishop's mitres. On the largest, Morro Grande, General Goméz had constructed a lighthouse over a hundred miles from the sea to send him news of insurrection amongst the plainsmen of the llanos. The ladders had long been removed, but even with them in place it must have been a harrowing climb. The curved windows were still intact and the gallery and handrails still showed signs of red paint. Inside the light itself had been removed and only the polished brass bed on which it revolved remained.

'Tell me more.'

'I've been trying to climb the Picacho de Galipan. The cliff you see to the left on the way down in the cable car.'

'And?'

'I don't know, I haven't managed to get up it. It's hard, and a long walk. One time it rained. I got halfway up it once, the second time I tried with Jerry.'

'What happened?'

'I got my hands on this good ledge—it was the first decent resting place for two hundred feet—and looked straight at this snake.'

'Poisonous?'

'Tigre Mariposa—the worst of the lot; so I had to climb back down. Jerry wouldn't go there again.'

'Why do you climb? Is it the danger?'

He thought for a moment. Often when he was asked this question he would say he climbed because he enjoyed it and leave it at that. How do you explain to someone who has never been climbing what it's all about? It's as if someone living in the tropics had heard about snow but never touched it—never made a snowball, never seen the magic white carpet that wondrously appeared overnight, nor felt the biting cold in fingers and toes from staying out till dark building a snowman.

'There's nothing like climbing. Did you climb trees as a child?'

'I can't remember. Yes, we used to climb the mango tree at my father's farm.'

'Do you remember the pleasure you got pulling up on the

branches, moving up, breaking the hold the ground had on you?'

'Yes.'

'Do you remember feeling frightened when you reached a certain height, when the ground looked uncomfortably far away? Do you remember how hard it was to keep going, how each move took longer than the last and how thrilled you were if you made it?'

'I remember having climbed the tree on my own once. My sisters weren't there for some reason and I couldn't get down. I sat in the crook of a branch unable to move with fear, determined not to call out for help. Eventually something snapped inside me and I was able to make the first move down.' She shivered, remembering the fear.

'You're cold,' said David. 'Let's go inside and have coffee.' He closed the patio doors and wrapped a rough blanket round her shoulders. She curled up in the chair while he lit the candles and poured the coffee.

'Tell me more about your adventures here,' she asked

'There was an old woman,' he began, 'who lived on the mountain above Guarenas in a ruined property called the Hacienda del Norte. We went past it, on the way to the waterfalls on the Quebrada Ayala. She lived all alone—she had one yellow tooth—it was hard to understand what she said.

'She made us coffee,' he said, lifting his cup. 'She collected the beans from trees growing wild on the hillside and roasted them in the sun on her patio—only one corner of which remained intact—the rest having been cracked by the ants. She ground them in a stone mortar and boiled the water in a blackened pot on an open fire. The coffee was thick and oily, without any trace of bitterness and she served it in small calabash cups.'

'How long had she been there?'

'All her life, she said. Only the walkers visited her. I asked her how she lived. She said: "Simply. I have my birds, trees and fresh water." The next time I went she'd gone.'

'Gone? Where?'

'Dead, I suppose. It was only three or four months later, but the forest was already growing through the roof. No one went there—she might not have been found for weeks. She had lived alone, contented, with few possessions. I like to think of her slipping back into the forest and disappearing in the earth and the rain. I can taste her coffee now, slightly smoky.'

Chelo came and sat next to him on the sofa. He put his arm round her and she put her head on his shoulder. They watched the candle flame for a while without speaking.

13

David began to feel more relaxed at work, more on top of things. He had to rewrite bits of the computer programme Jordi had sent from England but once he had it running they were able to start to use the information they had collected in Cumaná. Chelo was in charge of coding all the data: demographic statistics from the census and Joselyn's household survey, the areas of the zones they had decided on, the location of schools, shops and other services and the road pattern of the city.

Although Jordi was in England, he was still keeping in touch with the project, sending back comments on the material Alejandro sent him at least once a week. David had to admit it was a good working arrangement: Jordi defined the goals and set the pace, David invented the content and Chelo made sure it worked. He was even prepared to admit

Alejandro's role in fixing the bureaucracy. The arrangement worked so well, he realised, because Jordi was away. Had he been there all the time, his sudden changes of focus and energy would have been intolerable. Distance damped the oscillations and allowed them to finish each part of the project in an orderly fashion.

Jordi loved the energy generated by people working for him. He'd have been excited by the ideas and would have made suggestions, not just about what to do, but about how to do it. But David might have seen this enthusiasm as interference and would have resented Jordi pushing his nose in.

They were not all David's ideas though. Chelo made suggestions too, and was impossible to disentangle where her ideas ended and his began. Half the time he was unaware of the extent of her contribution because she did not get uptight if he did not use her ideas like Jordi would have done. She would ask him about it later, when he had time to think, whereas Jordi would have caught him immediately, when he was still emotional, and demanded an explanation. Faced with conflict David became inarticulate and their relationship would, inevitably, have gone sour.

Chelo's mind was sharp and incisive. She was rational, objective, analytic and helped him see the wood for the trees. David was inventing the stuff off the top of his head. The modelling was breaking new ground and without her he would have found it impossible to keep going. Chelo loved his inventiveness and delighted in the twists and turns that would appear almost magically as the work unfolded. She did not see herself as being creative, but loved being with inventive people. It was the process of creativity that fascinated her—that moment when something new was born out of someone's mind and you could almost see the sparks fly.

§

'I think we should go and have a look at the Tuy,' said David.

'It's cow pasture, there's nothing there,' said Alejandro.

'You know it, I don't. I've studied the maps of the area and now I need to go and walk the site and try and imagine a city there.'

'Walk!' said Alejandro.

'Yes, I think we should all go. It's all very well looking at the development plan with its artist's impressions and coloured plans. We need to feel what the place will be like with half a million people, a million cars and a lot of concrete.'

'Count me out,' said Alejandro. The last thing he wanted to do was to stagger about getting lost in sweltering thorn scrub.

'There is a fiesta in San Francisco de Charallave soon. Let's go then,' said Chelo.

'A fiesta!' Here we go again, thought David, gadding about when we're supposed to be working.

'Don't be so Puritan. You'll enjoy it, it's interesting. Indian grafted onto Easter—devils in the street. We can stay the night and look round early the following morning before it gets too hot.'

'All right...good...yes, that sounds a good idea, thanks,'

said David, thinking that this time he would be on his own with Chelo.

'How's the model coming along?' asked Alejandro.

'We've got it running and we're calibrating it with the 1960 and 1970 data.'

'And the evaluation?'

'The program's written, the main framework at least. It's a question of the criteria one uses. If I only use the outputs from the computer model, and the list of criteria Jordi sent, then the option with the most land nearest the capital will get the highest score. But other things are important.'

'Like?'

'Environmental factors, and the quality of life.'

'How do you measure that?'

'I have some ideas.'

'That's up to you then.' Alejandro didn't trust creative types with their novel ideas. He had to make sure they delivered what they had promised on time. Nobody read the full report, all that mattered was the bottom line. He wasn't sure David understood this or if anyone had told him how the line should read. 'Manuel favours the Tuy and he wants our report quick, so we have to meet the deadline.'

'But I want to make sure we are giving him the right advice. I'm waiting for the topographic and seismological data.'

'It's not what you want that matters. Manuel's paying—it's what he wants that counts.'

'But the brief is to test alternatives for massive government investment. It's important to get it right.'

'Manuel wants an unbiased view, that's right. He wants solid research and investigation to support the Ministry's proposals when they go to the President and Congress. But keep it simple. Take my advice: stop making a meal of it.'

§

The streets of San Francisco were thronging with people. It was easy to distinguish the visitors, they wore more expensive looking clothes. The shoes were the give away. But more than half the people must be locals, he thought, pushing through the crowd in front of Chelo. They had arrived late, after the procession from the church. Amongst the crowd were the blackened devils, some with straw masks and deformed wooden pegs for teeth, swirling, their pitchforks creating spaces in the throng.

Another performance began in the square and they moved over with the crowd. Chelo couldn't see.

'I'll put you on my shoulders.'

'No, you can't. I'm too heavy. My shoes are dirty.'

'Come on.' He steadied himself and raised her aloft, like the ferryman in Grimm.

'This is marvellous I can see everything,' she yelled over the noise. It was like a mystery play: a black queen and a white king, soldiers with scimitars, pantomime horses, princes in turbans, priests in purple and dozens of devils, their faces blackened, their costumes, once red, now pink from many washings.

'What are they saying, I can't understand,' asked David.

'Neither can I, it's the dialect, and some of the words are foreign. She's the Queen of Sheba and he's Solomon.'

The longer he watched the more he seemed to understand

of what was happening. It looked chaotic, but he began to see meaning. They were enacting an epic myth about spectacular wealth and power, about how this was nothing in the face of death. The king and queen, the princes, priests, warriors and merchants all went to hell to be tormented by demons. The great check and balance of religion.

The crowd began dancing to the thumping rhythm; everyone was stamping and gyrating. He danced with her on his shoulders. He could feel her laughing and clapping with the music. He tired, got his second wind, kept going. The weight dulled, became familiar, and her heaviness became part of him. Only his thighs ached but he could shut that out. He closed his eyes and danced in the dark.

He put her down. She turned and threw her arms round his neck and kissed him on the lips, laughing. Arm in arm they pushed through the crowd to find the hotel she'd booked.

'This isn't good enough. I made the reservations last week on the telephone. I spoke to you, yourself.'

The manager shrugged: 'The fiesta ... I'm sorry. So many came last night. I thought you might not come.'

'What are we going to do now. Oh David, I'm sorry. We'll have to go back home.'

'Let's have something to eat and then decide.'

They bought yellow corn pancakes and coffee in the street and found a bit of broken wall to sit on by the church. They were in the shade a large *Ceiba* and could enjoy the fiesta from a distance.

'We can come back tomorrow, early,' he said.

'I wanted to see it at dawn, and at night time,' she said.

'Let's drive round, have a look at the site and then decide.'

The Tuy was a sunken bowl, fifty kilometres wide. It was hard to see where they were in the rolling scrub and from the jeep they could see little except thorn bushes and tall dry grass. There were hills to the north and to the southeast, slate blue in the heat haze.

It was late afternoon and broiling hot. The track they were following was baked hard: crazed and broken slabs of concrete-hard mud. They had crossed another dry gully when David thought he saw a depression in the ground ahead, stopped and got out to look. Under the long grass and scrub there was a deep circular pit and what looked like a second further ahead.

'Sink holes!' he shouted to Chelo. 'You drive: I'll walk ahead.'

'No, let me sit on the roof and direct you.'

He shoved the gears into low drive and they ground forward at a snail's pace. Chelo's brown calfs framed his view through the windscreen. The vehicle rolled and tilted and she hung on to the edge of the roof, her bare feet wide spaced and firmly planted on the bonnet. He had the plan of the proposed city spread on the seat next to him and the best topographical plan he could find. He navigated by the range of hills to the north and by the line of the river than ran west to east across the site and was now, in the dry season, a series of muddy pools.

'This is it, I think.'

'What?'

'The city centre. Can't you see all the shops, the municipal offices? The main avenue runs down there,' he said pointing his arm. All she could see was dry scrub.

'How do you know?'

'We're on a hill, right? And, according to the plan, the centre should be somewhere about here, at the highest point.'

'What do we do now?'

'Make tea!'

'You're incorrigible.' She punched him on the shoulders. He grabbed her around the waist and kissed her.

'Let's stop here the night.'

'What! You're mad.'

'No, I've got everything we need.'

'Where?'

He showed her the lockers hidden under the floor in the back.

'I've got bed-rolls or you can have a hammock if we can find a tree.'

'I'm all sweaty. I need a shower.'

He could feel his shirt clinging to his back from the plastic car seat.

'Yes? Sorry I'm not thinking. I've got plenty of water—you could wash. I'll put the kettle on.'

He pulled his machete from its scabbard under the driver's seat and went to find some wood. Soon he had made a fire and got the water boiling. He unhinged the seats and plonked them upwind of the fire. Chelo stood watching the sun set and the mountains change colour.

'How come you're so well organised?'

'I just am. What do you fancy?'

'Anything! I'm starving. How much choice is there, anyway?'

'You'd be amazed.'

He cooked her a meal.

'Beer or wine?'

'Wine … Ah! you are a magician—it's cold!'

The Tilley lamp bubbled gently, casting a pool of light. The fire burnt low. He made coffee.

'Let's walk,' he suggested.

'In the dark?'

'Sure. We can take the lamp.'

'No, let's leave it. The moon is bright.'

They had walked a mile or so down the main avenue when she stopped and said: 'Can you feel it—a sort of trembling?' He couldn't.

'Is this a good site for a city?' he asked.

'It's hard to imagine,' she said.

'It could be a hell hole—its so low down.'

He rolled out the mattresses and put hers near the fire. He took off his clothes, folded them to make a pillow, and pulled the sleeping bag over himself. He could hear her singing to herself at the back of the jeep, humming while she brushed her teeth. She crossed in front of the fire, long bare legs in the firelight. She dragged her mattress next to his. As she kneeled to straighten her bedding he gently brushed his knuckles over the soft clad mounds of her buttocks. She turned and they kissed, tentatively at first, exploring each other's lips, longer, deeper, letting go, melting like ice in the spring.

In a village two Indian women were sitting on some worn steps, hunched over and sheltering from the wind. They were chanting softly, and in their hands they held small bowls.

The scene shifted, as it does in dreams. A storm was

brewing and a galleon was hauled in to the quayside, heeled over. A sailor shouted a warning, a cable broke free and the ship was swept away. A crack opened in the soft sandstone of the foreshore and the man was swallowed up. Looking down into the cleft, David could see a deep hole. Someone shouted: "Run!" and they all ran from the sea.

They were stopped by tall cliffs. They started to climb, but the rock was soft and crumbly. It was steep and one of the Indian women found a better way to one side. The boy ahead of David was too frightened to move and he had to help him by moving his feet to good holds.

As they reached the top the sea poured into the hole. When it filled they knew it would boil up and engulf them. They ran on through a garden of an hotel and found a car: a white left–hand drive Mercedes, like Jordi's. David pushed the man out of the driving seat and climbed in, but when he turned to look for the boy, he had gone. Then he saw him between the legs of marching men with spiked helmets and blind eyes. The Indian woman scooped the boy into her arms and ran to the car. But before they could get away the car began shaking violently.

'Chelo! What's wrong?' He struggled to wake. He tried to stand, to reach the light. He fell. The ground was shaking beneath them. She clung to him.

'What's happening?'

'It's an earthquake. Hold me, hold me tight.'

The movement lasted a minute, no more, but it felt much longer. There was a sound, deep in the earth, like an underground train. By the light of the moon they could see all the land rolling like a wave. There was absolutely nowhere to run. Senses, tuned to the still point of the turning earth

206

were upset, lost. The world was turned on its head. Clouds move, hills move as you walk, but the ground beneath your feet, that stayed fixed, steady. Not any more, the earth rippled like a jelly. It was as if land had turned to water but the effect, on the mind, was totally different from floating. This was unnatural, malevolent.

The world steadied, righted itself. They held each other for a long time without speaking.

He dozed, then felt her awake. 'Can't you sleep?' he asked.

'I'm too frightened.'

'Have you been in one before.'

'When I was little.'

'It's over now. I was having a nightmare …' He told her about his dream.

Chelo didn't say anything when he had finished.

'What does it all mean?'

'I don't know,' she said, holding his hand tightly.

'I'm thirsty, would you like a drink?'

'Yes, water.'

He reached over and filled a mug from the water bottle. It tasted deliciously cool. He lay down next to her and she snuggled against his chest.

'Do you get lonely—on your own?' she asked.

'Not really. I like the solitude. But it's lovely to get a visit from someone you like—like you.'

She hugged him.

'How long have you lived on your own?' he asked her.

'Three or four years. My father died when I was still at school and I went to live with an aunt. I had to leave school early and get a job … that's why I've no qualifications.'

'I had no idea. I thought you were an architect, like the

rest.'

'No … We were a very old-fashioned family. I met Jordi when we were children. We went to the same piñatas.'

'What?'

'Parties! The piñata itself is made in the shape of a boat or a doll, anything—you must have seen them, hanging outside shops. They're filled with sweets and toys and hung in the garden or patio. We used to have them on the first Sunday of Lent—before the fast. Now people buy them for birthdays or anything. The children have to bash it open with a stick. Even when he was small, Jordi always smashed it first. Then all the children scramble and grab as much as they can.'

'Sounds awful—like capitalism!'

'No, it's fun. Some get more than others and there are tears—Jordi always looked after me.'

'Does he still look after you?'

'No, by and large I look after myself,' she said, thoughtfully.

He looked up into the night. It was clear and dark and the sky was full of stars. But the patterns they made were still unfamiliar. 'I miss friends to climb with,' he said. 'Jerry's gone to Merida.'

'Jordi will be back soon,' she said.

'And?'

'You and he are great friends aren't you?'

'I don't know—I don't know him that well.'

'I thought you spent a lot of time together. He said you got really close.'

'I went to his home three or four times, and I saw him at work of course. I helped with the research project, for his dissertation. It was a simulation—we had to play roles—it was very exciting. Jordi was great, everywhere at once, you know. I saw things in him that I liked.'

'Is that all?'

'Yes and no. I invited him and Mariella to the Lakes, to a friend's cottage, but they always cancelled at the last minute. I wanted to show them something different, not the tourist bits. So, I don't know him very well. I didn't get to know him in England, and he's been away since I got here. But he's the sort of person I felt I'd known all my life, even when I'd just met him. We used to play squash, not often—but I enjoyed playing with him; he took it so seriously.'

'Did you win.'

'Sometimes. He was good at losing, he didn't let a bad patch get to him, and he could switch into top gear and go for the kill. I could never do that. If he was down I'd play him some easy balls. He wanted to win more than I did.'

'Do you never want to win that badly?'

'Not at squash! Other things … maybe. Things I believe in. And I'll fight for people I love.' She put her head on his shoulder and he caressed her hair. 'I miss some things.'

'Yes?'

'You get into bachelor ways … living on your own. I don't know what it is ? Women bring a home to life … Nikki used to fill the place with stuff : lumps of driftwood, pebbles, rocks , old plates she'd buy in Oxfam. It used to infuriate me … the flat cluttered with all sorts of rubbish. But I miss it now.'

'Oh! You're so infuriating!' she said, sitting up.

'What's wrong?'

'You were generalising.'

'No.'

'You were talking nonsense,' she said, smiling. 'Would you

like me to bring things home for you?'

It sounded true enough to him—why did she find it so infuriating? He wasn't sure she wasn't pulling his leg again. 'I'd like that,' he said.

'You're being very cautious!' she laughed. Then quietly she said, 'I love your place.'

'It's austere compared to yours.'

'It has a lovely feel to it.'

They woke early with the light and after breakfast drove to Cua, a hamlet on the southern limit of the Tuy. A straggle of decrepit houses with muddy tide marks and big brown rings where the plaster had fallen off. There was a Creole filling station. Slicks of gritty oil and a disorderly collection of abandoned cars and wrecked trucks disfigured the forecourt. They stopped to fill-up. There was a smell of rotting garbage and pig dung, heavily laced with diesel.

Stretching back along the rutted highway there was a line of billboards: Pepsi, Firestone, Cerveza Polar, Seguros Nacionales. Electricity cables hung haphazardly from leaning posts.

David asked about the earthquake: he didn't understand why they couldn't see any damage. The attendant said that they had felt the tremor in the night. It wasn't unusual, they often had them, but they were on rock; safe and sound.

'Did you feel it here?' he asked Alejandro the next day at work.

'Sure. It was just a tremor, we get them all the time.'

'What happened exactly?'

'I was working and the desk started shaking. I had my

head down and thought someone was fooling around. When I looked up the building was swaying.'

'How much?'

'A lot!'

'Was there any damage?'

'Very little, things falling and breaking, that's all.'

'How long did it last?'

'I guess it was no more than eight or ten seconds. But boy that feels a long time when you're on the sixth floor and the building's swaying around.'

'When was it exactly?'

'Yesterday, about two-thirty.'

'What about last night?'

'I was asleep.'

He rang the plan room at the Ministry and asked if they had sent the seismographic maps. He spoke to the head of the department who sounded evasive, saying that they were too busy to help. David said he would come in and look.

David steeled himself for a fight. He needed these plans, it was important. No petty official was going to stop him doing his job properly. But the man welcomed him quietly and respectfully. He lifted the wooden counter and invited him into the back. There were rows and rows of upright steel cabinets. The man took him to one of them and pointed to the label. It said seismology. The man said he should look for himself and pulled out the key national plan giving the reference numbers for each map. David went through the cabinet twice. The map for the Tuy was missing.

'There is no record of them having been booked out.'

'What about copies?'

'Missing too,' the man shrugged. 'I'm sorry I can't help. Try the Ministry of Hydrocarbons.'

He tried there and drew another blank. In the end, after ringing Jerry, he found someone at Creole, the American oil company, who gave him a copy of the plan.

14

Just as Mariella and Jordi appeared below them at passport control, Chelo disappeared. One moment she'd been there, withdrawn and short-tempered; he turned to say Jordi had put on weight, and she'd gone. He looked around but couldn't see her and decided to carry on waiting. The phrase 'parting's a small death' came to him. But reunion involved the resumption of ties. Leaving was sharper and clearer somehow. He'd anticipated Jordi coming back; he had hopes and expectations. He'd achieved a lot in six months and wanted to tell Jordi about it. Maybe we could have a beer together, he thought.

He looked across to where Mildred and Alberto were standing with Christina. They'd been cool when he and Chelo met them. He hadn't seen them for ages, he'd been so busy finishing the model.

Suddenly there was Jordi, full of energy, the centre of attention, and he was crushed in that familiar bear hug of an embrace. The jeep was packed tight with luggage. It must have cost them a fortune to bring back this lot. Why did Chelo leave? Alejandro said she had taken a taxi.

Jordi was opening duty-free carriers—handing out bottles of perfume and scotch.

After dropping them off, David sat in the car park for a few minutes, recovering. Then he went home and lay on his back on the bed and watched three flies. They flew just below the paper lantern, seemingly independent of each other, constantly changing direction, in zigzag lines. At intervals one or other would come too close and they would speed up, flying in spirals, as if in a dogfight, faster and faster until they flew apart.

After watching them for a while they appeared to form a single coherent shape, continually changing, like a mobile hanging from the ceiling, or electrons circling a nucleus. Then, as if to thwart him, one fly landed on the underside of the paper globe, for a moment or two defying gravity. Then, suddenly, it flew at one of the other two.

They flew locked together, round and round, in maddening circles, fighting or mating he didn't know; then apart again. Eventually there were only two flies flying lazily round the light and the pattern they made was less dynamic. He got up and shut the door on them.

Within a fortnight the office was transformed. Partitions went up and there were plans to convert the corridor into offices. Jordi hired a secretary called Magaly. She was a demon typist, loyal to Jordi, and made disparaging comments about other people in the unit. David didn't like her much and was surprised to discover that he resented the changes.

The unit was full of new people. Jordi was busy organising a conference to which he had invited half a dozen speakers from England. The theme was urban modelling and one of the main purposes, as David understood it, was to unveil the work they had been doing for Manuel on the Tuy. Felix, the director of the research centre in Cambridge which Jordi had visited, had agreed to come and was bringing a couple of colleagues.

Everywhere there was a whirlwind of activity in preparation. Chelo was in charge of a team translating and producing the conference papers. These, he learnt, would be bound into two thick volumes. An important element in running a successful conference, apparently, was to give each participant a fat tome at the end.

He tried to ignore the turmoil and to get some quiet he decided to start work an hour earlier, at seven. The first morning of his new regime he was surprised to find Jordi and Magaly there ahead of him. Jordi broke off from dictating.

'Hi, David. We need to talk. Just let me finish this.'

There were four new desks in his room and his had been moved away from the window. He had been working a while when Jordi came and pulled a chair up to his desk. 'Thanks for all the data—great job! We'll have to rework some of it, but …'

'Why?' asked David.

'We've had to fudge some things.'

'What things?'

'Oh, you'll see.'

David was upset. He had managed to get reliable data

despite the difficulties. It was the model again. If reality didn't fit, then the model was right and the data got fudged.

'Now, the evaluation model!' He got out the summary David had sent him.

'I assumed you'd want to change or add to the way I've designed it,' said David.

'No, it's great. Let's go ahead with this as it stands.'

'I have reservations about the model.'

'This is only a trial to demonstrate the principle.'

'And I've added some criteria to the list you sent.'

'Sure. But we need the results in time for the conference.'

'That doesn't give us much time.'

'You can do it. I'm counting on you. Don't let me down.'

His cedula, his ID card, had expired and he couldn't renew it until he had a visa. He had put it off for over a month. Chelo asked him about it, she was worried he'd get in trouble. She said there were firms that specialised in documentation: driving licence, identity cards, visas, passports, whatever. They could even get you a solvencia, the yellow card you needed to leave the country that proved you had paid your taxes. The going rate was five hundred bolivars.

'I want to do it myself. I resent paying middlemen, or maybe I just need a day out of the office. I'm not sure. I've been putting it off because I can't decide whether to renew the transit visa or apply for a resident's.'

'I don't understand you. It costs the same in stamps. So what's the problem?'

The problem was it sounded permanent and he felt unsettled. A three-year visa somehow committed him to stopping.

216

'I'm being stupid …' So it lasted three years—he didn't have to stay. 'I'll take the day off work tomorrow and do it.'

Extranjeria, the office that dealt with foreigners, was in the Avenida Baralt, next to the Opera House. The large hall was divided into aisles by tubular barriers and the queue wound round on itself many times. David joined at the back.

After three hours his feet hurt and he leant against the barrier to take the weight. The heat was stifling and he had taken off his jacket and loosened his tie. It was just like a cattle market. The smell of hundreds of people crowded into the poorly ventilated space was almost unbearable. It hadn't been so bad at first but as people got anxious—that they wouldn't make the front of the queue before the office closed for lunch—the stink got worse.

Many of the people were women, Colombians and West Indians. They looked frightened. He guessed they had been working illegally. To get caught on the street without an ID card meant jail and deportation. No woman would want to spend even one night in a jail here.

There was a large clock on the wall which everyone watched. As it got nearer to lunchtime he thought of giving up and coming back tomorrow. But each time he decided to leave, the queue made a surge forward as another batch of people were processed.

A black woman next to him asked if he was English. He found it hard to understand what she was saying: she spoke with a strong accent. She said she was from Trinidad. She was tall, at least six foot, and she was crying. Her teeth gleamed like piano keys in her tear-streaked face. She sobbed quietly like a lost child.

'Why are you crying? Can I help?'

She told him that she had just been sacked. She'd been working as a maid. The family she worked for were moving house and she had been cleaning the new place when she trapped her fingers in the swing door in the kitchen. The mistress phoned her husband and he came home from work and rushed her to the clinic. They had X-rayed her fingers and found that they were only bruised. The family gave her a week off with pay but her brother told her to claim compensation; if they had gone to all that trouble they must be admitting liability. So she asked them for two thousand bolivars and got the sack.

'Now I got no job and no references and me cedula expired. What me going to do?'

David didn't know. The queue moved forward a few yards and her nerve broke. She said she'd risk it until she could get another job and pushed her way out of the queue.

There were two women in front of him now. He couldn't help listening – they were having a row.

'They don't go to school any more. In the letter it says they don't go ... and I've been sending money back home ... every month ... to support your children! You knew ... and you never said.'

'It's all right for you, you work for a nice family with good wages. And you've got a flat for weekends with your fancy man.'

The first one burst out crying. 'He's no good ... last time he took the money I had and then he hit me when I tried to stop him.' The two women cried on each other's shoulders.

Women are imprisoned by invisible walls, thought David. Colombian maids without papers, women walking in the street—they were all fair game for men. In the market boys aged eight or nine pinched the women's bottoms, egged on by men who watched and laughed. It was almost as if the outside world were a forbidden land through which a woman had only limited rights of passage. A car allowed more freedom, but Chelo's red sports car was a challenge to male ego. David hated driving with her, men in big cars cut her up all the time in the traffic.

Exceptional women: Mildred, Christina and Chelo, had overstepped the traditional limits through their work, but there were many things they could not do alone. Women could go to shopping centres during the day, but not to a cinema alone at night, they could go to a cafe but not to a bar, they could go to the pool at the Sheraton but not to the beach. Many women accepted these restrictions without ever stopping to think how and why they had been devised. And the irony was that the structure was policed by other women—mothers, aunts, sisters, daughters. To escape women married and discovered new chains.

The queue moved again and suddenly he was there. He handed over his papers. They asked him why he wanted to take up residence. His fingerprints were taken, then his photograph. He had to wait a few minutes and received his cedula —an identity card the size and shape of a credit card.

'Good, you're back.' He was halted by Jordi storming into the corridor. Through the open door he could see Luis Carlos seated with the others. Hugo rose and closed the door on them.

'Didn't Chelo tell you I went to get my visa?'

'Oh, yes. How did it go?'

'Fine. I'm a resident. Is Chelo still here?'

'No she's gone.' David wondered why she was always running off, but before he could ask why she hadn't stayed for the meeting Jordi said, 'We're talking about the conference, I'd like you to be there.'

'I didn't know about a meeting, nobody told me.'

'The English are arriving Saturday week. I thought you might help show them round. We can take them to the playa, to the Andes, maybe even the Amazonas.'

'I wanted to talk to you about the conference. I'll be able to finish the results you need for your paper on the urban model but there isn't much time to write a paper about the evaluation work unless you can help me with one or two things. Will you have time to look through a draft?'

'There is no paper on the evaluation.'

'Yes there is, I've written one.'

'But the work isn't finished.'

'It is nearly and I wanted to use the conference to provide the impetus to finish it.'

'I haven't got time, I'm organising the whole thing! You are not in the programme.'

'But I thought that we would all be presenting papers on the last day. That's what Chelo said; the last day was when the unit presented its work.'

'The conference finishes early the last day so the English can catch their plane. There's no time. I didn't think you would have it ready.'

'But it's important to me. I'd hoped to give a paper. I'd like to publish and make contacts with some of the speakers.' David had to swallow. 'I'm going to the bathroom,' he said.

'Don't be long, I need you in the meeting.'

How did Jordi do it to him? He had nearly burst out crying with anger and frustration. He splashed his face with cold water, and looked at himself in the mirror, dripping. The work wasn't that earth shaking—it was simple, self-evident. Maybe Jordi was ashamed of it, it was certainly a lot simpler than most of the other papers—he couldn't understand half of them. Jordi was good at talk, a real bull-shitter, but when it mattered, where it hurt, he didn't deliver.

He thinks it's crap, thought David. Suspicion bloomed like cancer. He's just using me, who does he think I am!

In the meeting Jordi smiled at him across the table as though nothing had happened.

'I'm still not clear how we're financing this,' said Luis Carlos.

'It's self-financing,' said Jordi. 'The conference fees will cover it.'

'All the costs? How many people have booked?'

Jordi stood, belly thrust forward, left hand fiddling with the enormous brass buckle of his belt.

He must be nervous, thought David, enjoying his discomfort.

'The airfares, ten of them coming. The accommodation: the Tamanaco is not cheap. Parque Central, the most expensive conference centre in town. And now you are talking of taking them to the Amazonas, all expenses paid,' said Luis Carlos quietly.

'We must arrange a trip for them. So they can see something of the interior—Angel's Falls—it's one of the wonders of the world,' said Jordi, grandly waving his arms.

'Sure, but who is going to pay for all this. Surely you don't expect the conference fees to cover it all?' asked Luis Carlos.

'We agreed at the start of this that I was organising the conference, that I would have a free hand,' said Jordi.

'Within limits,' said Hugo.

'What were they then?' said Jordi glowering at Hugo. The others looked down.

'That there would be no call on our central fund,' said Luis Carlos.

'It's not coming out of the central fund,' he sneered. 'Manuel is going to bank-roll the lot.'

Only Luis Carlos seemed unmoved, almost as though he had anticipated the news. No one spoke.

Luis Carlos keeps so still, thought David. Cold and dangerous like a hidden crevasse. And Jordi, open like an oven door. But Jordi wasn't open. He was cunning and devious.

'And what does Manuel want?' said Luis Carlos finally.

'Nothing!'

'What is nothing?'

'I tell you he doesn't want anything. He's interested in sponsoring the conference.'

Luis Carlos was unconvinced. 'Tell us about the results of David's model and the paper you are giving about the Capital Region.'

'It's not finished,' said Jordi.

'Yes, but the outline, the thrust of the argument. Which alternative comes out the best? David?'

'I'm not sure we need a computer model to tell us,' said David.

'Nothing can stop the growth of the capital,' interrupted Jordi. 'It's the same throughout the world—London, New York, Paris.'

'Yes, we've heard all that before,' said Luis Carlos. 'But

what does the model tell us?'

'It all depends which factors you choose to do the evaluation.'

'The model demonstrates that the Tuy is the logical place for expansion,' said Jordi.

'Our agreed policy is to encourage development in the regions,' said Luis Carlos.

'Zulia and Falcon, Oriente, Guyana and los Andes, they are all crying out for development,' said Hugo.

'The evaluation model is not designed to work at a regional level, it is supposed to compare proposals within a city,' said David.

'But you could use it to compare different cities?'

'Yes.'

'And you've been running it for the Capital Region,' said Luis Carlos.

'In a sense, in the future say, one might envisage the whole region operating as a unified metropolis,' said David.

'And?' said Luis Carlos.

David could feel Jordi staring at him, that he had their attention. He was upset and confused. Clearly Jordi had planned to present a paper based on their work without consulting him. Why, what was going on? He looked round the table—they were all watching him, waiting to hear what he had to say. Alejandro was sucking the end of a pencil and Luis Carlos had his elbows on the table, his fingers on his lips in the habitual steeple. Jordi was fiddling with his lighter, turning it over and over in his hand. David was surprised to see how discomfited he looked. He wished Chelo was there. He needed her support, her logical perspective.

'I agree with Jordi,' he began, 'Caracas will continue to

grow. But so will the regions if there is sufficient investment. But as to the development of the Tuy, I'm not sure. You know I went there last month. It's just dry scrubland. Santa Teresa and Santa Lucia, they're sleepy villages and there's a bit of light industry near the autopista.

'I spent the night there, took a sleeping bag and slept out in a field under a bit of thorn scrub. The thing is it's so hot. At its highest it is only 200 metres and in August and September there is damn all wind—I've checked with the meteorological office.'

He looked at Jordi before continuing. Jordi was looking out of the window, ignoring him. 'Guarenas is much higher and gets the same strong easterly breeze that we get here. And of course it's nearer. Even after they build both autopistas the Tuy will still be over twice the distance. And there are other factors that I'm still researching'

'So you favour Guarenas?' said Luis Carlos, smiling.

'Yes, and I think commerce and residents might too.'

'Manuel has told me that MOP are planning a new autopista direct from Tuy to Lagunillas,' said Jordi.

'I'm surprised at Manuel—all that traffic past his front gate,' said Luis Carlos. 'My work makes the case for regional investment. There will be important people at this conference, people we need to convince. The press and television will come. We are talking about the next five year economic plan for the nation, not Manuel and his cronies making a killing on a bit of cow pasture in the Tuy!'

'I resent that,' said Jordi.

'Then I retract it,' smirked Luis Carlos.

Jordi seemed to pull himself together. Outnumbered, still he refused to give in. 'We can do both,' he said. 'Regional investment and growth of the metropolis, they are both possible with the increase in oil revenue. With OPEC we can ask what we want. Our national product will double, treble even.'

'That is a dangerous policy if I may say so. The West will not just lie down and take it,' said Luis Carlos.

'What can they do? They have to have the oil.'

'We shall see,' said Luis Carlos. 'The conference will have to go ahead, on the understanding of course that you are personally liable for any shortfall in funding. And after ... I've been talking to Americo about how we might reorganise the unit.'

Jordi looked round the table, including David in his contempt, and slammed out of the room.

15

About five, much to David's surprise, Jordi rang and invited him to go for a drink.

They sat on the same high stools at the bar they had been to when he had first arrived. They were on their fourth beer. David was feeling mellow, remembering friends in England, hearing about Jordi's work there. He'd felt at odds with Jordi earlier, but his resentment had evaporated as Jordi's warmth and nostalgia had won him over.

'How's your love life?' asked Jordi.

'What?'

'Don't be so defensive.'

'I'm not being defensive.'

'To get a woman to sleep with you, it's either easy or impossible,' said Jordi, loosening his belt. 'They take the decision, subconsciously, maybe, but it's their decision nonetheless. Something turns them on, something clicks inside, and they decide they have to have you. Not that they don't think about it a lot, they do. But it doesn't necessarily tip over into reality or action. They like to keep it as a fantasy. It's less threatening that way.'

David said nothing.

'All you have to do, if you've clicked, is invite them for lunch or something—set up the situation. Take the first step and they'll do the rest.

'What you can't do is ask a woman to decide intellectually or to take responsibility. That's your job. They want to fall into your arms: they want to be taken. Kiss them on the neck, their ears, their eyes. Talk to them—tell them the moon and the stars. You can't overdo it. But you can't say "let's screw". They don't take a cold decision like men do—unless they're like Aurora!'

Jordi must be drunk, he thought, why didn't he mind his own bloody business. 'I don't understand what you are talking about,' he said.

'It happens quick. If she wants you, and nothing happens, then she puts you in her fantasy collection, and there's nothing you can do about it. She'll flirt with you, but suggest you fuck and you can forget it.'

'What about affection, friendship, love?'

'Love? who's talking about love?'

'I thought we were talking about the closest relationship between two people.'

'I'm talking about screwing.'

'I don't screw around.'

'Don't tell me you're thinking of getting married!'

David wondered if he knew about his relationship with

Chelo.

'I'd have thought you'd relish your freedom, have a fling, sow your wild oats. I'm envious. You don't want to settle down until you're thirty or forty.'

David thought of leaving. Jordi put his hand on David's arm to stop him.

'I asked you here so we could talk. I've been looking at the results—you said you had introduced some new criteria.'

'I've been talking to someone about landscape. The Tuy is in a basin, as you know. The meteorological data shows very high temperatures from June to November, 35° and more, and low wind speeds. It's an inferno.'

'In the dry season!—it's like that in the interior.'

'Sure it's hot and dry, but not this bad!'

'So?'

'Tabori says you can use trees to funnel what wind there is, and have it flow over water, which would help cooling. But it wouldn't be enough.'

'The Tuy results need to be better.'

You mean you want me to make them look better, thought David. 'On the face of it the Tuy is not a good site for a new city. In fact it's a lousy site.'

'Why? What's wrong with it?'

'It's baking hot for six months of the year and, this is the clincher, there's a major fault line running along its main axis.'

'There are fault lines all over. All new buildings are designed to resist earthquakes.'

'Not this sort of fault. The geologists at Creole say they wouldn't build a hencoop on it. I'm trying to get more data.' He wondered too if Jordi knew he had spent the night there

228

with Chelo.

'We've been asked to run the model and test alternatives. I don't think we have to go into this sort of detail,' said Jordi.

'Oh yes we do.'

'It's not our job, the geologists are in charge of that.'

'It's part of the evaluation.'

'Manuel just wants us to compare accessibility and land availability.'

'Accessibility to what?'

'To markets, labour, employment.'

'That biases everything towards the capital. That's why the model is so limited.'

'The capital is a magnet, in any country you want to name.'

'That's the point—it's too congested,' David argued.

'Yes, but the amount of land available for development compensates for that.'

'But you have to weight the quality of the land.'

'How?'

'With this data. You take away the land the geologists say is too dangerous to build on, there's also an area of sink holes, and then you weight by quality of life.'

'What? How the hell do you measure that?'

'Environmental factors principally.'

'And?'

'Using the set of criteria I've developed the Tuy comes out far and away the worst.'

'Why didn't you use the list of criteria I sent you?' asked Jordi belligerently.

'I decided that they were inadequate.'

'You had no authority. Who's running this unit? I'm in

charge here.'

'I thought we were a team.'

'Like hell!'

'You weren't here. You told me to get on with it,' said David, hearing the strain in his own voice as he tried to keep cool and not get angry.

'I told you to program it and run it like I told you, with the data I sent, not to go off on a tangent of your own.'

'The data you sent were wrong. The land areas—we re-calculated them. Only a fifth of the area you gave us in the Tuy can actually be developed.'

'You're not getting away with this. We'll have to redo it. Manuel mustn't see this stuff. And I'm telling you, I want you to keep your mouth shut about all this.'

David got up and walked out.

§

It didn't take long, she was dressed, ready. She had been sitting on the divan all afternoon, feet crossed, reading and rereading the same page of a novel, trying to concentrate. She went to the bathroom and passed a brush through her hair. She hesitated a moment, her fingers playing with the glass stopper, then, with a soft sad sigh, she swept the curls from her neck and touched the perfume to her skin.

She climbed the marble steps and, as always, before her outstretched hand could push the heavy doors, Sebastian opened them and greeted her.

'Senorita Consuela! Good-evening.'

'Good-evening, Sebastian. How are you, how have you

been keeping.'

'Well. And you, Senorita, is all well with you?'

'I'm meeting Jordi. I'll be in the library when he comes.'

This was her father's old club. They used to come here as a family to concerts in the sala below and the library had always been her favourite room. As a treat, her father used to stop in the corridor a few minutes to allow her to look through the glass doors. Evening was the best time: the green lamps over the polished tables cast twinkling reflections in the glass fronted cabinets.

Now she moved through the glass doors from one room to the next, trying not to disturb the few readers' study. As a child it had seemed a fairy-tale palace and she imagined herself a princess walking down endless candle-lit corridors to the ballroom at the end. She had been here infrequently in the last few years since her father died. But the familiarity of the place: the smell of the leather chairs and furniture polish, the dying sun through the stained glass windows, was soothing now as she sat and waited.

'Let's go through to the restaurant. I'm starving,' boomed Jordi from the doorway. Heads lifted in disapproval.

Jordi ordered an arepa with chunks of roast pork. He hummed as he ate, clutching the bun in both hands. 'I don't trust anyone any more,' he said. She took one of his cigarettes and turned to blow the smoke away from him.

'And you and Mariella?' He didn't answer. 'You need her. It's not just the money. It's taken me until now to realise; you feed on each other's inadequacy. I'm too good for you, too difficult to live up to. I thought I … but you don't need me in that way.'

He shrugged and said, 'I need your help at the university,

at least until after the conference.'

'What happened today?'

'David tackled me about giving a paper.'

'And?'

'I'd forgotten to tell him I'd already written it. Then it came out in the meeting. They'd all ganged up with Luis Carlos ... and he sided with them. I needed you and Alejandro. Where the hell were you?'

'At home.'

'When I think what I've done for him'

'Don't you feel you've let him down?'

'I was never sold on this policy of regionalization. Even in London. Anyway Luis Carlos can look after himself.'

'No, David!'

'Felix is talking about inviting him to Cambridge. He's interested in the sales potential of the evaluation work. That was my idea you know!'

'Why's Felix involved?'

'Manuel needs the kudos of his consultancy work to swing things at the congressional hearing.'

'What will happen to David?'

'I got him his job here, everything. He can't just swan off and work for Felix. We'd be giving him the work on a plate. I need it to bargain with. He owes me.'

'He's worked hard for you—while you were away—collecting all the data you needed to run the model.'

'He was festering in England. He would never have amounted to anything. I rescued him from oblivion.'

'That's not the way he tells it. He enjoyed his job there, he liked the man he worked for. They respected each other.'

'He was retiring, it was a dead end—he told me. He

needed the push. Why else did he come?'

'He came for you. Perhaps it would have been better if he'd stopped there. He would have got another job.'

'Can we go back to your place?'

'It's over Jordi.'

'It's David isn't it?'

'No. When you went to England with Mariella—I would have gone with you.'

'You never said.'

'You never asked.'

'You're in love with him.'

'I'm fond of him.'

'He's a fool. Forget about him, let me come back with you, just this one time—I need you!'

'No, not any more. You have to leave me alone now.' Jordi stormed out. She sat awhile collecting herself. She felt immense relief now it was finished and an intense desire to be alone.

David had rung repeatedly since he got home but there was no reply. He was hungry, there was no food in the house and he had hoped to invite her out to eat. Finally the phone was answered.

She didn't want to go out again, she was tired. Could he come round to her flat then: he had to talk. Finally she agreed to meet him at Nueva Esparta, the Spanish bar behind Sabana Grande.

The place was packed and Chelo was nowhere to be seen. He felt agitated and hovered in the doorway, undecided whether to wait outside or crush his way to the bar. A party of students made a move to leave and he grabbed one of the tables.

The room was long and narrow and the bar ran along one wall. There were plates of Spanish tortilla and smoked hams hung from hooks in the ceiling. The menu, chalked on a board behind the bar, was extensive. His mouth watered. Where was she? He tried to listen in on the conversation at the next table but the men there were talking in Catalan or Basque, and he couldn't understand what they were saying.

'Why did we have to meet here?—it's too smoky and noisy,' he complained as soon as she arrived.

'I don't have to stay. It was you insisted we meet and you said you were hungry. I wanted to go to bed early.'

The bar was agreeable enough, but his intense feeling of irritation with Jordi transmitted itself to the muscles across his shoulders and he wished he could slough off the flesh and be rid of it. He closed his eyes and saw Chelo's head in silhouette, blood red, then soft Chinese green.

'I'm sorry,' he said at last.

'What's wrong?'

'I had a row with Jordi.'

'Rows with Jordi are like tropical storms: violent but soon past.'

'I can't take it, I'm not like that.'

'Do you bear a grudge?'

'Maybe. I hadn't thought of it like that. I just think people should be more careful with each other.'

'What do you mean?'

'They should be more considerate, more conscious of what they say to each other, of the words they use that can never be unsaid.' He told her about the meeting in the morning and about Jordi and the row with Luis Carlos.

She said, 'So you're feeling guilty?'

'Why should I feel guilty?'

'Because you owe him loyalty.'

'Why weren't you there then?' he asked.

'Don't shout at me!'

'I wasn't.'

'Don't you know what's going on? They're pushing Jordi out. It was inevitable from the beginning, of course. He isn't the type to run things by consensus and anyway Luis Carlos is too sharp. Jordi needs to be leader.'

'He leads with his gut!'

'Unlike you who lead with the chin! Yes, he's got guts. You know he's started a new company?'

'How's he done that?'

'With backing from his father-in-law. He's going to make a fortune.'

'I thought he was passionate about the research, that he wanted power to change things.'

'He's passionate about everything. Anyway, money is power ... not just here, the world over.'

'Luis Carlos despises money.'

'He can afford to, his family is one of the richest in the country.'

'But Jordi's family is wealthy.'

'He wants more.'

All this talk of money unnerved him. 'What about my paper, the paper I wanted to read at the conference?'

'So?'

'Jordi told me I couldn't read it, that I wasn't in the programme. He didn't tell me he'd written it already.'

'Jordi has plans of his own. There is a lot at stake in all

this.'

'I'm not interested,' said David. 'It's important that the development goes ahead in the right place. Jordi's paper is just a sales promotion for the Tuy.'

'You're peeved he hasn't included your paper,' said Chelo.

'Sure, but people are going to have to live there if it gets built. I have a responsibility—to tell the truth.'

'Come back to the flat. It's too noisy here.'

They pushed their way through the crowded bar and reached the pavement.

'Have you got your car?' he asked.

'No, I came by taxi.'

They reached her apartment and he parked. 'Come on then,' she said, laughing, suddenly feeling light-headed after the wine and the relief of breaking with Jordi.

'I'm not sure I want to. I want to be on my own. Maybe I should go home and sleep it off.'

'Come in—have a drink. I'll put on some music and cheer you up.' She grabbed the keys out of the ignition, skipped out and started to dance round the car park, singing at the top of her voice. He felt embarrassed.

'Come on,' she shouted. 'It's fun.'

'Chelo! I want the keys back. I want to go home.'

'Don't be a kill-joy, don't be a kill-joy,' she sang.

This is ridiculous, he thought. What am I doing here. 'Give me the keys,' he yelled.

'Come and get them,' she sang. He leapt out of the jeep and chased her across the car park. He grabbed her by the shoulders and she swung into his arms, kissing him.

'Don't mess about. Give me the keys.' She handed them to him, suddenly deflated. He walked back to the car and climbed in. She came to the passenger window and leaned in.

'Please come in,' she said.

'I have to go. I don't know why.' He had to go home and think it through quietly, what was happening, what it was all about, and what he should do. He loved Chelo. He looked at her face. He wanted to reach out and stroke her cheek, to run his hand through her hair, but his arm wouldn't move. He reached for the ignition.

'You don't know do you? she said. 'All this time you've been here—hasn't anybody told you!'

'What haven't they told me? What are you talking about?'

'Jordi! I'm talking about Jordi and me.'

David felt cold.

'I was Jordi's mistress.'

My god! I don't believe this, he thought. Jordi! Jordi and Chelo! What a fool he'd been. A couple of hours ago they'd been out together, drinking like old buddies. Jordi was giving him advice on lovemaking, telling him how to pull women! He felt sick. Jealousy roared through him like a tidal wave. Red hot, then cold, like a fever. 'I don't understand what you're telling me,' he said.

'That's where I was earlier, seeing Jordi. He rang and said he had to see me, and I went, like I always do. I'm telling you because it's over, finished!'

'You and Jordi … What about us?'

'Jordi's been away.'

'I know, you don't have to tell me that. So you needed someone to fill in for him, while he was away. But now he's back …'

'It's not like that! Listen … ' She opened the door and got in.

'Tell me what it's like? Go on, tell me! What's it like with Jordi? What does he do for you that I can't?'

She burst out crying. He was too angry to hold her.

'I love you,' she whispered.

'To think I trusted him. What made you do it—living like this?'

'When dad died there was nothing left. The house was a ruin. We had to sell to pay the debts. I couldn't go to university like you, able to get a good job, go anywhere. I haven't got a degree like the rest of you.'

'Your clothes, your jewellery? I thought you were rich, that you came from a wealthy family. I don't get it. You wear such expensive clothes, and this apartment—'

'I love beautiful things: I spend all my salary. The apartment—Jordi paid for it. It's in his name. He paid the deposit.'

'My god!'

'You don't know how difficult it is … how difficult it is to buy a place of your own, with no money.'

'Jordi pays!'

'He paid the deposit. The flat's mine: I make the monthly payments.'

'Have you no pride?'

'I loved Jordi. I fell in love with him almost as soon as we met again as adults. I'd never met anyone else like him. He literally swept me off my feet. We were at a dance …'

'I don't want to know! What the hell are you doing at the university, working with him?'

'He got me the job in the unit when it was first formed. I was working for the rector, but I had no qualifications and the pay wasn't very good.'

'But you're intelligent.'

'That doesn't count.'

'So Jordi bought this place.'

'Do you want a drink?'

'No! I don't want to go in there again.'

She lit a cigarette. Her hand shook.

Why couldn't he put his arm round her. She needed comfort, warmth, a shoulder to cry on. He felt trapped. Steel bands tightened around his chest, squeezing the breath out of him. He was so angry he could scream. Shit! Why? Why couldn't she have left him alone! 'I didn't know you were Jordi's woman,' he said. He felt like crying, but the tears didn't come. 'I can't see it. How could you fall for Jordi … when he was married.'

'There is a sensitive side to Jordi. My head doesn't rule my heart—sometimes I wish it did.'

'Why?' he demanded. Why had she chosen Jordi? Why was this happening to him? Why did he feel so hurt? Thousands of whys.

'Why what? Open your eyes, let your feelings out. Feel! feel me! Here take my hand. I'm warm, flesh and blood—a woman. Yours!'

'You're Jordi's. I'm not sharing you!'

'Jordi and I are finished.'

'Why didn't you marry him?'

'He was already married, to Mariella.'

'He could have left her. They have no children.'

'He married her for her money. Now he needs her father to bank-roll his new company.'

'And he wants you too. A greedy man.' Jealous bile rose into his mouth and threatened to choke him, pure poison. 'I don't want someone else's women!' he said, wanting to lash out, knowing he didn't mean it.

'What d'you expect: a seventeen-year-old virgin!' she yelled back at him.

'No!'

'It's you and Jordi—you're jealous; we had something you weren't part of.'

'Jordi's had you! Hasn't he?'

'I'm shop-soiled, second-hand; is that what you're saying? Well get out then, if that's what you feel, I don't want you. I don't want to see you again.' She threw open the door and ran to the building. He got out to follow her and stopped. Why had he said that? he didn't mean it—he could have cut out his tongue. She'd gone; it was too late. He could go in, apologise, hold her and tell her he loved her. Instead he turned and started walking, leaving the jeep where it was in the car park.

He'd been walking for hours. His feet hurt. His body ached with fatigue. Up and down, one avenue after another. Lights from cars, shop windows blazing. People of the night, a different world: bleak, black, despairing.

He felt excluded—jealous! Jordi'd gone off to England and left him. And now he'd found out that Chelo and Jordi had been lovers. He was just a temporary substitute while Jordi was away. Everything he believed in seemed to have been washed away. So much for his new life here! Jordi was a self-seeking bastard. How could he have been so blind?

There was a cinema advertising all-night movies. He paid without thinking and went in. The film was in French. He had come in halfway through and couldn't follow the plot. He felt himself crying; great salty tears running down his cheeks and into his mouth. He felt abandoned, alone. One thing he vowed—he wouldn't let it happen again.

There were empty spaces inside him. It was as if all his energy disappeared down a black hole, swallowing his hopes and desires and releasing nothing back. The enormous skin drum in his head went on beating, in slow motion, although hardly a whisper could be heard. It felt as if it would go on and on, without explanation, past exhaustion, until only the rhythm of the beating provided any reason for living.

Why did this always happen? Why couldn't he tell her? about how he felt and what he wanted? The only way he could cope was to ignore his feelings. But the black void inside him grew, cold and impersonal.

He began to laugh. It was ridiculous, pathetic. What a production! He had to pull himself together.

He reached home as it got light and fell asleep fully dressed. He slept on long after it was time to get up for work; the breeze billowed the curtains into the room, but he didn't wake until much later.

16

They sat looking back at the city unfolding like a map as they ascended. The English were fascinated by the motorway ribbons and skyscrapers and spent the time trying to identify their hotel and the university.

He'd been detailed to organise Wednesday evening and had booked a table at the fish restaurant Jordi had taken him to on his first night. Half of the party had been persuaded to travel to the beach over the mountain by cable-car. The rest had gone by road.

He hadn't been involved in greeting the English when they arrived. He'd also missed the formal reception when the guests had been introduced to the dean and members of the faculty. His first contact had been at the beach at the Macuto Sheraton.

David's eyes followed the red scars of new development

on the hills to the south where they were building new homes for the rich. Soon there would be houses as far as the eye could see. The shadow of the car lengthened on the hillside below them. There were gasps when the car fell as it left the last pylon to cross the deep chasm before the steep haul to the summit.

David had only ever been here before on a busy weekend when the place bustled with sightseers. Now the station was deserted and they had to wait for the last car going down to the beach. It was cold sitting on the wooden benches and the conversation became louder and more hearty as the three English tried to keep their spirits up. He hoped he'd got it right. There was supposed to be a car but Alejandro had been sceptical about the reliability of the service. The English all had light shoes, he noticed and it would be a cold night.

A man in work-clothes with a canvas bag over his shoulder arrived. David asked him if there was a car due and he said yes, he was going home on it.

The car pulled out of the confines of the station and the ground fell away below them as they descended into the gathering gloom. Looking back to the dark ridge was like looking up at the rim of a cauldron full of molten metal or a volcano about to erupt such was the glow from the light of the city beyond. Just below the ridge there was a horizontal band of mist cut clean above and below as if by a plasterer's trowel. Down, towards the beach, they could see the twinkling lights of San Jose de Galipan, the tiny hamlet of flower growers. The English speculated about the building of the cableway. The brass plate in the car named an Austrian engineering company. David sat in a corner and listened to their confident voices, answering the questions addressed to him, but otherwise keeping quiet. They identified the towers of the service cable and could just see the flat goods waggon stationary on its invisible thread. Snaking between the towers there was a narrow mule track, ascending and descending the verdant ridges, an endless squiggle, as if drawn in felt-tip by an enthusiastic child. The main pylons, carrying the cables their car hung from, were much more widely spaced, effortlessly spanning the dizzying void. The car slid down into the gloom.

We'll be down in ten minutes—Chelo and the others should be there by now, he was thinking. The car came to a quiet halt. They were suspended in mid-air and dimly they could just see the ground perhaps five or six hundred feet below. It was quite dark, the lights of the littoral obscured by the bank of low cloud. The car swung gently in the breeze. Conversation ceased.

'Jordi was right when he said we'd get stuck up here,' said Crispin. They all laughed and the tension broke.

'What happens now?'

'We wait—they're probably disconnecting the previous car,' said David. A minute or so later the car moved.

The English were quiet now, savouring the atmosphere of the place. This is what space travel must be like, he thought. It reminded him of a drawing, in a book about relativity, of a man looking out of a spaceship at a passing rocket and wondering whether he was being overtaken or going backwards. But for the hum of the cable over the guide-wheels as they approached a pylon and the click-click as the car slid over the guides it was impossible to know that they were moving.

One of Jordi's new assistants met them and drove them

to the restaurant. The party had already filled one of the big tables. He could hear Felix's voice, penetrating, commanding, with a foreign cadence. He saw Chelo, and then Jordi, sitting near her, looking relaxed, expansive. Evidently Luis Carlos hadn't come, he hated socialising and resented the whole idea of the conference anyway.

David guided his party to a table next to the water and helped them order. The restaurant seemed changed, larger somehow or was it that he now noticed more detail—how the bleached timber of the roof beams fitted together with crude lap joints, the peeling paintwork. For some inexplicable reason he felt a sudden rush of affection for the effrontery of the place, for the cock-eyedness of it all.

He'd changed in the eighteen months he'd been here. He had only to observe the English to see how stiff he'd been. Crispin, uncomfortable in his dove-grey tropical suit, doubtless bought for the trip. It was now creased and had an oily fish stain on the lapel that he dabbed at constantly with a paper napkin. Richard in pin-stripe shirt and wool socks, dark jacket trailing from the back of his chair on the sandy floor, his only concession the removal of his tie. Had he really been this English? Jordi must have thought him a pain—new jacket, shiny shoes. Things had happened to him during his time here, changes of which he was only dimly aware.

It was not so much that his own values had been undermined, if anything they had been strengthened, but previously he had been disposed to believe the best of people. From now on he would try not to pin his own needs onto others, not believe promises that flattered his secret hopes. He hadn't changed that much, he realised. As his dad used to say, when he came home and found David's mum had bought a load of new brushes from the door-to-door salesman: she was always a sucker for a good salesman.

He still didn't fully understand what was going on between Manuel and Jordi. Maybe they stood to make a lot of money, but it did not concern him. It was part of life here, the way of the world. He did not want to know about it, it did not affect him. He had just got to do his job as well as he could and try and ignore the rest. But that was easier said than done when he was involved, when his work was part of the plot.

Felix came over and introduced himself. 'Have you thought about coming back to Britain or are you planning to stay here? ' asked Felix.

'I haven't thought about it,' he said.

'You're not planning to settle here are you?' said Crispin.

'When I left England I had no fixed ideas. I didn't know what was going to happen … it was like starting afresh. In any event I thought I'd stay a couple of years—it takes that long to learn the language and see the country properly.'

'How is your Spanish?' asked Felix.

'Sounded all right to me,' said Crispin.

'I was thrown in at the deep end but it took six months to be able to get by.'

'The reason I asked about your Spanish was that I may need some help here, on the ground so to speak,' said Felix, leaning across the table to talk to him. 'I've been approached by someone in the Development Corporation for the Andes, the director actually. He is at the conference and has asked us to tender for some work. I wonder if you'd be interested?'

'What does it involve?'

'Going to Merida, talking to people, finding out what they think they want exactly,' said Felix.

Crispin and Richard said they wanted to get to bed. David asked if someone could drive them back. Jordi threw him his keys.

They had just gone through the empty tollbooths at the start of the autopista when there was a whistle. David looked in the driving mirror and saw soldiers run into the road behind, drop to one knee and level their machine guns at him. Instinctively he braked, pulled the speeding vehicle round in a sharp U-turn and drove back to the sentry post. Somehow he had never realised this was a police checkpoint, everyone always sped through. One of the sentries opened the car door and motioned them out with the point of his gun. The corporal examined their papers. David told them they were important speakers at a government conference. Gradually the militia lost interest; only the traffic cop refused to let them go.

'What does the obnoxious little man want,' asked Crispin.

The man was waving his notebook, saying they had gone through a roadblock without slowing and were driving the wrong way down the autopista.

'What's going on?' asked Crispin.

'It seems there was a robbery in Maiquetia and they had a report of a vehicle like this on the radio. They thought they'd caught us making our escape.'

Another car stopped and Alejandro got out. He listened to what the cop had to say, smiled and suggested they settle it in the sentry post. Crispin said: 'He's going to bribe him. It's all the same in these Latin American countries.'

They got in the cars and David turned round carefully, feeling shaken by the incident.

'What happened, why did they let us go,' asked Crispin.

'Alejandro told the cop that his father was a general who would have his balls cut off if he didn't stop playing the smart-arse,' said David.

§

David lay on a canvas lounger, watching a little boy and girl jumping in the deep end and doggy-paddling across the corner of the pool, gradually increasing the distance as their confidence grew. Then, as the toddler climbed the ladder to the high diving board, David noticed his mother had fallen asleep.

The boy reached the end of the ten metre board: he looked tiny. David had to screw his eyes against the sun; not daring to look, unable to take his eyes off him. He jumped, and seemed to fall forever. There was a splash, he disappeared and then, magically, bobbed up like a cork. He was out of the water and climbing again, calling to his sister to come too.

Most afternoons the English spent at the pool. The Tamanaco was the best hotel in town—a pyramid covered in vegetation on a hill at the end of Avenida las Mercedes. The department was empty and there was little for him to do. Chelo was busy at the conference hall, providing a calm centre in the chaos. It was a big production—in the foyer outside the large theatre there were three copiers and at least a dozen typists churning out bilingual transcripts—and Jordi striding about like a general. David found the sessions boring.

Everyone else appeared to be drunk and having a great time. At the reception last night, Richard had peed into a potted palm in the corridor of the hotel. Standing next to him, David had watched it appear from under the pot and spread over the red carpet as guests came out of the dining room toward them. Crispin had worn a Mickey Mouse T-shirt to the reception, stayed out every night and done the first slot in the morning on pills. Was everyone mad or had he dreamt it.

Unexpectedly, Aurora appeared, put her towel on the grass and lay down next to him. She had been at the reception, looking sensational in a black wool dress, hair tied back—with Americo—the first time he had seen her for ages. David introduced her to Richard and Crispin.

"Would you give me a lift?' she asked.

'Where to?'

'Sebucan, it's not far out of your way.'

'See you,' said Richard.

As they pulled out of the car park, Jordi and Chelo were just arriving.

'Enjoy yourselves,' shouted Jordi leaning out of the window and waving a hairy arm at them.

At her home, a large quinta in a quiet street, she invited him in. Her breasts showed through her unbuttoned shirt.

'No, thank you, but no,' he said. She leant across the bench seat and kissed the corner of his mouth.

'Goodbye then, David.'

He watched while she opened the iron gate, then drove away.

§

That night he dreamt he was on an expedition with a group of armed men to the Caroni River. There were waterfalls, a mile wide, rising in terrace upon terrace and producing a great mist. The mist created hundreds of rainbows festooning the falls in colour and light like immense illuminations.

The scene changed. They left the boats and marched across the flood plain, climbing more and more steeply through dense forest, hacking a way through the rotting vegetation. It rained incessantly and they were plagued by clouds of insects.

Near a great rock they caught sight of a woman on a pale horse with a bow slung across her naked chest. She looked back at them, then disappeared round a shoulder in the mountain. They had all laughed.

The march became easier once they reached the upland savanna. They forded swollen rivers chest deep and men and horses were washed away and drowned or swept over rapids. Finally they caught sight of the table mountains. Occasionally, as they hauled the pack-mules up the mountain slopes, they sighted women warriors in the distance.

They camped under the cliffs where the mountain came to a point like the prow of a great battleship. The rock was gold in the evening light. A waterfall spouted out from the face of the rock some way below the summit edge as if from a gargoyle in a thunderstorm. Morale was high as they pitched camp.

The women came on them in the night. Some were killed in their sleep, only one man escaped.

He ran for the river, the women in hot pursuit. He clambered down the rocks all slippy in the spray and reached the waters edge but the river was too deep and fast. He could hear them behind him, cursing as they slid. In the moonlight he saw a path and followed it. It lead upstream to where a waterfall curved across the flood forming an amphitheatre, trapping him. He pushed on in desperation and found a natural passageway behind the falls along a narrow ledge. The thundering water formed a curtain, the noise deafening. He was soaked instantly but raced on, congratulating himself on his escape. He clambered up the opposite bank and emerged over the rim to a ring of women with drawn bows. Strong arms gripped his biceps and he was lead away.

They tied him to a tree; his arms outstretched, the sharp buttress-like rib of the tree bore into his back and he felt he was being wracked. One of the warrior women, naked but for a thin string of pink coral beads round her waist, took his sword and thrust it into the coals of a fire. When she turned he saw it was Aurora.

The women danced and sang, glistening with sweat, ignoring him. He tried to break free but the rope was tied too well. He watched them by the light of the fire and tried to divine meaning in their movements and the shapes their dancing made. Women's magic against the mechanics of men, wooden bow against sharpened steel.

He could see his sword glowing in the fire, and Aurora dancing. As if reading his mind she leapt and pulled it free, running at him, yelling. He wanted to shout: No! this is wrong. It wasn't meant to be like this, this split between man and woman. We are supposed to be one: to touch, hold, love; not to torture and maim each other. We're on the same side, he wanted to shout, but his mouth was as dry as sand and no words would come out. He stared, fascinated, at the rushing blade, pulsating cherry red. As the tip touched his chest a tall woman appeared from the shadows and the women turned in unison. It was Chelo.

His eyes said: Look at me! I'm flesh and blood like you.

No! Men are beasts, she said. You will betray us, you will destroy us; but we won't let you. She dropped her hand and Aurora laid the red steel on his eyes and he woke screaming.

The sheet was wrapped round him in a sweaty rope, his back was a fiery knot of pain and his chest slick slippy. He got to his feet, shaking, and staggered to the bathroom in the dark, struggling to remember the dream.

§

After the conference Jordi was seen less and less in the unit; then Chelo left, having got a job in Conahotu, the Tourist Board. The workload increased as work came in from Luis Carlos's contacts in OMPU.

Manuel asked to see David at the Ministry. 'I've had this letter from the Minister of Foreign Relations requesting the loan of your services as a climber,' Manuel said, peering over the top of his heavy black spectacles.

David had met a Dr Perez at the excursion club who had invited him on a trip to mark the frontier and he jumped at the chance to get away.

'What does it involve? Why has the Frontiers Commission asked for you?'

'I'm a rock climber—the section of frontier they are working on has a lot of cliffs and they want me along for technical support.' That should do it, he thought. Keep it vague; there wasn't much else he could do, he hadn't been given any details.

'Will this interfere with the evaluation work on the Tuy?'

'No, the draft report is ready now. There's just a couple of things I need to do when I get back.'

'Well, I'm delighted,' said Manuel, beaming. 'How long will you be away?'

'Two weeks.'

'Fine. No problem. Jordi tells me that the evaluation's gone well.'

'I wanted to talk to you about that,' said David, steeling himself. 'I'm worried about the earthquake risk in the Tuy.'

'Yes, so Jordi tells me. I'm extremely grateful to you for doing such a thorough analysis. Of course we knew all about the fault line through the valley and our geologists have produced an exhaustive report. They will be working very closely with Jordi in the submission to the Congress.'

'Is the report available?'

'Naturally.'

'Could I have a copy?'

Manuel took a document from the top of a pile on his desk and pushed it across the table. 'I'm pleased you are doing such a thorough job,' he said. David wondered if he had misjudged him.

Later, back in the university, he was bent over his work when someone sat on the end of his desk and said hello. He looked up and saw Aurora.

'So this is where you've buried yourself,' she said with the same amused, almost scornful smile she had the first time he'd met her at Alberto's farm. She crossed her legs. He saw she was wearing a short, mini length, leather skirt.

'Hi! What are you doing here?'

'I thought you might like to take me out for lunch.'

'Sure, when?'

'How about now?'

'I'm busy.'

'Leave it, it won't run away. Come on!' She took his hand and pulled him up. He picked up his jacket from the back of the chair and shouted 'Ciào' to Alejandro. As they walked through the entrance lobby to the car park she slipped her arm through his.

'Your car or mine?' he asked.

'I came by taxi.'

'Where do you fancy?'

'You choose.'

He decided to take her to the Porton, in the old part of the city, where he'd been with Keith Pinder. He parked and she couldn't open the car door. He lent across to help and as his arm touched her breasts she let out a sigh. This is corny, he thought. What's she playing at?

During the meal she must have kicked off her shoes because suddenly he felt her bare toes rub his calf under his trouser leg. Hardly crediting it, he turned sideways and moved his leg away.

Leaving the restaurant they strolled down the hill.

'Walk me to the Urdaneta,' she said. 'You can go back for your car, I'll get a taxi.'

'Sure.'

'The beard, it suits you. When did you grow it?'

'While I was away. Why? Do you find it sexy?' he said, fingering the stubble.

'I think you're sexy with or without the beard', she said, completely unruffled. 'Come round this evening, I'll cook you something. I owe you a meal.'

'Where? When?'

'Early, after work. Here, this is the address.' She handed him a card printed in flowery script.

'What about Angel?'

'Don't worry, he's not invited.'

'But … '

'He's away on business. In the States, like always. Don't forget, about eight. See you. Ciào!' And off she strode, high heels clicking on the paving of the avenida.

Along the street there was a man selling stuff off a wooden tray slung from a strap round his neck. As he drew level he saw the Durex label and asked how much. He paid without thinking. Further on he realised he'd paid too much and opened the bag. It was a pack of a hundred. That'll keep me going a while, he thought wryly. What am I doing, he wondered, angry with himself.

He got to the address soon after eight. She let him in and kissed him on the mouth.

'Sit down,' she invited. There was a table laid for two and a bench seat.

'Whose is this place?'

'A friend's. A girl friend. She's away. She lets me borrow it. Let me take your jacket? You're sticky,' she said touching his back.

'It's hot outside, and the traffic was bad.'

'Before the rains it gets humid. Have a shower while I fix a meal.'

'Yes?'

'Go on. I won't bite. It's through there.'

He crossed through the bedroom. The low bed had a red tasselled cover. He tried to sing in the shower but his mouth felt dry and his voice was off-key. He turned the tap round to cold and threw back his head. The icy water brought a sense of sharp reality and again he questioned what the hell he was doing there.

He reached round the curtain for the towel but it wasn't on the rail. As he climbed out and she was standing in the doorway holding it. He dripped on the stone floor. 'Here,' she laughed, and threw the towel at his chest.

They ate in silence. He found it difficult to enjoy the ratatouille and rice she served.

'Are you on a special diet?' he asked.

'It's macrobiotic. Don't you like it?'

'It's fine.'

'I'm not the best cook in the world,' she giggled.

He felt queasy after the strudel and cream and wanted to brush his teeth to get rid of the taste of the ratatouille. He started to talk about work and Jordi, but she put her fingers to her lips and led him to the bedroom.

She unbuttoned his shirt and rubbed her fingers through his chest hair. He fumbled for the catch at the back of her skirt and it slipped to the ground. She stepped out of it and unbuckled his belt and unzipped him and pulled him down onto the bed.

'You won't need that!' She burst out laughing when he reached for a Durex.

'Come on, fuck me! Do it now!'

Without preamble she pulled him into her, grasping his buttocks in her fists.

'Harder,' she yelled, and he attacked her body as if he were clawing his way up an ice-cliff and his life depended on it.

'Good boy,' she crooned as he slumped beside her.

He slept and woke a while later. She was leaning on one elbow looking at him. She reached for his crotch and squeezed his balls. It hurt.

'I know, don't tell me, you want to join a monastery,' she said.

He lay back on the pillows and she knelt over him. There was sweat on her breasts and a sharp musky smell from her armpits. When he licked her she tasted salty and sweet. It was longer this time, and he pleased her.

Fastening his shirt buttons, looking out at the night, his sense of desolation and longing grew ever more bleak.

'Certain smells are so distinctive,' he said, realising how different Aurora smelt from Chelo.

'Like?'

'Mmm. Oh I don't know—the digestive biscuit smell of rugby kit. Climbing gear smells fishy.'

'Not very flattering,' she said, standing and looking at herself sideways in the mirror.

'Doesn't Angel mind?' he asked.

'Angel! He's impotent. He used to make me dress up, when we were first married. Ugh! the endless hours trying to make him excited enough. Now he's too busy making money to notice.' She unhooked a dressing gown from the back of the door, put it on and sat on the sofa with her legs crossed under her.

'What does he do?' asked David.

'He's into development. His family owns great tracts of land.'

'In the Tuy?'

'Yes there too. They're hoping to develop there with the proceeds from government expropriation.'

'Isn't there a problem with that—about what price should be paid?'

'That's right. It goes to the Congressional hearing.'

'Is it definite that they intend to go ahead and build a new city there?'

'According to Angel.'

'I'm supposed to be evaluating different alternatives for Manuel.'

'It's all fixed. That's for show. Drink?' she asked, getting up.

She was telling him his work was a sham, that it was cover for a government fraud. He couldn't make himself believe it, even though he'd known it intuitively for a long time.

Driving home he tossed the Durex out of the window. He felt guilty, as though he had betrayed Chelo. That was it, never again, he decided.

But he did see Aurora again and, as the days passed before the Frontiers trip, he found himself thinking about her with an obsession that accompanies relationships based solely on lust. He found it difficult to concentrate at work. He thought about her blouses with their gaping buttons and about her underwear, which was frilly and French. He thought about her gorgeous bum and how she told him she often went without pants. He thought about how she liked to look in the mirror while she fucked and he could hear the words she shouted at the height of passion. More and more images of her interposed themselves between him and his feelings about

Chelo. But he knew it was Chelo he wanted still.

After ten days of seeing Aurora every night he met Dr Perez at Maiquetia airport and flew south with the expedition. They were away nearly three weeks. To David it seemed much longer and he came back lean and tanned and somehow purged. Like breaking a bad habit, he managed to stop seeing her.

17

David knocked on Luis Carlos's door. The offices had been partitioned since Jordi had gone.

'Come!'

'David! Good to see you. How are you?' Luis Carlos's attempt at affability made him seem colder, more calculating.

'What do you want to see me about?' asked David, directly.

'Good!—your evaluation report. Why Guarenas?'

'There's plenty of land, it's nearer to the capital and it will develop anyway, with or without government investment. The climate is good and non-polluting industry could be sited there. And, as you know, I don't think that the Tuy should be developed as a city, it's too dangerous.'

'I'm not interested in the Tuy. It's your proposals about Guarenas that concern me. It does considerably better than the five regional centres the unit is advocating.'

'Why not develop both?'

'Because I believe oil revenue will drop dramatically and if the government is committed to creating a new city, regional programmes will be sacrificed.'

'Why not spread the investment proportionately?'

'You don't understand. We either win or lose; there can be no sensible compromise. There are powerful factions in Congress, one of which wants Guarenas developed with as much investment as they can squeeze, regardless. There is a lot of money in all this.'

'What's all this got to do with me?'

'We want you to change your report.'

'What do you mean? It's not finished yet.'

'I've seen the draft results. I want the final version to show at least three regional centres doing better than Guarenas.'

'What! You want me to fiddle the results?'

'Merely adjust the criteria, change the parameters. You can do it.'

'Sure I can do it, but I won't.' Luis Carlos might have good reasons for wanting to develop the regions—it would help create a more balanced economy less dependent on oil, and also mean a more equitable distribution of resources to the less rich parts of the country. But he'd be hanged if he was going to cheat. If you could just invent the data to suit yourself then all the hard work was meaningless.

'I thought you might say that,' said Luis Carlos, pursing his lips. 'From now on, Alejandro will be co-ordinating the evaluation work. I expect you'll give him any help he needs.'

'Like hell,' said David, straightening up in his chair, readying himself as if for a fight.

'I understand you're doing some work for Felix in Merida. I'd play my cards in that direction if I were you. Never know when you might need a job back home.'

Although David had not liked Luis Carlos much, up to now he had thought he was one of the good guys. Things were getting vicious. If only Chelo were still around, he would have someone to talk to, someone to help him see what to do.

David spent the next couple of days collating the information he'd gathered on earthquakes.

"Transverse breaks in the crust separate segments of overriding lithosphere," he read. "Many large cities in Latin America have developed in these zones of active crustal slippage. The degree of structural damage depends above all on the extent of soil liquefaction—where water-saturated layers of loose sediment are overlain by impermeable layers … Such earthquakes have repeatedly destroyed Guatemala City (9 times) and San Salvador (14 times), as well as razing Managua to the ground this year."

He opened the report Manuel had given him on the Tuy. A photo-geological study by Aeromapas Seravenca CA noted the presence of major faults, but concluded that they were unable to determine if the faults were active and that they needed to be studied further.

A soil study by Ingeneria de Suelos SA said: "The Tuy presents no difficulties for urban development." But in the appendix David found a note saying that bore holes 14, 17, and 18 showed liquid clays at a depth of four metres.

He went back to see Jerry's friend, a geologist with Creole, and showed him the soil survey.

'The crux of the matter is the nature of the subsoil,' said the geologist. 'Superficially the area is fine. There are two types of subsoil in the Tuy: alluvial terraces of red stone and clay, which don't pose any problems—the existing settlements of San Francisco, Santa Teresa, Santa Lucia and Cua are built on this; and gravel and conglomerate.'

'Is there a problem with this second type?'

'In the presence of underground water, yes.'

'How much of the area they propose to develop is of the second type?' asked David.

'At first sight, not much. Most of the bore holes were done in areas with the first type of subsoil. But if you examine the geological map of the valley it's clear that over half the area is composed of a 10-foot mantle overlying deep beds of slime and mud. Bore holes 14, 17 and 18 were in these areas.'

'What does that mean?'

'It means that anything built there is likely to collapse in an earthquake.'

Joselyn's office looked different. There were tourist posters on the walls, which made the place look like a travel agent's. But the same bored faces were working behind the same grey metal desks.

'*Olá, coma estas?*' He attempted the social niceties and failed in the face of her frigidity.

'Hello, Christopher Columbus!' Keith stood and gave a sardonic bow. Joselyn shrieked. David wondered what he was talking about.

'We heard about your voyage of discovery. Can't the Frontiers Commission find the way in their own country?'

said Keith.

'I was insurance, in case they needed a rock climber.'

'We're not interested in your tales of derring-do,' said Joselyn. 'What do you want?'

Fine, he didn't want to talk about the trip. Why risk spoiling a memory with cheap sarcasm. 'I came to ask for help,' he said.

'Help with what?' asked Joselyn, belligerently.

'I need some data on the Andes, from the MERCAVI survey.'

'I didn't think Luis Carlos was doing anything in the Andes,' said Joselyn.

'No, it's not for him. It's for Felix. He's doing some consultancy work for the Corporacion de los Andes. He met Carlos Garcia at the conference.'

'Our data aren't available for private consultancy work.'

'Why not?' he blurted out.

'It's not our job to help English consultants make money.'

'It's for the development corporation!'

'Then they can contact us direct.'

'I'm asking as a favour.'

'If it was mine to give, then fine. But we have to guard our professional integrity. We don't do private work or swan off for weeks buccaneering.'

Professional integrity, my eye! thought David. 'Good God, even Manuel does private consultancy.'

'Never!'

'Well, for a start, he's involved with developers in the Tuy.'

'How do you know that?' asked Keith.

Why don't I keep my big mouth shut, thought David.

'That's slanderous,' said Joselyn, triumphantly. 'There is a Congressional hearing to decide the future of the Tuy and Manuel, as Minister of Planning, has to be completely impartial. It is inconceivable that he would have retained an interest of that kind.'

'Are you going to let me have the data?'

'No.'

'Okay, I'll go to MERCAVI and get it.'

'They won't let you have it.'

'They said they would, but I should try you first to avoid paperwork. I'd thank you not to repeat what I just said about Manuel.'

§

The card was edged in black and signed by Mildred. So the grandfather had died, thought David sadly, missing him, and he was being invited to the wake at Manuel's.

David had the strange sense that he had been through this before. Maybe it was the strong similarity to Jordi's leaving party. Apart from the black dresses of the women, nothing had changed. People stood in the same positions, saying the same things. It was as if time had been frozen, like in a photograph of lost friends. Yet to David it seemed such a long time ago.

He found Mildred in the hallway with a group of women. Her back was turned and he observed them for a moment before interrupting. They were talking about Jorge Manuel and they were giggling. He realised that they were enjoying themselves. The sombre mourning lent them an elegance they obviously relished. Recollections of Jorge Manuel's romantic exploits were clearly thrilling.

Mildred turned. 'David! I'm so glad you could come.'

'I'm sorry about your father,' he said. He lifted the flowers he'd brought. They were pale gold chrysanthemums. They looked plain against the banks of gaudy bouquets and ornate wreaths. A maid appeared. Mildred handed them to her, then changed her mind and asked her to fetch a vase. She made a fuss of cutting the stems and arranging them. David was touched.

'You liked him,' she said.

'Yes. He was so full of life.'

'And now he's gone. He lived with us for so many years, I got used to him being there when I came home. I go into his old room and expect to see him still.'

'Like a phantom limb.'

'Yes.'

'What did he die of?'

'A long life of over indulgence. He was ninety-three!'

'Where is he now?'

'Only God knows.'

'I mean the body.'

'Why?'

'I'd like to see, if the coffin's here.'

'Yes?'

She took him through the house to a room in darkness. The coffin was shiny, like a concert piano, with big gold handles. On top there were pasty white lilies in a pair of grotesquely ugly silver vases.

She left to attend to the other guests. He stood in silence, trying to remember Jorge Manuel and his gravel voice, but his mind wandered imagining how the family mausoleum might look. In his mind's eye he envisaged it: pink marble topped with a pair of black angels with pitchforks.

When he had gone to look at his dad laid out in his best suit it was as if he was no longer there. In sleep a person retained their animation, but his cold body was more unreal than a waxworks. Yet it had been hard to believe that his father's larger-than-life personality no longer existed. His body was just a vehicle, no more or less than his Hillman car.

He couldn't remember his mum and dad ever kissing or even holding hands. Yet he was sure they had loved each other. His dad was away all week and every Friday evening, as a treat, his mum would cook one of his favourite meals: white belly tripe or pigs' trotters.

His mum was a fastidious woman, prudish even. He remembered that she loved to watch the waves on a pebble beach at Fleetwood where they went for their holidays when he was little. If there was a high sea they would drive to the front and park facing into the storm. Dad would have his paper, David would be in the back of the van reading comics and his mum would just sit and watch the waves.

He went out onto the terrace. A waiter offered him a drink from a silver salver. Whisky. He refused. He saw Manuel with some men, sitting on the sofas in the salon. He acknowledged them with a wave. Manuel smiled and said something to the men, who gave him a close look. He came over and, linking his arm in David's, guided him a little way into the garden.

'Tell me David,' said Manuel relaxing his grip, 'How is the evaluation proceeding? I'm most concerned to avoid any delay.'

'I had to do a little more research,' said David.

'This preoccupation with earthquakes … it's a distraction,

an irrelevance.'

'The report will be ready next week, on time, as promised.'

'Excellent. I'm relying on your independent assessment. In my position, you must understand, that there can be absolutely no trace of self-interest ... a whiff of impropriety and ... who knows! I have to be seen to be impartial, disinterested. So, tell me David,' asked Manuel mildly, swinging round to face him, 'what did you mean by telling Joselyn Calderón I had a personal involvement in the Tuy?'

Startled, David wondered what had she told him. Why couldn't he keep his big trap shut! Without thinking he said, 'She must have misunderstood me, I wouldn't dream of saying such a thing.'

Manuel smiled and walked away. David was furious: with Manuel, with Joselyn, but most of all with himself. He hated Manuel now: for having power over him, for making him lie. The hypocritical bastard!

He heard Jordi before he saw him and had to stop himself hiding. He appeared, shoving a way through the jam of guests, arm and arm with Angel, strutting, boasting. He was smoking a long Cubano. David had never seen him smoking cigars.

'David?' Jordi didn't give him the usual bear-hug.

'Olá,' he said. It came out like a croak; he was trying to sound relaxed. Angel made for the doors to the salon. The cigar smelt like a bonfire of wet leaves.

'I need to talk to you. Have you got a minute?' said David.

'What about?'

'The Congressional hearing.'

'Haven't got time now. Have to see Manuel.'

'It's important.'

'Ring me at the office. Ciào for now.' He gave David his business card. There was an abstract design with red and black dots. It read 'Diseño 2000—Jorge A Cardona'. There were a lot of letters after his name. Prince Jordi, thought David, Lord High bloody everything else.

He felt someone's arm slide through his.

'What's with you and Jordi?' It was Christina. He was momentarily disconcerted. 'Come into the garden and tell me about it,' she said. They sat on a bench under a mango tree well away from the house. 'What's it all about?' she asked.

He poured it all out: his anger and uncertainty; his anxiety about the Tuy.

'Have you tackled Jordi about this?'

'Some of it.'

'What about Manuel?'

'I don't know. Is it some kind of fraud?'

'Have you talked to Chelo?'

'Why?'

'What are you going to do?'

'I don't know.'

'Don't worry about Jordi, he'll be all right.'

'I'm not worried about Jordi.'

'Jordi's not got much sense of right and wrong.' She looked angry and David found himself, ludicrously, wanting to defend Jordi.

'When I first met him I thought he must be destined for something great.'

'Like what?'

'I don't know … liberator of Latin America from Yankee imperialism, Nobel prize winner … who knows. D'you think he has heroes too.'

269

'Simon Bolivar, Bertrand Russell and Che Guevara,' she said without hesitation.

That figures thought David. 'I see him as Napoleon … in his uniform, all gold epaulets and leather boots. Wouldn't he love all the strutting about, and the destruction.'

She smiled wryly.

Where's Julio?' he asked.

'I thought you knew.'

'Knew what?'

'Julio and I have split up.'

'Why? I'm sorry I shouldn't have asked.'

'Lots of reasons. I was busy with my work and, if I made an effort to get home early, Julio was always out playing dominoes with the boys.'

'I'm sorry.'

'I didn't see much of you after I got married.'

'I suppose I thought I'd be in the way.'

'Are funerals like this in England?'

'How do you mean?'

'A travesty.'

'Maybe. We were late for my dad's funeral. We went to the wrong place. The gates were locked with chain and padlock and there was no-one to ask. We had to race across the town to the other crematorium.'

'That's appalling!' said Christina.

They had got there half an hour late and the funeral director rushed them to their seats. Looking at the strangers on the other side of the aisle, David had the idea that they were at the next cremation and that the coffin sliding behind the mustard plush contained someone else's father.

His dad hated being late, but he would have appreciated

the joke. It didn't really matter: he'd gone and they'd come to see him off. His aunts wept. David nearly burst out laughing imagining him telling the tale to St Peter.

§

Jordi sat behind a big desk, smoking. The office looked like a film set. David didn't mind him smoking cigars—he smoked them on climbing trips, bowling along the long straight potholed roads in the interior, hot wind roaring in his hair, smoke pouring out of the window like a steam train—it was the pose he objected to. 'What's Luis Carlos up to?' asked Jordi.

'How do you mean?' said David.

'What will his submission to the Congressional hearing contain?'

David was thrown. He'd come to Jordi's office to tell him what he'd found out about the Tuy, not to reveal what little he knew of the opposition plans. He said nothing.

'Does he agree that there must be some investment in the Metropolitan Region?'

He knows I think there should be, thought David. 'He thinks all public investment should be in the regions and that the capital can take care of itself.'

'How's he going to justify that?'

'He's run the model with different parameters.'

'He has his supporters.'

'OMPU want to discourage development all round the capital to keep traffic volumes down.'

'What are you going to do? Are you going to recommend

Guarenas?' asked Jordi.

'I won't be called by the hearing.'

'You might be.'

'I want to convince you that the Tuy is too dangerous.'

'I've heard all that before,' said Jordi impatiently.

'I've finished the report for you. I've sent a copy to Manuel.'

'Yeh! I read your draft while you were away.'

'But I've got new evidence. The final report's different.'

'Leave it with me then.'

'Will you read it?'

'Sure. Listen, have you thought about leaving the university. Consultancy, that's where the money is, that's where it's all happening.'

'I don't know what I'm doing. Maybe I'll go back home.'

'Don't be stupid, England's had it. The IMF have pulled the plug. Why don't you stay and make a million. You could be a millionaire in five years.'

'Sterling?'

'Maybe, with your brains and application. I don't see you as an academic, you're too pragmatic. There could be a job for you in Diseño 2000. If you are going to settle here, you'll need friends.'

David kept quiet. He hadn't come here to help the rich get richer.

'This country needs people like you. In twenty years time a new generation will take over, people like me and Angel.'

'What about Luis Carlos?'

'A rival party!'

At least he can still make a joke, thought David.

'Why don't you help us?' asked Jordi.

'I'll think about it, if you'll think about the Tuy.'

Later, he realised that Jordi had been more interested in his support of Guarenas than in Luis Carlos's submission. It wasn't what he'd said, so much as the tone. Jordi had been welcoming enough; had taken him round the office and had introduced him to the architects working at drawing boards and to his vivacious PA. It was more impressive than he had imagined. There were drawings for at least half a dozen office blocks and shopping centres they were developing. He'd put himself out, been more friendly than he had been for ages. But he'd changed. He'd moved into a different league.

He's not the man I knew in England. He's left me behind. He's not interested in research any more, or in improving the life of the poor. He's only interested in satisfying the elite; in getting rich.

He looked at himself in the shaving mirror; lifted it from the window-ledge and brought it closer to his face. He stood very still, holding the mirror about a foot from his face. A stranger looked back at him. Dead eyes, frightening.

He knew he'd changed, but not this much. He smiled at his own stupidity, and the movement broke the spell, recreating the familiar mask of how he thought he looked.

18

David had time to kill before the hearing. He knew that the British Council had a library and had been meaning to try it for months. The flower-seller on the corner was busy selling wreaths to mourners coming to the funeral parlour next door. The open doors were so wide David wondered if the building had originally been a garage. He could see the men in white and black standing around, looking bored. Some had slipped out for a smoke and a chat. From deeper inside he could hear the wailing as the women grieved.

The road was lined with almond trees. The trunks of the trees were scarred and the once elegant avenue choked with parked vehicles. Most of the large houses had been converted into commercial premises of one kind or another. A single-storey medieval castle had been built to the edge of the sidewalk and a neon sign in Gothic lettering said

'Restaurant Henry V'. Only the British Council retained any of its former grandeur. There was a garden with tall trees and the old house looked cool and graceful.

Inside, a tiny dark woman sat at `a desk.

'What do you want?' she snapped.

'I'd like to use the library.'

'You can't.'

David just managed to stop himself saying why not.

'I'm working in the university. How do I join?'

'You have to fill in this form and get it signed by two sponsors.'

'Fine. Can I just have a quick look round?'

'No, not until you're a member.'

'Hello.' A tall young man emerged from an office. 'Archie Campbell, deputy director.'

'Hello, David Anthony.'

'Let me show you round.'

The woman glared from behind her desk.

'Not exactly a sparkling collection. The Georgette Heyer and Dick Francis get snapped up.'

'I expect I'll find something of interest. Anything on South America?'

'Very little. The trade's the other way round. We're here to bring English to the natives.' David said nothing. 'Where do you live?'

'La Florida.'

'How about coming round for a drink? We're in Las Palmas, the square at the top of the avenue, Edificio Tiuna. The penthouse.'

'When?'

'How about this evening? At seven then.'

David felt pleased. Archie might be from the diplomatic set, but it would be good to speak English and catch up on the news from home.

He was shown in by the maid. The large room was almost empty. Archie got up to greet him.

'Nicole?' called Archie. A tall woman with a boyish hair cut came in from the balcony.

'You are at the university?' She spoke with French accent.

'Yes, in the School of Architecture.'

'What would you like to drink?'

'A gin and tonic, thanks.' Archie went to the drinks cabinet.

'What time do you finish work?' asked David.

'Four-thirty most days.' Although Archie held it well, David suspected he'd been drinking steadily since he got home. A paperback of Pablo Neruda's poems lay face down under his chair. Maybe they could be friends—it would be good to have someone to talk to.

'Are you based here long?'

'Two years,' said Nicole. 'Just over a year to go.'

'We get moved around. The idea is not to get too settled. We were in Dubai last. This isn't so bad. You can drink for one thing.'

'Have you been to the tennis club in Altamira?' asked Nicole.

'No.'

'You must come one weekend as our guest. There's a pool. It's pleasant,' she said.

'It's Queenie's birthday party on Friday. Want me to get you a ticket?' asked Archie.

'Is it worth going?'

'Fascinating! The whole British contingent will be there showing the flag.'

'How much are the tickets?'

'Singles are three hundred bees.'

He couldn't afford it, but he liked them both. He was pissed off with Venezuelans and the idea of spending more time with English appealed to him.

'Do come. We're starved of interesting company,' said Nicole.

'Would you like the money for the ticket now?' he asked.

'If you've got it on you?'

'The Thompsons are short of men on their table. We'll put you with them.'

'I thought I'd be sitting with you,' said David, feeling cheated.

'We'll be on high table with the Ambassador. Very boring!'

'Have you explored the country while you've been here?' Archie asked, looking across at Nicole.

'We collect butterflies,' she said.

"And moths,' added Archie.

'Where?' asked David.

'At La Mariposa, on the old road.'

'We saw the name on a map,' said Nicole, 'and, since it means butterfly, we tried there first.'

'And are there many?'

'Yes,' said Archie.

'But it's very hot. It's in a bowl in the hills, and there are lots of other insects. Archie has been horribly bitten. Show David!'

Rather shamefacedly Archie rolled up a trouser leg. His

calf was covered in sores. 'Can't resist scratching them I'm afraid.'

'Can I see your collection?'

Archie thought a second as though conferring a great honour. He took a key from his pocket and unlocked a tall cabinet. Almost reverentially he slid out the first drawer. Fifty butterflies were pinned through the thorax. Archie paused before withdrawing the next drawer.

'It's taken over a year to nail this beauty: "Morphidiae: Shocking Blue!"' It was the same butterfly David had seen with Jerry.

'Do you go too?' he asked Nicole.

'Yes, we caught this together.' David had an image of them loping toward each other through long grass, their nets held aloft like standards.

'We have a cabinet from each of our postings: Dubai, Mexico, Thailand, Canada.'

§

David was bored. Bored by the whining about maids and about the traffic, the endless harping back to England. The speeches were hollow and mawkishly sentimental. The waiter placed the fourth bottle of whisky on the table and once again David refused when the host offered to pour him a drink.

Maybe the evening would be more bearable if he were drunk. He only had a hundred bolivars left. Fifteen pounds to last him till pay day. Why throw it away on some ten-year-old blend he'd never heard of.

'The people in the ranchos are savages,' said a woman

across the table. 'They don't know how to live. It will take generations for them to learn to live decently.'

'I think they should paint the ranchos white. They'd look rather chic from a distance,' said a young woman who was rather tipsy.

'They're spoiling the environment. We have a beach house. It's beautiful but lots of people are building shacks near us, it's terrible,' said Mrs Thompson.

'The government should turn the place into a national park and stop all future building,' said her husband.

'They might demolish all the existing houses,' said David.

'We must educate them,' said Mrs Thompson. 'You're at the university Mr Anthony. It's up to you educate these people.'

'What do you do exactly?' asked the tipsy woman's husband.

'I work in the School of Architecture. And you?'

'I'm with an international firm of accountants.'

'Is it right that some people should earn so much more than others?' David asked with feigned innocence.

There was a hush round the table. 'I think professionals should charge as much as the market will stand. Supply and demand. That's the only way to establish a fair price,' said the accountant, looking round the table for agreement.

'When the oil runs out the only way to pay for education and health care will be through taxation.'

'As long as it doesn't come out of my pocket!'

'Why?' He could see that the accountant was getting angry, that the others round the table wanted to take the conversation back to the trivial and the safe. But they were also fascinated. For a moment etiquette seemed suspended, anything could happen.

'I had to work hard for my education,' said the accountant, his vowels beginning to slide. 'I see no damn reason why I should support riff-raff and layabouts who are too lazy to take advantage of the vast opportunities here.'

'People find it impossible to break out of their poverty.'

'I'm more intelligent and work harder than people in ranchos. So I qualify for a higher salary.'

'I'm not sure you work harder,' said his wife, rather surprisingly siding with David.

'What happens when everyone's got a university degree, there'll be no one to sweep the streets!' the accountant protested.

'We must be talking about different countries,' said David. 'If you'll excuse me I must go.'

Mr Thompson caught up with him in the foyer. 'Anthony, hang on old man. Small question of the cover charge.'

'I didn't drink.'

'Not my fault, old man. Swings and roundabouts. Redistribution of income, what!'

'How much?'

'Hundred bees.'

David handed over the last note from his wallet.

§

In the week before the hearing David went to Merida to do the work for Felix and go climbing with Jerry.

'People like us can't do much. Keep your head down, stay out of trouble and do your best, that's my motto,' said Jerry.

But what is my best? thought David.

'Step out of line and they open a file on you.'

They were lying on the only flat bit of snow on the route. He looked up at the stars, cool, far away. He had his sleeping bag pulled up over his head with only a small breathing hole open. They shared the bivi bag, snuggled up together for warmth. Tomorrow, at dawn, they would climb Pico Bolivar, the highest mountain in the country. It would be easy. David could have walked up it, but, for Jerry, he would cut big steps in the hard snow and belay him with the rope.

He'd told Jerry something of his dilemma. Should he stick to his principles and so betray his friend?

'Why don't you pack it in and move out here? You could get a job teaching in the university. It's a great life—all the climbing you could want, no traffic, no aggro. Why don't you?'

'I don't know.'

It would feel like running away. Something had happened that he was meant to come to terms with, even if he didn't know what or how. He felt frightened, not of the climb tomorrow, that was straightforward, he only had to be careful and look out for Jerry. No, it's people who are really dangerous, he thought.

'Do you think I'll be able to get up it tomorrow?' asked Jerry.

'Sure.'

'But I've never done any ice-climbing before.'

'It's not really an ice-climb. It's steep firm snow. Ideal. I'll cut steps, it'll be like climbing an easy ladder.'

'But there are cliffs at the top.'

'Yes, but don't worry, everything looks impossible from

below. Wait till we're there if you can. Trust me. Vinci did it solo in the thirties, so it can't be hard. Then we drop down the other side and we're back on the tourist track.'

'When did you start climbing?'

'When I was fifteen.'

For years he had climbed with the same partner, although they were quite unalike. He could remember every detail of a route, while David forgot the individual moves. Some bits of routes remained, like snatches of a song, and he could remember the quality of the light and the soft, springy grass at the top of some crags.

His friend climbed slowly. He could hang around for hours on a move. David liked to move steadily. If he couldn't get up after a few attempts he usually came down.

'What about the danger?' asked Jerry.

'I always reckoned the most dangerous time was walking down the path after finishing the climb.'

He remembered a day, soon after he started climbing, on a cliff in Wales, when he had tripped on a root, had fallen five feet, landed on a ledge and rolled off. He fell eight or ten feet to the next ledge and would have fallen down the whole cliff if he hadn't taken the shock in his right arm.

'If you haven't climbed for a while your body feels stiff and awkward, and you're filled with doubts and fears. What if this hold breaks just as I'm pulling on it? Is the next pitch too hard? From below everything beyond the next ten or twenty feet tends to look impossible, especially if you're out of practice. You have to restrict your vision and concentrate on the next moves.

'Some days, magical days, you climb well: your mind stays sharp and doesn't race ahead. I used to think climbing made you confront the inevitability of death. I now believe it brings you up sharply with life. When you're afraid, really afraid, fear takes over and you're paralysed. When you climb well, sights and sounds, the smell of rock and lichen, the finger tip touch of a small hold, are so intense you feel most of life is just a pale shadow of the real thing. On some climbs there is such delight at the top that, for a few moments, the world seems a beautiful, uncomplicated place.' If only the rest of his life could be as simple as climbing.

The following morning they woke early and got to the top soon after midday. By eight that night they were back in Merida and the following day he began the work for Felix, settling into a round of interviewing during the day and writing up his notes in the evening in the hotel bedroom.

Felix rang from England to see how the work was going. 'Have you thought any more about returning home?' he asked.

'Why?'

'Frankly I'm impressed with the evaluation work Jordi showed me. I think you would be a useful asset to the company. If you're interested I'll talk to my co-directors.'

David said yes, he might be interested. He felt flattered and it would solve a lot of problems. He'd only meant to stay a couple of years anyway, he told himself.

On Friday night Jerry picked him up from outside the hotel and took him up to his house in the mountains. The following morning Marta went shopping, leaving him and Jerry looking after the two small children. They played in the meadow by the side of the stream at the bottom of the garden. The water was icy and they skinny-dipped until they were blue then played tag and wrestled until they warmed up.

'Have you tried the hongos?' Jerry asked.

'Hongos?'

'Mushrooms, like this.' He stooped and picked a tiny mushroom the size of a jacket button. 'Far out, man,' he said popping it into his mouth.

'You mean they're psychedelic!'

'Sure, try one.'

'I don't take drugs,' said David.

'These aren't drugs,' said Jerry, laughing.

One won't do me any harm, he thought. It seemed so innocent: the meadow, the wild flowers, the children playing in the stream. He ate a few. They played Frisbee until lunchtime, going up to the terrace when Marta rang the bell for lunch.

After their meal the children had a lie down. David said he would go for a quick walk on the mountain behind the house and be back by supper.

At first he wandered through meadows, following whichever way took his fancy. He'd felt no effects from the mushroom over lunch and had forgotten about it until the path he had chosen got narrower and steeper and he had to breath harder.

In the valley there had been lots of trails, now there was only the steep narrow ridge and, to make progress, he had to push aside the lush undergrowth. He felt melancholic: he could go on or go back—two options, both equally depressing. It was a metaphor for his life. He wanted to stay; he wanted to go home.

He was tired and asked a trailing vine for help as he pulled on it to help him up a steep bit. Talking to the plant seemed quite natural, yet part of his mind knew what was happening

284

and monitored the process dispassionately. But the rational voice felt distant, detached from the pumping machine that carried him along. It would get dark. It was stupid to go on. Then, magically, he realised he could lie down and rest. He chose a soft hollow on the crest. The earth was warm and he lay flat on his face, his head too heavy to lift, and felt the energy in the ridge. He observed an ant climb a stem of grass. So basic and yet so mobile. What simple pleasure one got from movement, in the rhythm of the muscles in motion, when the brain shut down.

He could hear a waterfall, faintly at first, on the wind. It sounded beautiful and seductive and he decided to go on until he reached it. The waterfall became the aim of the climb—the reason for living. When he reached the falls, there was only a small stream cascading one or two feet over smooth stones.

He sat down and dangled his hands in the cold water and for a moment felt refreshed. But the thought entered his head that the stream was wearing away the rocks over which it flowed and would eventually wear away the whole mountain. The thought was profoundly depressing; he had lost sense of scale and proportion.

After he had been sitting some time it seemed as though the stream sang as it ran over the rocks: 'You are mountain: I am water.' And David thought of himself as the mountain and Chelo as the stream.

He'd been walking six hours, he calculated. Fit, he could climb two thousand feet an hour. How far had he come? Twenty miles or half a mile? He had no idea. If a two foot piddle can sound like a cataract, how long is a piece of string?

He should have gone back then, it was getting late, they

would be worried, but he pushed on to where the ridge began to level out after the steep climb. The sun had gone and sombre shadows fell across the path. The bird song had ceased—the world had gone strangely quiet and there was a foreboding chill in the air. He slowed, knowing something terrible was about to happen. A lance hit him in the chest, went through his body and his heart exploded. He fell forwards, onto his face. He thought he'd died. There was a bright light in his head.

Finally he opened his eyes. He could see a tiny grain of earth: crystals the size of boulders, dead leaves like skeletal cathedrals. He had met his death. He levered himself upright and realised he had trodden on a bamboo stem that had whipped up like a garden rake.

He decided to go back, he couldn't go on after that. But he found, to his surprise, that he was carrying on. Suddenly he was running downhill. The ridge dropped to a col before rising again. He was going on, going down. How easy, how enjoyable! That's it! his drugged mind thought. He could do the same at work—keep going, but make it easy for himself— don't tackle the hardest things head on all the time, coast down the easy bits and enjoy life.

For a long time he continued climbing, forgetting everything, concentrating on the rhythm of placing one foot in front of the other, pushing with his hands on his knees to help him up the steepest parts.

The vegetation began to thin and he realised he was coming to the top of the mountain. That's the answer, he thought. Up there, at the top, there will be lots of ways to go, no more climbing, no more agony. That's the point of the climb: the meaning of life—the top will be paradise.

He came out onto the flat. It was dark; he was frightened of getting lost. He left markers: broken twigs, piles of stones, overturned pitcher plants. But he was uncertain whether he would be able to see them in the dark on the way back. If I miss the way on the return journey, I could easily end up on the wrong side of the mountain. Going down there are many choices; so unlike going up.

He continued across the gently rising rock plateau, expecting to reach the top in an hour or less. But the plateau went on and finally terminated in a ring of jagged cliffs, like a great amphitheatre. They were high and black against the night sky. He thought he could climb them in the light, but in the dark, tired and hungry? He could stay till morning; curl up under a boulder and sleep. But the effects of the drug had worn off, leaving him chilled and hungry.

He resigned himself to going back, and not reaching the top. There was no purpose to the journey just as there was no meaning to the riddle of life. It was all a waste of time. He turned around to retrace his steps and saw two snow covered peaks in the distance. Pico Bolivar! It hadn't clicked at first—the mountain he'd climbed just a few days ago—and Pico Espejo—Mirror Mountain—with its lake! A cartwheel moon painted the slopes pale pink. He stood watching until the colour faded. And a new thought entered his mind, hazy at first, then clearer, of two people, a man and a woman, walking together in the mountains as if at the beginning of time. That was it! Now he knew what it was. He had to see Chelo.

Some way down the ridge he stumbled over a root and nearly fell. When he started walking again, he found he had hurt his ankle. He limped a few paces, his legs felt loose and rubbery and about ready to go AWOL. Ahead, in the moonlight, a rock showed up like the hump of a surfacing whale. David kept going until he reached it and sat down on one end, hunched over, with his arms between his legs, resting.

He lost track of how long he sat there, gathering his strength, drifting pleasurably in and out of sleep until a dawning realisation shook him into wakefulness. With the clarity that only comes when one is totally spent, he understood why Chelo was so important to him and was able to admit, perhaps for the first time in his life, the depth of his longing for someone to love—someone to help him reach himself. Inspired, he realised she needed him too. Nonsense! Chelo was together, she knew what was what. The hell she needed him.

He knew he missed her badly: the way her dress swung as she walked, her incisive objectivity, her uninhibited lovemaking. If he had attempted to describe his true feelings about her he would have said that he woke up in the night with loneliness clawing his insides out. It was awful how totally he needed her to be at one with him.

And Chelo? She would, he thought, use earthier, more robust words to describe her feelings. He imagined her at home, asleep. She might dream of him sitting there on the rock and fly over the mountains in 'her private jet' and parachute down and drown him with love.

The sky lightened, it would be dawn soon. Jerry and Marta would be worried if he was not there when they woke up. How comfortable they seemed with each other, and how at home they made him feel. He did not have to pretend with Jerry and Jerry did not play games with him, or try to manipulate or control him. Although not particularly suited—Jerry was pedantic and unadventurous—he spoke

English and they understood each other.

He got to his feet, put his hands to his hips and stretched his tired back. The first few steps were hard but he got into a rhythm, counting—One, two, three, O'Leary. Four, five six… For a while the dialogue inside his head stilled.

He relived the embarrassment of not understanding what Chelo had said the first time they met and then pushed the memory away. Sometimes language was an impossible wall and misunderstanding could loom unexpectedly. Speaking a foreign tongue day in, day out, continually failing to appreciate shades of meaning, to communicate precisely, produced a dull strain that wore away the spirit. The nuances of speech and convention were a trap rather than a source of amusement and delight. What things he had been through since he came. How long ago? A year? More like a lifetime.

With hindsight the first few months, while Jordi was away, seemed to possess the innocence of childhood. His vocabulary had been limited to a handful of words, but he had the same quiet confidence he had as a child. The world was strange and new but he was able to draw on internal reserves of strength. After Jordi's return, the world became a larger, more threatening place, filled with uncertainties and confusion. It was if he was seventeen again and experiencing all the old inner turmoil and lack of confidence.

David was only dimly aware of how people saw him. Like the society he was living in, his personality felt disjointed and uneven. David struggled to comprehend the dilemma: how his own mental state was intertwined with the development of the nation. Was it like that because that was how he saw it or was he like he was because that was how society saw him? How could he hope to help, divided from himself, out of touch with his own unconscious? How could any human being pretend to solve this disharmony? He felt melancholic and it took a supreme effort just to keep putting one foot in front of the other. There was mist in the valley and the drop in temperature felt like entering a cold store. His wet shirt clung to his back making him shiver. On he walked across the meadows, dog-tired. Then hope came with first light. The only thing that mattered, he realised, was the meaning people discovered in their own activity. What did he value? Climbing, being with people he loved. He had to find out what he was meant to do and get on with it. Find Chelo! That was it, that's what he had to do. He had to see her and tell her he loved her.

He could see Jerry's home and he crossed the stream into their garden. There was no sound from the house, it was early still and everyone was asleep. He took off his boots and socks and bathed his feet in the cold water.

19

He had only been back in Caracas a couple of days when Jordi rang one night, out of the blue: 'There's a weekend party at the farm, Chelo's coming. Want to come?'

He felt utterly confused. He'd been puzzling about how to make contact with her; their paths didn't cross any more. He'd wondered about sending her flowers, or telephoning and he'd thought about writing, but he couldn't be sure the letter would arrive, and he didn't want to take it round himself.

This wasn't how he had imagined it. He'd pictured the two of them somewhere quiet and private, not in a great crowd, and especially not with Jordi. He was tempted to say no.

'She wants you to come. She told me to invite you.'

'Okay.'

'Want a lift?'

'No. I'll make my own way there. See you.'

He felt excited, as if at the start of a race. It was not only the prospect of seeing Chelo after so long, but Jordi's voice was warm and he had a sudden rush of affection for him.

Then fear rushed in; of being humiliated, of seeing them together. He wouldn't go. But then, he argued, she said she wanted him to go.

Güigue, a small town about 15 kilometres away, supplied the farms in the bottomlands on the south side of the lake. They'd gone in early that morning to get spares for one of the tractors and were in a bar having a second breakfast of corn cakes and coffee.

Aurora flirted with the waiters; Mariella egged her on. Jordi, loud and unpredictable, ordered a third bottle of beer. David held himself together by mentally crossing his arms over his chest and hugging himself. Chelo wasn't expected until the evening: he doubted she would come.

They left the bar. Outside a man was beating a dog with a stick. He didn't look angry, perhaps it was just something to do in a place where nothing happened. Men stood around, drinking and watching. The dog crouched flat on the road and whimpered. David walked up to the man, took the stick from his hand and threw it away in a high arc. The man raised his fist. Jordi said No! The men outside the bar laughed and went back inside and bought more beers. David felt his upper arms start to tremble.

'What the hell was I doing?'

'Don't worry about it. Let's get back to the car before he comes back with a gun,' said Jordi laughing.

Jordi was roaring drunk by the time they went down to the stables after lunch to see the mating. They could hear the crashing and banging from the house and David realised it was the stallions kicking the doors of their stalls. They walked on and came to an enclosure surrounded by a high thorn hedge. The hedge was covered in sweet smelling flowers and the circular grass plot, watered by the overflow from the water tanks, formed a lush oasis. Vincente held one of the mares while the vet made a quick inspection. Jordi mounted an oil drum and, belly thrust forward over his wide leather belt, stamped in time to a song about seducing maidens.

The stable lads carried down a large cool box filled with crushed ice and cans of soft drinks and bottles of beer and Jordi shouted for one of them to throw him a bottle. He took the top off with his teeth.

One of the lads slipped padded straps over the mare's rear fetlocks and Alberto lifted two fingers to his mouth and gave a loud piercing whistle. Minutes later the stallion, snorting and pawing the earth, dragged the two lads into the arena.

'Look at the size of it, it's practically touching the ground!' Aurora bit her lower lip with excitement and, absent-mindedly stroked Jordi's thighs. The stallion reared up, tall, terrifying. Its sharp hooves struck the mare's shoulders. David watched the soft mud squirt through Vincente's bare toes as he struggled to hold her head. The stallion gripped the mare's neck, wounding her with his teeth. David felt giddy with the noise and the violence. Unexpectedly it was over and the stallion slid off. Great gouts of semen poured on to the earth, the oystery smell drowning the perfume of the flowers.

David woke from a nightmare—he was trying to shout and heard himself whimper. His back ached: he was in a hammock, curled like a foetus. He remembered he'd come back to the house on his own. He turned over and tried to recapture the dream.

He'd been back at school. Duggan had him by the throat, bent back over a chair, unable to move. From then on, he'd been one of Duggan's favourite victims. He told his father, who took him into the garden and demonstrated how to block a punch. David knew it wouldn't work, but it made him feel better that his father had wanted to help.

Aurora had wanted to come back to the house with him, but he'd shrugged her off. He could hear her now, with Angel, in one of the bedrooms.

Then, like floodgates bursting, he remembered another boy at school. He was just as big as Duggan, but docile and gentle. On finding a piece of chalk in his blazer pocket, David had drawn neat white lines on the black lapels of the boy's blazer. As the boy had smiled uncertainly, David was swung round and punched in the face. He lashed back and Duggan knocked him down, smashing his nose; someone said it served him right.

He lay on his back looking at the roof beams to which the ropes of the hammock were tied. The beams appeared to rock from side to side while he remained absolutely still.

In retrospect, his cool, almost clinical, cruelty seemed more cowardly and malevolent than Duggan's bullying. He'd discovered his dark side and experienced the pleasure of abusing a fellow creature, but, by good fortune, the thrill had been exorcised immediately by the punch in the face. From then on it had been more important to him to control his own impulses than exercise power over other people.

He sensed her arrive; smelt her perfume invade the veranda. They were alone for a few moments. He made to climb out of the hammock but she came and knelt beside him and took his hands in hers. They didn't speak, they just looked at each other.

'Olá, mi amor!' Jordi came in, yawning. Chelo stood and Jordi threw his arms round her. 'Good, you made it. Come, I want to talk to you. Let me get you a drink.' Jordi whisked her away, leaving David wondering and anxious.

'Come and dance,' said Aurora. David had been for a walk down to the gate to watch the horses being brought in from the paddocks and had just come in up the veranda steps. Angel was launching her round the room in a samba. They danced superbly.

'I can't do that!'

'You dance all right with your eyes shut!' Aurora yelled. David saw Chelo, at the other end of the room with Jordi, give him a look to kill.

'Caramba! You women have really gone to town,' said Alberto, coming into dinner and sitting at the head of the table. They had dressed as if for a formal banquet and the candle-light made their earrings and necklaces sparkle.

Thank God Alberto's here, thought David. He had felt under-dressed compared with the others, but Alberto was still in his work clothes. They had been seated at the table half-an-hour, waiting. David had already drunk two glasses of wine and felt woozy. Jordi was well into his stride at the other end.

The maids Aurora and Mariella had brought with them

began serving. 'No, the other dish! estúpida,' scolded Aurora. 'I told you he doesn't like vegetarian.'

This is all I need, thought David, sensing Chelo's hostility.

Angel was giving forth about oil revenue and prosperity, encouraged by Mariella who was flirting with him. He was the life and soul of the party; David hadn't imagined he could be like this. As if reading his thoughts Aurora leaned over towards him and whispered: 'Amazing what an afternoon in bed will do for a man.' He felt her trying to play footsie again and tucked his legs under his chair, out of reach.

Jordi stood up; the chair rocking back perilously. 'I want to make a toast,' he said refilling his glass to overflowing with the blood-red wine. 'To David and Chelo!' David felt his ears burn. 'Loyal friends who steadfastly kept the department going while we were all in England.'

He watched Chelo looking at him, coolly, appraising his reaction. 'And all thanks to David who wrote the evaluation model which will be so crucial next week. It allows us to make an objective assessment where previously we were guided only by self-interest.' David felt his flesh on the back of his shoulders creeping with exasperation and fury.

'By the way Manuel is very pleased with our report,' said Jordi, rubbing salt in. 'To loyal friends!'

'Salud y pesetas!' shouted Angel.

What is a friend? thought David; someone you could count on. Well he hadn't stuck by Jordi, who clearly felt he should have. He was David's patron: David was not supposed to do his own thing.

Alberto was describing how he had been trying to fix the hydraulics on the tractor without a manual. In his quiet, unassuming way he had defused the tension and made them laugh. 'Life is more exciting if you don't read the instructions,' said Aurora, enigmatically.

Jordi had got up from the table and was dragging an iron bedstead onto the veranda. It was late; the air was thick and muggy as if threatening a storm. David, almost asleep at the table, stood and said goodnight to everyone. He collected his hammock from the living room and went to the veranda to sling it outside in what little breeze there was.

'What are you doing out here?' challenged Jordi.

'Slinging my hammock, why?'

'You'll be better off inside where you were: there's going to be a storm,' slurred Jordi.

'It's too hot. The rain won't reach, the roof's too deep; anyway I'll move if it does. I thought that was why you were moving the bed,' said David, reasonably.

Jordi muttered something and stumped off back to the dining room.

Much later David woke to whispering. He recognised Jordi's voice cajoling, hectoring, and a woman's refusal. He heard the bed springs groan and the iron feet scrape on the concrete as the bed moved under someone's weight. Jordi's tone grew more coaxing, more insistent. There were sounds of struggle from the bedclothes.

David reached out from the hammock and found the end of the bed in the darkness. He touched the metal bars and reached further and his hand found her foot and closed around her bare ankle. He let his fingers follow the shape from the prominent ankle bones, along the bridge, to the tips of her elegant toes, and back by the soft uncalloused pad to measure the width of the heel in the palm of his hand. She shifted in the bed and he sensed her respond.

There was a faint light from the corridor and he could just make out Jordi's bulky shadow. Maybe Jordi could see him holding her. There was a crash; she had pushed Jordi off the bed and he'd stumbled trying to keep his balance. He was cursing under his breath as he staggered back into the house. David fell asleep still clasping her foot.

He woke as it got light and rolled out of the hammock to have a pee. Chelo stirred and woke. She put her fingers to her lips, telling him to be silent, slipped on her shoes and skipped down the steps into the garden.

It was a misty damp dawn and they walked to the dam, oblivious of the heavy dew and the possibility of snakes in the long grass. On reaching the dam Chelo pulled off her shift and dived in. David took off his shorts and plunged after her.

The mist had cleared by the time they stood on the dam wall rubbing each other down with their bare hands to get warm. They sat back-to-back in the sun. David felt oddly reflective after the euphoria of the cold swim and the emotion of the previous night's vigil.

'Why?' she asked.

'Why what?' he said obtusely.

'Why did you have an affair with Aurora?'

'It happened, that's all.'

'How? How did it happen?'

'A look, that's all. You know!—a look passes between a man and a woman; you know because it's happened to you.'

'It happened to us!' She could have killed Aurora then, she hated her so.

David said nothing. He thought about Aurora and realised that she had made him conscious of his own sexuality. But sleeping with Aurora had made him feel bad, the obsession was too cold-blooded. With Aurora, sex was unconnected with feelings of love and affection; her relationships were divorced from any kind of loving, that was not what she wanted. She came from an obsessive family—she was fascinated by sex in the same way Mariella was obsessed by money. The detachment lent her lovemaking an erotic excitement, an extra spice. David's sexual feelings had been heightened precisely because their affair was without commitment, because his brain was aware that, at a deep level, it meant nothing to him. He had been choosing to do it, for kicks, and because of the jealousy and anger he felt about Chelo and Jordi.

With Chelo, in the Tuy, it had been different. It was hard to define, to pinpoint the elements that made it special. It was like on a climb, one of those rare occasions when it all came together: the situation—a big isolated crag, the route—bold yet intricate, and the climber—pushed to the limit but, seemingly, with all the time in the world, flowing up the rock-face like oil on glass. Yet it was on these occasions, more than any others, that memory failed him. The action was so smooth, so right, that no imprint seemed to be left of the detail, only a feeling of well being and fragmented images of bilberries and sunlight. Something remained though. It was as if the movement left a tracery of coloured light in the mind, something films of climbing came nowhere near discovering.

Looking at her, wondering what to say, he finally said, 'I'm sorry.'

'I don't want your sorrow!' She was furious. 'Why Aurora? a woman of such excessive tastes. No, don't tell me! the simple explanation is sufficient. You wanted to, so you did, and to hell with the consequences.'

'You're no one to talk.'

'I loved Jordi, and I stopped seeing him when I knew I loved you. You went with Aurora from lust.'

'Why on earth did Jordi invite me?' he asked, as the craziness of it all hit him.

'Maybe he wanted you to make me happy.' She thought about how Jordi had been ringing her for weeks, at the office as well as at home and about how she'd refused to see him.

'But he loved you!'

'That wouldn't stop him taking chances. He loves risks—the bigger the risk, the greater the excitement.'

He worked a lump of shale loose from the earth and heaved it into the dam with a splash. They said nothing for a time, while he struggled to get control of his emotions.

'If you get lost, do you retrace your steps or do you go on and hope to find the way?' she asked.

Is she trying to change the mood, he wondered. 'It depends,' he said.

'On what?'

'How soon I realise I've gone wrong.'

'So?'

'What?'

'What of us?'

David turned and looked at her. Her long hair was still damp from their swim.

'You know this isn't a rehearsal, there is no second chance.'

'For us?'

'Maybe not; maybe yes.' She stood and pulled him to his feet. 'Take me to Choroni,' she said.

'When?'

'Now, immediately, as soon as we can pack!'

§

They were packed and ready before anyone had risen, but as they were leaving, Alberto arrived from Güigue with hot bread and they stopped to have breakfast with him in the kitchen.

He came down to see them off, but the jeep wouldn't start. David was under the bonnet when he heard Jordi ask if there was petrol in it. He thought he remembered filling up in La Encrucijada on the way but couldn't be sure. The needle read empty and he felt foolish; sensing Chelo's impatience. Alberto fetched a can. Jordi stood, impassive, bleary eyed; only Alberto waved as they left. As they drove away he had the idea that someone might have syphoned off the tank.

Their spirits rose as they left the flat lands and climbed over the mountains to the coast.

On the beach at Puerto Colombia, men with sieves, their forearms bulging with the effort of swirling the huge trays, were grading pebbles into piles. There were seven piles, each with stones smaller than the last, so that the smallest pebbles must have been sieved seven times. Chelo told him that they were for water filters, and that the men went out in rowing boats to collect them.

Having found a man who would take them out to the islands and parked the jeep at his house, they climbed aboard with their stuff and the man pushed the heavy skiff into the breakers. It rolled free from the beach and a wave seemed to lift him effortlessly over stern and into the boat. The outboard coughed and burst into life, the bow came round, he opened the throttle and they headed out to sea, leaving a foaming curve across the bay.

They sat facing each other in pleasurable silence. David steadied himself against the swell by tucking his legs under the thwart and gripping the frame with his toes. Where the paint had worn from the gunwale the water had brought back the colours of fresh cut timber to the bleached wood.

'Feels good,' he said, noticing the sudden change in the colour of the ocean as they crossed into the deep.

The island appeared as a grey smudge, then as a line of palms. As they got nearer they could see birds at intervals along the beach, moving in unison. They might have been flamingo but for their colour, which was bright blue. It was not until they got quite near that they could see that the birds were plastic rubbish bags dangling from posts in readiness for the long weekend of Corpus Christi, when people invaded from the mainland. But, with luck, they would have the island to themselves for a day at least.

As soon as the boat had disappeared over the horizon they made love. Later he left Chelo asleep in the hammock he had slung between a pair of sea grapes and slipped away for a walk along the beach. The sun and wind were fierce and unrelenting after the shelter of the trees. The breakers roared and boomed on the coral. For a while, as he counted the rhythm of his steps on the damp sand, his mind stopped whirling.

He turned at the end of the beach, where the narrow sand spit disappeared into the ocean, and ran back, the wind behind him, legs pumping, bare feet slapping on the hard sand, foundering on the soft margin of the water line, correcting, stretching forward for the distance.

Chelo stretched in the hammock, and woke. David was

gone. She looked up and saw him, a long way away along the beach, running back towards her. She was pleased he was still there, that he hadn't gone out of sight. She felt they were still together, that the connection between them hadn't been severed. She was drowsy, conscious of the well being of her body, relishing these moments alone—giving her emotions time to adjust. She thought of getting up and joining him, but continued rocking gently from side to side in the hammock. Her eyes closed, she could see the bright patterns left by the dappled shade of the leaves. She felt light-headed, drunk almost. Her fingers danced the shape of her body and she stretched her hands above her head. She wanted him inside her again.

She heard him arrive, panting, and sat up in the hammock, holding her arms out. He pulled her to her feet and they ran down the beach into the warm shallow water; falling together with a splash, rolling over in each other's arms—making love.

They lay next to each other in the water, sensing the gentle insistent rhythm of the tide. Dolphin and tunny played beyond the reef, leaping out of the water chasing flying fish. A mob of pelicans were flying slow bombing runs over the lagoon, folding their wings and plummeting into the water, emerging dishevelled with silver fish in their beaks.

How wonderful to be able to swim naked, to feel the wind on their bodies, to have the island to themselves; Chelo hugged herself with the pure luxury of it all.

Later he lit a fire and made coffee, and they sat in the hammocks eating fresh rolls and marmalade. Her smell—the scent he'd grown to love—seemed more intense, and her lips softer, more expressive.

'I'm happy, truly happy,' said David. 'I feel as if the bands have broken.'

'What bands?'

'It's a fairy story.'

'Yes?'

'A prince is cast under an evil spell, and his old coachman forges three iron hoops across his chest to prevent his heart from breaking. The prince escapes the spell with the help of three servants who each perform an impossible feat: eating a mountain of bread, drinking a lake and walking through a fire. As the coachman drives the prince away, at the end, there are three loud cracks as each of the iron bands snap.'

'I love fairy stories. Why are there bands around your heart?'

He was silent for a while, trying to think it out.

'You remember the night I told you about finding my mother? Well when you held me I knew you were going to be special to me. Then I found out about Jordi ... I said things ... I put steel bands round my heart ... so I wouldn't get hurt again. Well now the bands have snapped.'

Chelo got up and pushed the burnt logs further into the fire making the flames spring up. She walked down to the water's edge and stood looking at the horizon for a while, then she came back and unlocked his arms from around his chest and hugged him. 'Perhaps we'll find your mother together,' she said.

After a while she suggested he climb a palm to collect the young green coconuts. He made a clove hitch in a length of cord cut from their improvised washing line and passed it over the hand grip of a machete. The other end he tied round his waist, so that the blade dangled below his feet.

'Do you know what you're doing?' asked Chelo, amused

by his preparations.

'I know the theory; I've seen village kids do it.'

He grasped the trunk, put his feet on and climbed. He'd chosen a palm that leant more than its neighbours, but, at half height as it straightened to the vertical, he ran out of steam.

'Are you all right?' she shouted nervously.

'No!' he laughed, looking down. It was too far to drop, and he might land on the machete. 'Don't worry, I'm just having a rest.'

His forearms ached, his shoulders ached, his back ached, the backs of his calves ached and, above all, his bare feet ached on the rough bark. He gritted his teeth and climbed. His hand closed with relief on a thick leathery stem and he heaved himself up and wrapped his legs round the tree. A shower of ants fell on his head and shoulders, and he tried to beat and scrub them off with his free hand.

'It's not like this in the adverts,' he shouted, finding that the machete was too unwieldy to use.

Chelo watched him. He was crouched in the shade of the canopy, thighs gripping the trunk, fifty feet above the ground. She watched the way the muscles on his back rippled as he reached to twist a nut free and let it fall, with a thud, to the sand.

'How many should I take?'

'Five or six.'

He threw them down, holding each by the stem, and they thumped, one by one, on the dry sand.

'Look at you!' she said, when he had shinned down. There were wide red marks on his chest and thighs and he was covered in dirt.

'Let's swim,' he said grasping her hand and running with her into the breakers.

Their idyll lasted two days: they explored the island, walking right round the coast; they sat in the shallows of the lagoon, legs entwined, talking for hours; they waded out to a wreck and sat on the fore-deck in three feet of water and watched the sea anemones that covered the ship, like a vast miniature city, opening and closing with the push and suck of the swell.

And Chelo taught him to swim properly. He'd been able to swim before, after a fashion, doing the breaststroke and a passable crawl for a short burst. But that was only locomotion, on the surface, to get from one bit of water to another. She taught him to appreciate the sustaining buoyancy of the sea—to trust that it would hold him safe, and she showed him how to go below the surface and explore its depths.

They swam on the lagoon side of the reef; diving down the steep wall of coral into aquamarine and peacock light. Shoals of brightly coloured fish turned in unison, and delicate creatures clung to the living rock.

They swam out through the channel, where the waves crashed on the barnacled outer wall of the reef. The old fear gripped him, until she turned and came back for him and they dived together. And swimming thus, he saw the underside of a wave—a sleek curve, as elusive as mercury, perfect, slapping the rock and shattering in streams of glinting silver bubbles.

Swimming back she pointed to a brain coral—white, deathly, convoluted, five or six feet across, sitting on the sea bed. It was the fissures that petrified him, so deep and penetrating and unbelievably complex. Safe back in the air, on the beach, he tried to remember its shape, but as he began to recapture the details he pushed the image away knowing that it was something exposed that should be hidden, like intestines or the inside of a bone ...

David had broken his leg in the gym at school. The bone had stuck out through the flesh, white and pink, snapped like a stick of rock. He stared at it in astonishment, struggling to relate the bare bone to himself. His eyes focused like a microscope on the fine holes entering the marrow, seeing a world which lacked the familiar distinction of surface and interior, of entity and environment. It was this that terrified and made him retch.

His mind turned to the Tuy—new roads slashed through the earth, the scrub removed by fire. No wonder Jordi longed to clothe the naked earth in concrete and smooth green grass.

Ninety per cent of the population was crammed into the mountainous fringe of Caribbean coast that had the most benign climate and had been settled first. The interior was harsher and its raw untamed character attracted David. He knew that if you walked away from the road, even a mile or so, you could see the true nature of the country. Travelling at speed along a highway was corrupting. Fleeting impressions of faces, people and places, meaninglessly joined together in a strip cartoon by the travelling windscreen.

But the population was expanding and people had to live somewhere—not everyone could live on the over-crowded margin and the interior was bound to be developed. Jordi was not alone in wanting to tame the wilderness, to develop the land and make money.

In the afternoon of the second day boats began to arrive, bringing increasing numbers of people, and after an hour or so of loud music and screaming families, they asked one of the boatmen to take them back.

They stopped where hot food was cooked by the side of the road: arepas, sizzling meat, butter-yellow corn pancakes, crayfish, fried pork crackling, oranges, bananas, avocados and mangos, coconuts that floated in ice-filled oil drums and all kinds of fruit drinks: guayaba, guanabana, tamarindo.

'What shall I do about the hearing?' he asked after they had been driving an hour or so. There was heavy traffic because of the holiday and the queues on the motorway began at La Victoria. He felt frazzled, agitated at the prospect of the impending congressional hearing and half-wished they had stayed away until it was all over.

'That's up to you,' she said.

'You must have a view.'

'You must do what you think is best.'

'Yes, but what's that?'

'What have you done to date?'

'I sent my report to Manuel, and I've tried to talk to Jordi, and Luis Carlos.'

'And?'

'They aren't interested. They couldn't care less. I just don't understand Jordi. When we were in England … '

'You're not in England now!'

'You know, despite everything I love the man. I don't know why.'

'It's his warmth. It's a physical thing—you feel you could warm your hands on him.'

'He found me when I really needed someone to take an

interest. He made me feel that I had something worthwhile to contribute.'

'That's his greatest talent—catching people when they're vulnerable,' she said, wistfully.

The traffic slowed to a crawl as they approached the landslide where the autopista had caved in again.

'What a waste,' said David, beating time with his hand on the steering wheel. 'All that talent and energy harnessed to self-interest. In England he had such breadth of vision, such generosity of spirit.'

A traffic cop waved them through and they entered the tunnel and speeded up.

With a wry smile Chelo said, 'He reflects back what people want to see.'

'He certainly needs an audience,' he said, feeling better, sensing the cool air as the road climbed the mountains guarding the western approach to the city.

'Jordi isn't just a person,' she laughed. 'He's an event—like a travelling circus—you're supposed to enjoy the show, not look behind the scenes.'

'We worked as equals in England.'

'Here he's your patron: you should be dutifully grateful—favours demand loyalty and gratitude,' she said in the sarcastic tone that was intended to make him laugh but which he invariably found irritating when they were talking about Jordi. No, he thought angrily, it's not that automatic. He thought about Jordi, and all his family had done for him. Finally, he said, quietly, 'My pride got in the way.'

'You did what you thought was right,' she said, reaching for his hand.

'I resent being made a fool. I'm just as egotistical as he is really. So what can I do about the Tuy?'

Chelo said she knew someone on the committee. If he wanted, she would have a word and tell him that there had been a report on the earthquake risk.

David suddenly felt safe. He had asked for her help and she had taken it on. He trusted her and knew that whatever happened it was going to be all right; he was not alone.

'Felix offered me a job in Cambridge. It might be good. I need to go back, I feel battered by it all,' he tried to explain.

'You're running away,' she said, grabbing her cigarettes off the dashboard.

She was right in a way—part of him wanted to return to the familiarity and security of England. He needed a rest— what bliss to speak English again, to hear his feet scrunch on autumn leaves. He remembered all sorts of things he missed—sausages and English beer, cricket and the Sunday papers. Back in Britain he could forget about it all and make a fresh start. He could forget Jordi and the whole cursed lot of them. But not Chelo.

In a sense, he had been running away a year ago when he'd come here. He felt pulled apart. He couldn't keep running away, starting again whenever things got difficult, whenever he got hurt. He could stay and make a new life with Chelo. They might have children, settle down and build a house. Here you could buy a plot of land and create something exciting. Not like in England with its planning permissions and building control. He imagined a timber house in a mountain valley. There would be a stream and a meadow with wild flowers.

But if he stayed he would always be a foreigner. The children would be Venezuelans, but he'd always be English.

Could he stand that sense of not belonging?

South America was different. You thought you knew where you were and then bang! some subtle shade of meaning misunderstood and you were lost. Would he ever learn these conventions? Maybe they were in the blood— transmitted through your mother's milk.

Take kissing. Nobody kissed in England, unless they were lovers. Here even the men kissed each other, with bear hugs, like Russian politicians. A whole morning could be disrupted at work when someone came back from holiday abroad and went round kissing everyone. At social functions, as an honorary member of Jordi's family, David was expected to kiss all the female relatives. Women would point their faces at him, waiting for the two pecks—left cheek, right cheek. Or was it right then left? He could never remember and continually bumped noses.

The fine detail of life eluded him. It was like a village: any two people could find a link—within the upper class of course! Nobody ever said no; yet what shades of maybe could be encompassed in the word yes! The older generation, Jordi's parents, believed saying no was discourteous, but the younger generation said yes to keep their options open. Appointments and invitations were provisional—only kept if a better offer failed to turn up.

He longed to put down roots, to do something useful with his life, to make friends and have a family. England was where he belonged, where he felt at home. He'd miss the tropics, the newness and the adventure. But Scotland was wild enough.

'I know what you're thinking,' she said. 'You're feeling all English. Well fine … take the job, let's go and live in

England for a while. Or we could move to Merida. It doesn't matter... let's try something and see how it feels.'

'I don't know what to do, all I know is that I want to stay with you,' he said, reaching over and touching her arm. 'God, I'm sick of this planning business. I'm going to pack it in ... do something else, anything. And I'm tired of living in Caracas ... you can keep the big city life, I've had enough of the noise and the traffic. You know what I'd really like to do is to go back to England for a bit. Maybe we could go and visit my mother together.'

'What's to stop us going? I'd like to. Let's book a flight for after the hearing.'

She came home with him and after showering together they went to bed and fell asleep in each others' arms.

20

'Señor Romero, Estimado Doctor,' began the chairman after Manuel had sat down, 'We would like to ask you certain questions concerning the geology of the Tuy, specifically the ability of the site to resist earthquake movement. We understand that you have commissioned certain studies.'

'That is correct.'

'Could you give us the main conclusions.'

'Certainly,' said Manuel suavely. 'Firstly, the geological survey of the area by Seravenca found no active faults whatsoever. Secondly, Ingeneria de Suelos conducted an exhaustive analysis of the subsoils in the valley and concluded that the Tuy presents no difficulties for urban development.'

David, looking down from the public gallery, unable to contribute to the proceedings, wanted to shout liar, but was constrained by the formality.

'Thank you Sr Romero, that seems quite conclusive. Are there any questions?'

'Yes, I have one,' said one of the Congressmen. 'Is it true that you have had an evaluation report from Mr Anthony?'

'That is true,' said Manuel, who turned and looked up, momentarily, towards where David was sitting.

'And is it also true that this report suggests that the Tuy is far from free of earthquake risk?'

'That is so. However, it is also true that the report is flawed.'

David gripped the rail in front of him and leaned closer.

'I am afraid the facts presented in the report are wrong. This so often happens when amateurs have the temerity to make judgements about specialist and highly technical matters,' said Manuel looking along the line of committeemen arranged opposite him.

How can he be so self-assured, thought David.

'No part of the region,' Manuel continued, 'indeed no part of the country, can be deemed to be entirely free of earthquakes. Nevertheless, the geologists, and they are the best people to judge you would doubtless agree, have assured me that the Tuy is no more earthquake prone than the Capital itself.'

'But, Sr Romero, with all due respect, is it not true that a major fault line runs right across the centre of the valley,' the Congressman pressed.

'Irrelevant! There are faults all over the region. There is nothing to suggest that the fault in question is active. In any event, if it were, a zone within twenty kilometres would be at risk. I repeat, the Tuy is no more at risk than the Capital.'

'I'm sorry Minister, but I must press you on this. Was

there no evidence of severe earth movement in the Tuy during the recent series of tremors we have experienced.'

Manuel smiled like a cat. 'What is clear, with respect, is that no buildings, I repeat not a single building, collapsed in recent series of tremors. Our engineers have been and examined the adjacent villages of Santa Teresa, Cua etcetera and have found no evidence of damage whatsoever.'

'That seems quite conclusive,' said the Chairman, showing irritation at the continued questioning by his colleague.

'In fact,' said Manuel, rubbing salt in, 'there hasn't been any major destruction anywhere in the Capital region since new codes of building practice were introduced in 1959. We have the technology to handle earthquakes. I can therefore assure you that the geomorphology of the Tuy valley presents no significant difficulties for urban development.'

David stayed at home the following morning and missed the session when economists from the Central Planning Unit at the Treasury were cross-examined. He spent the time lying in the hammock, enjoying the breathing space to think and to sort out his emotions.

People like Jordi and Luis Carlos were quite exceptional, he realised. It was not just the wealth, although that was part of it, but more their confidence in their natural role as leaders. They were members of the elite from birth, but, in addition, had the energy and intelligence to see their world as something to enjoy, command and exploit. They accepted the structure and worked within it, strengthening, braiding and amplifying their influence, but never breaking or challenging the system.

David wondered if he had missed the point. For Jordi communism was all or nothing—he was waiting for the revolution but, meanwhile, he could enjoy wealth and privilege to the full—social justice and equality could wait. But wasn't that the way of the world, didn't the powerful always enjoy the fruits of power? Why exactly did it make him feel uncomfortable? He did not begrudge Alberto his farm or Manuel his big house. Was it envy? Maybe he wanted some of the good life for himself?

If you professed to change the world, surely there had to be some integrity? But there was a complete lack of consistency in their behaviour. He accepted that people were paradoxical—that they could quite happily say one thing and do another, but in this case the discrepancy—between rhetoric and practice, between ideals and life-style—was too huge. What he resented most, he realised, was their total absence of guilt. They never once apologised for, or even commented on, the contradiction. If they had been more self-aware he would have branded them hypocrites. As it was, he was left with an ill-defined resentment, which occasionally erupted into suppressed anger.

Each time David was faced by some moral dilemma in his own life he had to think things out from first principles. He thought about the network of social relations and influence that existed here and of which he was a part. He realised he had been naive. He had thought to flout the system, that the rules did not apply to him, that he could ignore them. He had even secretly believed he would help overturn the structure. In reality he realised he was as bad as those he had branded as phoney communists. Ideals withered as society ground you down and remade you into what it demanded, not what you wanted. He had failed to act on any of his early intentions and had lost sight of the contributions he had naively hoped to make.

He found he was studying a web stretched between grass stems, shaking in the wind, heavy with tiny droplets like the beaded doily his grandmother used to put over the milk jug. A fly beat its wings violently, threatening to break the web. The tiny spider advanced and strengthened the thread that held the fly. The fly beat its wings and the spider scuttled away, only to emerge again a few moments later. David found a dry stalk and intervened in the natural order by detaching the fly from the web. He brought it nearer, examining it closely. Its wings were enmeshed and it would never fly again. Gently he rehung it by the single thread. The spider came once more and bound its legs to the one beating wing and left it hanging for later.

David got back after lunch in time to hear Jordi and Luis Carlos speak. Jordi was brilliant; making a convincing case for developing the Tuy by citing examples of satellite cities from many parts of the world. He touched on the evaluation by the team, under his direction, at the University, and talked at length about Felix and the consultancy work in Cambridge. He had a pair of slide projectors showing plans and photographs to back up his argument and had the committee eating out of his hands. David found it hard to concentrate on the detail of what he was saying. He sat, fascinated by Jordi's delivery, feeling sad, hearing the familiar crack as he clicked his fingers to emphasize a point.

As Jordi sat down David had the impression that he'd been championing Guarenas as well as the Tuy. He couldn't understand it.

'What's Jordi up to?' he said in a voice that carried and

made some of the committee glare at the gallery.

By the end of the day it was clear that the committee would decide in favour of the Tuy. On leaving he was stopped by a man in the foyer and found himself facing a television camera.

'Excuse me, Mr Anthony?'

'Yes?'

'I am reporter from Metrovision. We would like to record an interview with you now.'

'With me—what's this about?' David was still preoccupied, thinking about the hearing, annoyed by how both sides had distorted his report and misled the committee. But it was Manuel's callous disregard of the potential risks that was so outrageous.

'We understand, Mr Anthony, that you were responsible for developing the technique used to evaluate the alternative planning proposals being considered by the committee?' asked the interviewer.

'Yes, I helped write it,' David said, wondering what was coming next.

'Could you explain briefly how the program works and what it does?'

David did his best to keep it simple.

'Both the proposals seem to use your program to support their arguments. What do you favour Mr Anthony?'

'Neither!' said David without hesitating.

'I'm sorry?' said the interviewer.

'I favour the development of Guarenas, as a satellite to the capital, together with investment in three cities in the regions: Barcelona, Barquisimeto and Acarigua.'

'And the Tuy?'

David said nothing and crossed his arms. The interviewer looked anxious. Finally David said: 'Ten metres under the Tuy, right where they intend to build the new city centre, the ground is liquid mud; anything built on it will collapse in an earthquake.'

He'd done it. Just when he'd thought it was all over he'd been given a chance to say what he believed. The cameraman stopped filming. The reporter thanked him and went off to find other people to interview. Walking away David had the sensation of sailing through the air, ecstatic. On top of the world, he felt he could do anything.

Then he saw Jerry on the edge of the crowd of people, moving away and heading out of the building. It didn't make sense Jerry being there. He couldn't have come to provide moral support or David would have seen him earlier. Feeling confused, David tried to catch up with him. Outside, Jerry had disappeared. Opting, on the spur of the moment, to turn right David ran round the end of the building and saw him climbing into a car. Not stopping, he rushed up to the car and stood in front of it. Through the windscreen he saw Jerry looking anxious.

'What are you doing here?' he asked, as Jerry got out.

'I was in town on business,' said Jerry.

'Great, let's go for a drink to celebrate.'

Jerry wasn't keen, but David, still feeling euphoric from the interview, insisted. There happened to be a cafe just across the street. Jerry locked the car and they walked over. David ordered Cuba libres at the bar, and they went and sat at one of the round tables on the sidewalk.

David asked about Marta and the children. Jerry said they were fine. He seemed agitated and uncommunicative. David told him about the hearing. Although Jerry knew some of the background a lot had happened since he'd seen him in Merida. But Jerry was preoccupied and didn't seem to be paying attention. The cafe got busier and as the tables filled up, it seemed to David that Jerry scrutinised everyone as they came in.

Finally, more out of exasperation than anything else, David asked, 'How come you're here?'

'What?' said Jerry.

'How did you know about the hearing?'

'You told me.'

'No I didn't.'

'Someone must have told me.'

'Sure,' said David. 'Is there something wrong? Jerry, why are you here?'

'Why?'

'Call it intuition.'

Jerry looked uncomfortable. His head was bobbing back and forth, like it always did when he was nervous, and he kept looking round.

'What it's all about Jerry,' David asked. Jerry still did not answer. 'I've been fighting my own little battles here, but it feels there's something else going on.'

'How's that?'

'Something's obviously bugging you.'

Jerry didn't say anything. Despite the noise in the street, David could hear the ice cracking as it melted in their drinks.

Jerry was sweating and his glasses were slipping down the bridge of his nose. Tell it your own way, thought David, take your time, but tell me about it.

'Marta ... she was expecting ... Michael. I was in Nam,'

Jerry blurted out.

'What happened?' David coaxed. 'Did you come here to escape the draft?'

'Sort of. I got invalided out.' In a rush at first, Jerry began his story. Three drinks later, David was able to piece together what had happened.

Jerry had been in the infantry. His platoon was ambushed and most of them killed. Jerry was captured and then, incredibly, he'd been rescued by helicopter. In hospital he was interviewed by a captain from military intelligence who discovered he could remember every detail of the action and his period of captivity. A note was made on his file.

Later they ran some tests and made him an offer. He was propositioned by a man with a crew cut: return to his unit, which was taking heavy casualties, or sign up for special training back home. After he'd get a honourable discharge and a posting abroad, probably in Central America.

When he'd finished it took David a minute or two to take it all in. 'So what you're telling me is that you're an agent!' Different images flashed through his mind. Jerry shirtless, wearing an identity tag that was just like Jordi's. Him timing their walks, making notes in a little black notebook.

'It's nothing. Just low level cover. There are thousands of us, hundreds of thousands worldwide. Anyway, I'm sick of it, I want out. That's why I went to Merida,' said Jerry earnestly.

'You're CIA?'

'They were worried about a revolution, man! Two, three years back, nobody knew what was going to happen. They had a regular little army out in Falcon. We thought this might be another Cuba. You wouldn't believe the money invested here. It's not just the oil either. Rockefeller alone owns most of Guarico; it's as big as Idaho. '

David leaned back in his chair, sorting it out in his mind, giving his emotions a chance to catch up. He called over a waiter and ordered more drinks. His first reaction was to laugh. Jerry a CIA agent! with his little black book. It was all so crackpot.

The way Jerry told it, he'd had a breakdown. And Marta was pregnant. Maybe they were bluffing; maybe they would have sent him home anyway.

'You were targeted from the beginning,' said Jerry.

'Why on earth?'

'You're a communist aren't you?'

'No!' said David, loudly enough for people on the next table to look round.

'But you were.'

'I used to go to meetings, at university, for a year or so.'

'Two years eight months,' corrected Jerry.

'And I was also a member of the mountaineering club and the chess club.'

'Don't make me laugh.'

'I wanted to see if communism offered a better way,' said David.

'To what?'

'Social justice.'

'And?'

'It doesn't.'

'That's what we figured,' said Jerry.

So he had been watched. Old conversations, questions Jerry had asked, took on a new significance. 'What about Marta?' he asked.

'She likes you—said we were wasting our time. I was sure we'd get nowhere with you and as far as I was concerned that was just fine. Then the powers that be got excited over the congressional hearing. They couldn't figure the angles.'

'What now?' asked David.

'It depends what I tell them.'

'And?'

'They brought me out of retirement for this operation. They decided ages ago that you weren't a subversive. I want out, and the best way of achieving that is to prove you're still no threat. So you'll get a clean bill of health from me. I want to go back to Merida and forget about it all again.'

David stood and asked, 'Will someone else pick up where you leave off?'

'That depends. I guess not,' said Jerry as they said goodbye.

Chelo didn't appear to find his news about Jerry anywhere near as remarkable as he expected. To her, it was self-evident that the United States would have agents in the country and, if David had an American friend, it was entirely feasible he could be one of them.

Later that evening they watched the news together, sitting on the sofa, holding hands. Suddenly David saw himself on the TV screen, just after a piece about an earthquake in Nicaragua, hesitant, then answering the fateful question. Afterwards he sat silent, feeling a bit shocked at seeing himself on television. Chelo kissed and hugged him and told him he'd been good. Laughing, she said she'd wondered if he'd forgotten his lines when he hesitated.

§

At work, his position became increasingly untenable, as Luis Carlos failed to give him useful work and the other members of the unit treated him as a pariah.

A week later the congressional hearing published its findings. When he met Chelo she said: 'Have you heard? ... they decided on Guarenas, and that's not all. I found out from Alejandro that Mariella's father heads up the consortium that owns the land.'

David tried to take it in. 'And Manuel?' he asked.

'Who knows?' she shrugged.

www.ingramcontent.com/pod-product-compliance
Lightning Source LLC
Chambersburg PA
CBHW060946030726
47503CB00003B/746